20TH CENTURY CASANOVA

C G GIBBS

INTRODUCTION

The greatest gift of all is life, and with that gift many individuals are further gifted to outshine or perform superior to others.

Giacomo Girolamo Casanova was one such man. He had the gift of being one of the greatest Womanisers of all time, but this was three centuries ago.

The gift has now regenerated to a modern-day Casanova.

PROLOGUE

From a table outside the nearby café, a thirty-year-old man watched the strange gathering with interest, sipping his coffee as he took in the scene before him. His hair was a little long and unkempt, and he sported a full beard. He looked like any normal tourist on holiday.

Of course, he wasn't a normal tourist at all. And he wasn't on holiday.

The man smiled, feeling a little sad as he watched the memorial. They were always sombre occasions, of course, meant to celebrate a person's life but more often than not managing to focus on the sadness of their passing.

But still the man smiled, watching as the mourners exchanged stories and wiped tears from their eyes.

In another world, in another life . . .

Everything would have been so different.

CHAPTER 1

England, 1965

Julian looked down at his shiny black shoes as he stepped out of the car, reminiscing as he did so about the young saleswoman who'd sold them to him when he and his mum had visited the shoe shop. His mind lingered on the way she'd walked, the way that she'd smiled, the way her hand had lifted his foot to the measurer, both gently and expertly.

"Size four, madam," she had informed Julian's mum, before lifting a shoe from a nearby shelf and slipping it onto his foot.

"Perfect," Julian's mother had said.

Julian smiled, directing it at the pretty-looking woman who was staring down at him.

"Just right for school," the saleswoman had told him. "You're going to break some hearts, young man!" she added, ruffling his hair.

His stomach had lurched then - a good lurch, not a bad lurch - and those words had been swirling around his head ever since: "You're going to break some hearts."

Julian was jolted back to the present by his mum, who placed her hand on his shoulder as she began guiding him up towards the school gate. He noticed there were tears in her eyes.

"Have a good day," she said with a watery smile, once they'd reached the gates.

"OK," Julian replied, trying to ignore how upset she seemed to be. "Bye, Mum."

He watched as she turned and headed back to the car, fumbling in her handbag for a handkerchief as she went.

"Name?" a voice above him asked, and Julian looked up into the face of a tall, dark-haired, clipboard-carrying lady who was currently towering over him, peering down at him rather sternly.

"Julian," he replied automatically.

She rolled her eyes. "Julian *what?*" she asked.

"Oh, sorry," Julian said, embarrassed. "Julian Foster."

She nodded and began scribbling on her clipboard. "Follow Joyce," she instructed him, nodding towards a blonde girl who was standing a few feet away, watching them both. "She will take you to your class."

Julian nodded at the woman, then turned towards Joyce. She was tall and thin, with short blonde hair, and she wore an air of superiority and maturity that left him in no doubt that she was his senior. She looked two years older than him, at least.

"This way," she said brusquely, before turning quickly on her heel and marching off into the depths of the school. Julian had to walk as quickly as he could to keep up - at some points he was almost running, scuffing his brand new shoes along the ground in his desire to not be left behind.

"Is that your new boyfriend, Joyce?" someone asked, as they marched along one of the school corridors. Joyce and Julian turned in unison to locate the owner of the voice.

It was a girl who looked about the same age as Joyce, though not at all similar physically - she had long brown hair and an amused expression, as if grinning and giggling was what she did most. She was standing in the doorway of one of the classrooms with another girl, and the two of them giggled as Julian turned to look. He felt his face colour immediately.

"Don't be mean; you're embarrassing him!" Joyce retorted.

By now, Julian's eyes were fixed firmly to the floor in front of him. Despite dreaming about coming here and all the funny and witty things he would say when he got here, he couldn't think of any words right now. None at all.

"Take no notice, Julian," Joyce said kindly. "I'm sure they're just jealous. Come on, we need to get you to your class or you'll be late."

With that, she took his hand and continued to lead him through several corridors towards his class.

It seemed to take forever, and just as Julian was wondering if they would ever arrive, Joyce came to an abrupt halt.

"This is your classroom," she told him, pointing through the door. "Have fun!" Without saying another word, she turned quickly and headed back the way they'd come, walking quickly as though she had somewhere far more important to be.

Taking a deep breath, Julian reached up and patted his hair down, suddenly self-conscious. Then, after only a few more seconds of hesitation, he pushed the classroom door open, trying to remain calm as he entered.

The teacher greeted Julian warmly, then introduced him to the class before pointing at an empty seat.

He sat down obediently, looking around at the rest of the class as he did so. There was a more or less equal mixture of boys and girls in the room. The girls sat on the left and the boys on the right, and there was a wide aisle running up the middle, effectively separating them.

Julian's seat was on the aisle, and by the end of the class, he knew at least a couple of his fellow classmates' names. The boy sitting next to him was called Richard, and the girl immediately across the aisle was called Linda.

It seemed to Julian that he had only just sat down when the bell rang, signalling that it was dinnertime. The class immediately stood up and started packing their things away in a rush, but when they came to leave the room, they filed out in order, such a practised and smooth movement that Julian assumed they must have to do it at the end of every lesson.

Julian had no idea where he was going or what he was doing, so he just followed the person in front of him, looking around him curiously at his new surroundings as he went. When they reached the dinner hall, he picked up a tray and proceeded to the brightly-lit counter, where a warm dinner plate was pushed towards him by a grumpy-looking woman in a hairnet.

"Meat pie," she stated, barely looking at him as she put the plate on his tray.

Julian nodded his thanks then progressed down the counter, where he received a dollop of mashed potato followed by a small portion of peas and gravy.

It all seemed so straightforward and easy that it wasn't until he reached the end of the counter that the panic started to set in. Where was he supposed to sit? He knew no one, but he didn't feel like sitting on his own. What if there was nowhere he *could* sit on his own, anyway? What was he meant to do then? He could feel his face burning again, powerless to stop the rush of red that he knew would right now be blossoming on his usually pale cheeks.

Frantically, and with his heart pounding, he looked around, trying to figure out where he should go. He spotted Joyce on the other side of the room with her friends, and briefly considered going over, but he soon realised that she wouldn't want him annoying her at dinnertime, especially considering the age difference. Just as he had decided not to disturb her, Joyce looked up, caught his eye, and waved him over.

He approached Joyce's table joyfully, feeling grateful that he would have somewhere to sit and that he wouldn't have to spend his first dinnertime sitting by himself.

He was feeling good as he headed over, but just as he got to within a few feet of Joyce's table, something clipped the back of his ankle and he stumbled forwards, watching in horror as his plate flew off his tray and landed in front of Joyce, splattering food and gravy all over her cardigan and white blouse.

There was a moment of horrified silence, and then Joyce let out an almighty scream - it reminded Julian of Olive screaming at Popeye in the cartoon.

She rose quickly from the table, pulling off her gravy-splattered cardigan and glaring at him as she stalked off, presumably to the bathrooms.

Julian stared after her as she went, open-mouthed and unable to speak.

He couldn't believe it - what a great first impression to make. Miserably, he turned away from the table, wishing he'd gone and sat on his own. Better a loner than this!

ONE YEAR LATER

Richard's house was situated at the end of the school playing fields. It was an easy place to escape to during school hours, and the ideal location to set up what quickly became known as a 'booby centre'.

Richard took on the role of lookout and would make sure the coast was clear, Julian acted as cashier, and one of the girls - normally Joyce - would lift up her jumper to the paying guest. They would split the money three ways, and Julian and Richard quickly became frequent patrons of the local sweet shop.

Julian, it has to be said, was not the brightest of pupils. His school reports featured the same comments time and time again - 'Julian must pay more attention in class', 'Julian is easily distracted', 'Julian needs to work on his concentration'. His parents put it down to a poor attention span, but the truth was that there was nothing wrong with Julian's attention span - it was just that his attention was directed elsewhere. Julian had very little time for his lessons, and felt that his time was much better spent admiring the prettiest girl in the class.

Julian's teacher, Mr Shaw, could be in full flow on the topic for the day, but not a word would permeate Julian's mind. No, instead of focussing on the teacher, Julian's eyes would be fixated on Linda, studying every minute detail of her face. Linda would often glance across the classroom to catch him staring at her intently. Whenever this happened, he would always direct his eyes quickly towards the desk or chalkboard, and she would turn away, knowing that he'd be looking again within moments.

He just couldn't help it; it was as if there was some kind of invisible force making him cast his gaze in her direction.

Julian's affection for Linda grew each time they played this game, and he felt an unbelievable thrill run through his body each time he looked at her. This sensation grew and intensified each time Julian and Linda spent time together - and this they did quite a lot, so Julian's feelings had plenty of time to continue growing. As did his charms and his ability to talk to girls in general.

It turned out that Linda lived just a couple of roads away from Julian, and they would walk home together most days, timing their kisses and trying to beat the record they had set the day before. They would quite often amble home behind an older schoolboy, who was normally accompanied by three or four girls, and he would kiss each one as they departed through their front gates.

Julian studied the older boy in fascination, attempting to emulate him as much as possible. He even tried to copy the boy's Scottish accent, but as it always ended up sounding more like an Indian accent, he soon abandoned that idea.

Instead he focussed on the way the boy moved, so when Julian practiced the walk behind the older boy, they ended up looking like two ducks, waddling in a row.

"What are you doing?" Linda asked one day, staring at him.

Julian's face turned the colour of beetroot. "Nothing," he mumbled, returning to his usual stride. "I was just . . . well . . . copying him," he admitted, nodding to the boy in front.

Linda quickly realised why. "You don't need to change anything about yourself," she told him.

Julian snorted and sat down on a nearby wall, looking dejected. He knew this would only make Linda more sympathetic towards him, wanting to comfort him.

It worked.

Linda perched close to him and looked into his eyes. "You have something very special," she told him, "and you don't even know it."

Julian smiled shyly. The truth was that he *did* know it, but his gift had now been confirmed.

CHAPTER 2

1968

Julian's mum fumbled in the side pocket of the car, eventually producing a crinkled tissue, which she clasped in her hand as she looked at her son. "Now, be a good boy, won't you? I'll see you in the holidays," she told him thickly.

Julian nodded. It hadn't quite struck home what was happening to him until his mother had said 'in the holidays', and feeling heavy with dread, he stepped out of the car.

It was that time of year again. Time for a new school, time to meet new people, and - more importantly - time to get to know some new girls. That was the bit Julian had been most looking forward to.

Nervously, he loosened his tie and looked up to take in the grandeur of the buildings that stood before him.

There was a wide stone stairway in the centre of the building that led to a magnificent two-story frontage, with buildings extending to the left and right; Julian couldn't help but feel trapped by the sheer size of it all.

It was all a little bit overwhelming, and although he knew he'd be able to handle it, he still felt anxious.

A loud chime sounded in the air as the clock tower struck one, and Julian jumped. He heard giggles from nearby, turning left just in time to see a group of girls being led past by their teacher. Some of them had seen him start at the sound of the clock and were tittering among themselves.

Julian watched them stroll away, their skirts swaying as they went, and allowed himself a sly little grin.

First impressions were important, sure, but he knew he'd soon be able to talk those girls - and any others - round. After all, he had a gift. And he sure as hell was going to use it.

His class introduction was held in the common room. It was the usual stuff: the boys were all asked to introduce themselves and to tell their classmates where they were from.

Julian was overcome with nerves; the rest of the boys looked much older and more confident than him. If he'd been in a room of girls, he'd have no problem, but with all these males staring at him and judging him, he wasn't sure he could handle it.

His hands shook as the boy next to him introduced himself.

"Philip Edmonds from Carlisle," he said, in a strong, confident voice.

The rest of the class turned their eyes on Julian, and when he opened his mouth, he was surprised by the nervous, squeaky voice that came out of it; he'd never once sounded like that in his entire life, he was sure of it. "My name's Julian Foster," he said breathlessly, "and I'm from here."

Laughter echoed all around the room. He had meant that he was from the county that the school was in, but now his classmates all thought he was an idiot.

Once the rest of the class had introduced themselves they were taken on a tour of the school, and after being led through the dining room, the boys were then shown the washroom and the showers.

The sound of laughter and splashing water greeted them as their teacher opened the door to the changing rooms, and Julian saw a group of older boys lined up in the shower. They were messing around, throwing shampoo bottles backwards and forwards and ribbing each other good-naturedly about the outcome of the football game they had just played. Julian immediately realised how immature his own body was in comparison to theirs, and was filled with dread at the thought of one day sharing the same showers with the other boys.

After all, you could have all the charm and charisma you liked, but if you didn't have the goods to back it up with, what then? He suddenly felt very self-conscious.

"This way," the teacher said briskly, marching onwards towards the dormitory block. The boys trailed behind in a straggling line, with Julian bringing up the rear. He was deep in thought.

The dormitory block turned out to be a long stone passageway with rooms coming off on both sides, and while the teacher directed some of the boys through the first door on the left, he pointed Julian and the rest of the group through the door opposite.

Each dormitory was separated into three sections - with five beds in each section - and Julian immediately spotted his silver trunk placed next to his new bed and wardrobe. It was the nearest one to the door.

"Forty-five minutes to unpack, boys," the teacher told them as they filed into their rooms.

Julian set about unpacking quickly - anxious not to be late - but just as he opened the lid of his trunk, he felt a presence behind him. Turning around, he found himself confronted by three of the boys in his class, all of whom immediately began to mimic his earlier squeaky voice.

Great. This was just what he needed - more members of the same sex to make him feel small and not good enough.

He turned back around and tried his best to ignore them, but a second later, another of the boys in the dorm grabbed a shoe from Julian's trunk and began waving it in the air. Julian made a grab for the shoe, but the boy tossed it over his head and across the room towards the rest of the group before he could even try and reach it. A tall, hard-faced boy with mousey-coloured hair snatched it out of the air with ease.

"Come on then, squeaker," he taunted. "Come and get it if you can!"

Julian felt a rush of fury, and before he knew what he was doing, he had dived for the shoe. He missed it by a considerable margin, however, as the boy gleefully lifted the shoe above his head.

Blinded by rage, Julian grabbed the boy around the neck and wrestled him to the ground.

"Fight, fight, fight!" the rest of the boys chanted.

Julian had never been in a fight before, and therefore, he had no idea what to do next. What he *did* know was that continuing with the brawl would get him in no end of trouble. So, deciding that it would be much better for him to be the bigger man, he released his hold and stood back.

"Submit?" he asked.

The other boy clambered to his feet and Julian saw immediately that he had no intention of submitting.

Clenching his fists, Julian felt a rush of air whoosh past his head as he skilfully sidestepped his opponent's fist. He grabbed the boy around the neck and wrestled him back to the floor.

"Submit!" he said again.

"Yes, yes!" the boy finally screamed, clawing at Julian's arm as it slowly tightened around his neck.

Julian released his hold before picking up his abandoned shoe and continuing to unpack as if nothing had happened.

"Shake on it, Julian," a choked voice said from behind him.

Julian turned to see his opponent, massaging his throat with one hand with the other outstretched towards him. He took the boy's hand without hesitation and shook it firmly.

"The name's Philip. Nice to meet you."

Once Julian had finished unpacking - and once he was sure that the other boys in his dorm probably weren't going to mess with him again - his mind turned, as usual, to girls. This happened a lot, probably more than with other boys of his age, and that was saying something.

He was just wondering where their dorms were, and how he could get there, when their form master returned to continue the tour.

"Follow me," he barked, leading the boys further down the long stone passageway to a large, solid, wooden door, upon which was a notice detailing the bath days for the boys and girls.

Julian tried not to think about the girls' bath days too much - he thought it probably wouldn't be a very good idea while he was surrounded by classmates and the form master - though he filed away the mental image for later.

Instead, Julian made himself focus on the matter at hand.

Reaching into his pocket, the teacher produced a large brass key, which slid effortlessly into the lock and produced a satisfyingly loud clunk as it turned.

On the other side of the door, a long row of cubicles formed a semicircle that led to another identical door. Behind it, Julian could hear voices.

"Girls!" he and Philip said in harmony as they walked past, hoping they would come out in response.

"You two!" the teacher shouted, "Come away!"

Julian and Philip scuttled on quickly, though they did share a brief smile with each other as they went.

This was going to be fun.

The two boys quickly re-christened each other as Jules and Phil, and that evening, they sat outside the dining room together while they waited for their evening meal, finding out as much as possible about each other.

He had already sensed that Phil was different to most of the other boys there, and as Phil told him about his life, it occurred to Julian that this was probably because he was from such a hugely different background; unlike most of their classmates, Phil did not have a privileged upbringing, and he was attending the school on an academic scholarship.

Julian got the impression that Phil was pretty streetwise and knew how to handle himself - after all, he had two older brothers and five older sisters, so he'd obviously had plenty of practice. His mother had died some years ago, and his dad had spent most of the intervening years in the pub, leaving his children to fend for themselves.

Julian, on the other hand, was an only child from a middle class family, and his mother ran the family business, something that she had taken over from her own mother years before.

His father was a powerful, influential man who governed the family, ruled the finances, paid the bills, and made all the decisions. Julian didn't know it, but his father had bribed the Headmaster of his junior school to secure Julian's entry - he'd helped him with his mathematics, and had copied English papers from the school's top pupils, all so he could meet the entry exam standards.

Julian's feelings towards his father were indifferent at best. He was a hard man - an ex-para - who rarely showed any emotion, recognition, or appreciation for anything. Julian couldn't remember his father ever sharing a caring word or loving embrace; it simply wasn't the kind of thing he did. His mother, on the other hand, was the complete opposite - she never stopped praising Julian, never stopped telling him how great he was, how handsome he was. He didn't find this particularly strange - he was just used to it.

He had left Julian's mother a few weeks before Julian was due to start at the school - another reason for Julian to board away from home - and she was still coming to terms with everything.

Overall, Julian and Philip couldn't have come from more different backgrounds, and in Julian's mind at least, that was the reason they went on to be such good friends.

Opposites attract, thought Julian, and this was true in friendship, also.

Julian's first introduction to the whole school community was the following morning in the assembly meeting house. The school followed Quaker principles and he found the experience of sitting in silence until something inspired you to speak quite bizarre. Even with hundreds of people in the massive room, you could still have heard a pin drop, and the slightest cough or snuffle immediately drew the eyes of everyone in your direction.

Julian couldn't stop his eyes from roving over the rows of girls at the front of the assembly hall. After all, he knew that if he was to experience any form of inspiration while sitting here, it would come from examining his female classmates. They just oozed inspiration, at least when it came to inspiring his private thoughts.

While he enjoyed what he was seeing a great deal, however, nothing in particular moved him to speech, so he kept his lips pressed tightly together and did everything in his power to ignore the furious tickling at the back of his throat. The last thing he wanted was to draw negative attention to himself with so many girls nearby.

After they had finished the assembly and eaten breakfast, the students were sent off to their first classes, and while Julian's father had managed to secure a place for him, he had not been able to miraculously improve his son's academic prowess. This was soon to cause problems for Julian.

Based on his 'excellent' exam results, Julian had been placed in the top performers class - along with Phil - though it soon became apparent that he was not able to keep up with the work, and within a week, Julian found himself demoted from the top classes.

"Don't worry about it, Jules," Phil told his friend when they were back in the dorm. "It doesn't mean anything."

Julian was sitting on his bed, feeling utterly mortified. It wasn't that he was particularly bothered about being in the top set - stuff like that never really bothered him - it's just that he didn't want any of the girls to think he was stupid. It would have been better to have started in a lower set in the first place, rather than starting high and being brought down to a lower class. It was like he'd failed before the term had even got going.

"It's probably just a blip," Phil continued. "You're off your game because of starting the new school and everything; that'll be it. You'll soon be moved back up to the top class when the teachers realise."

Julian nodded despondently, though he appreciated his friend trying to help. Quite apart from his worries about how girls would perceive him, a true downside of being moved out of the class was that he was no longer in any of the same lessons as Phil. There was nobody in his new set that he liked as much as Phil, which just made the classes seem all the more boring, and less inclined to take part. If he'd had trouble concentrating before, that was nothing to how he felt now. He just couldn't be bothered with it all.

Julian knew that he would never get his marks high enough to get back into the top set; he hoped his female classmates wouldn't be worried about trivial little things like his intelligence. After all, he had other things he could dazzle them with.

"Look at that," Julian said, pointing across Jane and into the distance. They were sitting on a grassy bank in the school grounds, and Julian had spent the last few minutes studying her face - it was a bit chubby in an adorable kind of way, her nose a little button, her eyes a piercing blue. Some of her curly blonde hair was falling down around her eyes, the rest of it tied back in a messy ponytail. She was the epitome of 'cute'.

She turned her head to follow his hand, and Julian moved his face closer to hers. When she turned back to Julian, their lips met. It was only the briefest of kisses, and moments later they were both lying back down, staring into the endless blue sky.

Julian had felt a small but very tangible thrill rush through him when their lips had met, and he knew he wanted to feel more of that little tingle, no matter what it took.

"We should go," Jane said a few minutes later, checking her watch. "We don't want to be late."

Sighing, Julian stood up, before stretching both hands out to Jane - who grasped them tightly - and pulling her to her feet. The momentum propelled Jane into his body, and Julian felt her small breasts pressed against his chest. Another little tingle rushed through him.

He kissed her again, but after a moment she pushed him away firmly, though not unkindly. "I think that's far enough, Julian," she told him, before setting off towards the school.

It would have to be enough for now, but he was already looking forward to the next time they'd be alone together.

CHAPTER 3

When he'd first started at this new school, Julian had been at a difficult age. His growth spurts were so sudden and intense that his trousers, which had been an inch too long one week, were two inches too short the next. A few weeks after he'd arrived at the school, he discovered his first pubic hairs, and his voice cycled through everything from tenor to bass and back again within the space of a few minutes. It was pretty unsettling to say the least.

As his body changed, Julian found himself spending more and more time comparing his development to that of his classmates. Phil, for example, was well ahead of Julian in terms of growth and development, and one day, when he was feeling particularly courageous, Julian asked Phil what it was like to be more developed.

Phil thought for a moment before shrugging. "It's just nice to fill your pants."

Julian nodded - it would be nice.

Although Julian was now in his teens - and although he could charm a girl and talk smoothly and suavely - he was a late developer, physically. His mum had told him that the later he developed, the younger he would look later on in life, but this offered little consolation to Julian right now. All he wanted was for things to start growing down below, and as soon as possible. Then he could really get going, where girls were concerned.

As the months passed by and Julian's body continued to mature, his confidence began to grow. He had ample opportunity to compare himself to the other boys - the after-games showers and the all-boys swimming lessons saw to that - and he was thrilled to realise that while it wasn't the biggest, it also wasn't the smallest.

He was getting there, slowly but surely.

The bell sounded suddenly, ending the maths lesson and jerking Julian out of his reverie. He had been staring intently at the back of Jane's head, reliving the moment two years ago - though he couldn't quite believe it had been that long ago - when he had felt her breasts pressed against him. He thought of it often, and most of the time, it was when he was supposed to be concentrating in class.

There was a flurry of activity around him as his classmates began packing away their stuff, and as Julian gathered his books together, he looked up in time to see Jane leaving the classroom. He was momentarily mesmerised by the sight of her skirt, swaying as she walked. That happened quite often, too.

"Jane!" he shouted, jogging down the corridor to catch up with her.

She turned towards him expectantly. They had exchanged little more than the occasional polite 'hello' since their encounter on the grassy bank that day, and Julian was starting to wonder why he hadn't pursued her more. He supposed it was because of all that time he'd spent being unsure of his body. Well, now he was more sure, and he was willing and raring to go - if she was.

"Would you like to go for a walk together later?" he asked confidently.

"OK," she replied coyly, her eyes twinkling with mischief. "Meet me later in the girls' wing."

Throwing him a smile, she turned on her heel and strode off towards her next lesson, leaving Julian staring after her with a broad grin on his face.

The girls' wing consisted of a large common room and several classrooms on the ground floor, with a grand sweeping staircase that led up to the dormitories.

Julian made his way in stealthily, knowing that if a teacher spotted him, he would be swiftly ejected. He sat in the window seat opposite the staircase - hoping that no staff members would come through while he was waiting - and after a few moments, he heard voices and giggling sounds coming from the landing above him.

Looking up, he saw Jane, accompanied by several of her friends. She smiled as she made her way down the stairs towards him, and his eyes ran up and down the length of her body as she approached.

She looked amazing.

They said very little to each other as they strolled through the corridor, and when they reached the main entrance, Julian opened the door and stood back politely.

"Thank you," she murmured.

As they headed across the grounds, Julian tried to remember all the advice Phil had given him during their endless talk about girls. Most of it had been passed on to Phil from his older sisters, so Julian thought that the advice was likely to be pretty sound.

With his 'gift' he probably didn't need the advice at all, but he was slightly nervous, and he figured that he could do with all the help he could get.

"I like your outfit," he said, suddenly remembering Phil's advice on complimenting girls. It came out sounding stilted and fake, and Julian cringed in embarrassment, but Jane took his hand, squeezing it gently.

"Thank you," she said again.

His compliment had broken the ice between them, and as they walked across the grounds and along the river, they chatted as if they'd known each other for years. It felt comfortable, and safe.

It took a while, but eventually Julian plucked up the courage to place his hand around Jane's shoulder. He half thought she'd pull away from him, but instead she snaked her arm around his waist in response, and he scooped her towards him, kissing her passionately. The next second, they fell to ground together in a tumble of arms and legs, their lips and tongues meshed together, exploring each other, as Jane's arms tightened around him.

Julian could feel the blood rushing all around his body as his hands travelled the length of Jane's torso before slipping through the gap in her blouse. His fingers slid over her ribcage, entering the warm cup of her bra, and he groaned as he felt her erect nipple, Jane letting out a muffled murmur in response.

Jane's legs were wrapped around him, and Julian could feel her pubic bone pushing against his manhood. His hand travelled down her body, clasping the soft underside of her thigh as her hips gyrated against him. He could feel his body stiffen and tremble as his senses continued to overload.

He wasn't even thinking that someone might see them - in truth, he wasn't thinking much at all.

"Ohhhh," he groaned. Pressing his hand against his crotch, he felt a warm wet patch seeping through his trousers. Quickly, he pulled down his jumper to cover his embarrassment.

"I think that's far enough, Jane," he said earnestly.

Together, they laughed out loud.

CHAPTER 4

It was all planned out. Philip had purposely left his towel in the bathroom, and while the form master was attending to Julian (who was being sick, or was at least pretending to), he gave Philip his key so he could go and retrieve it. It worked like a charm.

Phil carefully unlocked the door, letting himself in, and once he was on the other side he placed the key firmly against the bar of soap, making gentle rocking movements to release the key and leave a firm impression behind.

Satisfied with his work, he washed the key to remove any traces of soap and then dried it off with the 'forgotten' towel. Once he was done, you couldn't tell that anything untoward had happened to it at all.

In fact, everything had gone so according to plan that he didn't quite believe it, and he smiled as he slipped back out of the bathroom. Phase A had worked a treat. Now it was on to Phase B.

It was a Saturday afternoon, and that meant there were no lessons. The students used these hours as 'free time', meaning they mostly either played sports or escaped the school entirely to venture further afield.

And this was exactly what Julian and Philip planned on doing.

They had the impression of the pass key, and now they needed to hatch a plan to obtain a blank key that they could work on until it matched it perfectly. They'd been thinking about this for a while, and they knew exactly what they needed to do next.

A previous reconnaissance mission to the local shops had given them some much-needed information, and they were now sitting on the village bench across from the cobblers store, waiting for everyone to clear out.

They knew from their recon trip that the shoelaces were hanging at the back of the counter, and that the blank keys were on a board to the left of the door, and by using this information they'd been able to come up with their plan.

They waited for a few more minutes, occasionally catching each other's eye and trying not to start laughing - they both felt far more nervous than they thought they would, and laughter would definitely ease the tension, at least a little bit.

When finally the last customer came out of the shop, the two boys stood up and strode over, entering the store together. They tried to look normal and casual, though that was easier said than done.

Philip edged gingerly into position next to the keys, while Julian marched up to the main counter, behind which the shopkeeper was eyeing him, only slightly suspiciously.

Clearing his throat, Julian asked, "Could you show me some black laces, please?" hoping that his nerves - or the slight crack in his voice - wouldn't give him away.

The shopkeeper didn't reply, but simply turned to the display of laces to pick out a selection. At the same time, and without missing a beat, Philip grabbed a blank key from the board next to the door and shoved it into his pocket.

The shopkeeper turned back to face the shop a second later, holding out the laces under Julian's nose.

"How much are these ones?" he asked, pointing at the laces nearest him.

"A shilling," replied the shopkeeper, in his bored-sounding drawl.

Julian pretended to think about this for a moment, then shook his head. "OK, thanks. I think I'll have to call back, thank you."

The shopkeeper let out a small grunt, his gaze flickering slightly to Philip near the door before turning to put the laces back.

The boys hastened towards the door while his back was turned, and once they were outside, they ran the whole way back to school. Only when they were on the other side of the school gates did they stop, leaning over to catch their breath.

They were shaking - both from the exhilaration and the adrenaline rushing through their bodies, and from the very real fear of being caught.

"Good work," said Julian, grinning.

"Right back at you," replied Philip.

Later that night, Julian slipped the blank key under his mattress, the safest place he could think to put it. Soon it would be time to go on to the next phase - he only hoped it would go as smoothly as it had gone in the cobblers shop.

Julian had had an instant dislike for his metalwork teacher; he found him extremely irritating, not to mention the fact that his technical drawing lessons were far too hard to understand.

Philip, on the other hand, was Mr Canning's star pupil, so it was decided that he would distract the teacher while Julian did the 'dirty work'. It was time for Phase Three.

"OK, boys," announced Mr Canning to the class as he glanced at the clock on the wall, "you can put your tools away now."

Once most of the equipment from the lesson had been put back in its place, Philip headed over to the teacher.

"Can I ask you a question, Sir?" he asked nervously.

"Yes, of course. What do you want to know?"

While he was distracted, Julian moved over to one of the workbenches, pretending to put something away when in reality he was leaning over and picking up one of the files that had been left out on the top. He slid it into his boiler suit pocket and then quickly turned to make his escape.

Unfortunately, he'd turned around too quickly and hadn't noticed one of his classmates who was in his way. In his haste to leave the classroom, Julian accidentally pushed him over, and before he could run off, Mr Canning rushed over and grabbed Julian by the arm, stopping his escape in mid-flow.

In reflex, Julian kicked out, catching his teacher on the shin with his steel-capped boot.

Julian's eyes widened as Mr Canning let out an ear-shattering scream, but he took his chance and sped off out of the room so he could hide his prize. He knew he'd be in trouble for running off, but that was nothing compared to what would happen if they found out he'd been stealing from the school.

Julian had spent the whole rest of the afternoon worrying about what his punishment would be, but when he finally found out, he was delighted with the result: not only had he been banished from the awful metalwork classes, but he'd been relocated with the girls in their cookery class - brilliant!

That night, Jules and Phil sat at the window seat of their room, dressed in their darkest clothes and looking out at the full moon that lit up the grounds with an eerie glow. The noises coming from the semi-darkness were eerie too, the whole thing adding to their sense of unease and anticipation.

Finally, the clock tower struck twice, and Julian turned to Phil, his face illuminated by the light from the moon. "Time to go."

Earlier that day, Julian had arranged a plan with Jane and her friend Sally: they were to raid the tuck shop and take the booty up to the girls. On top of this, Jane had given him a drawing of the dormitory layout for the boys to follow, which he now had tucked into his inside pocket.

It was time.

CHAPTER 5

As quietly as they could, Julian and Phil crept over to the door, pausing slightly to make sure no one else had woken up.

The night before, they'd both gone on a little recon mission, a scary yet thrilling journey through the school in an attempt to figure out where they could and couldn't go - basically, where there wouldn't be anyone on watch, waiting to catch them out and get them into a whole heap of trouble.

Julian had been picturing teachers and other staff members lurking around every corner, and every time they got to the end of one corridor and peered past the wall, his heart started hammering in his chest.

But there was no one at the end of the first corridor, nor the second, nor the third. It would seem that Julian's idea of the school crawling with staff at night was the exact opposite of what happened in reality: everyone was probably tucked up in bed, enjoying their sleep - which was the last thing on Julian's mind.

Forcing his thoughts back to their present situation, Julian stared at the vague silhouette of Phil's head while they listened, but the only sounds coming from the other boys in the room were the faint noises of snoring and the occasional bit of mumbling. One of the boys turned over in his bed, the duvet rustling as he moved, but that was it.

Once he was convinced that all was well, Julian reached out for the handle and gently pulled on the door, his heart thumping loudly in his chest as it creaked slowly open.

Just then, a loud snort escaped from one of the boys nearest the door - James, probably - but then the sleeping form under the covers returned to its gentle, rhythmical snoring.

Julian's heart - which seemed to have completely stopped at the sound - started beating again, and breathing out a silent sigh of relief, Julian flashed Phil a look - *how close was that?* - before slipping out into the corridor.

All was quiet outside their room, the only light coming from the low, emergency-type strip lighting on the ceiling, and for that Julian was truly thankful; there was no way they'd be able to even attempt this if the school's main corridor lights were left on all night - they'd be seen in an instant.

Julian watched as Phil carefully pulled the door shut behind them, then he turned left, peering down into the depths of the dark hallway.

"You good?" he whispered to Phil, trying to keep his voice as low and as quiet as possible.

Phil nodded: all was good.

Together, the two of them crept down the corridor, slowing down their pace whenever they passed a door to one of the dorms. It was an agonisingly slow way of doing things, and Julian was beginning to think it would be morning before they even made it to the girls, but they didn't have much choice.

The thought of getting to Jane - of seeing her in her room, in the middle of the night - kept Julian going, kept him (relatively) level-headed.

After about ten minutes, the boys got to the door that led to the kitchen and dining area, and as slowly and as quietly as he could, Julian reached out and pushed on the handle.

At first it wouldn't budge - as if it were locked - and he glanced at Phil, his worried face eerily illuminated in the dull glow of the ceiling lights.

Moving closer to his friend, Phil joined Julian at the door, and together they leaned against it, pushing as hard as they could.

With the extra weight, the door slammed open in a flash, hitting the kitchen wall with a bang as it crashed into the plaster, no doubt making a dent - Julian just hoped no one would notice.

A split second later there was a loud crash at the other end of the room, making Julian freeze on the spot. Was there someone in there? What were they doing? And were they about to catch them out?

Just as Julian was preparing to run and get the hell out of there, something small and dark darted over to them, rushing through the open door and out into the corridor with a hiss and a meow.

Phil breathed a sigh of relief. "It was a cat! I thought we were about to get it. I thought we'd bumped into the headmaster having a midnight snack or something!" He held his hand over his chest, as though reassuring his heart that everything was fine and that it could, in fact, carry on beating as normal.

Julian had to smile - to think, he'd been terrified of a tiny feline!

After pushing Phil into the kitchen and carefully closing the door behind them, Julian punched his friend on the arm. "Be quiet! If no one heard the door or the cat, they might hear *you*."

After taking a deep breath, Julian slipped out a small torch he'd been hiding in his sleeve.

It didn't give off that much light, but the little it did give off they very much needed - apart from a small amount of moonlight pooling in through the large kitchen windows, it was totally dark in here.

Walking slightly quicker now, the adrenaline that was rushing through their veins starting to get the better of them, the two friends hurried over to a door in the corner of the room. It looked like it could belong to any old storeroom or pantry, but Julian knew better, and after sliding the copied key into the lock and giving it a quick turn, they opened the door onto the tuck shop.

OK, so it basically *was* a storeroom (though much bigger, and with a counter where the 'business' was carried out), but it was the *things* that were stored here that made this place so special. All those delicious things, so much better than the three square meals they received every day.

Julian grinned as he shined his torch onto shelves and shelves of chocolate bars, bags of sweets, packets of crisps, and cartons of juice. In a corner at the back of the tuck shop was a small freezer, which Julian knew was full of ice creams of all flavours, and in the other corner there was a huge stack of pop bottles, just waiting to be consumed.

After heading inside the small shop and pulling the door closed behind them, Phil nudged Julian in the side, grinning just as much as his friend was. "So, what do we take?" he asked, his voice full of anticipation of all the sugar he was about to eat.

"We need enough for the girls in Jane's dorm, but we shouldn't take too much - we don't want it to be obvious."

Phil nodded, pulling his drawstring P.E. bag from his pocket and placing it on one of the empty shelves. Julian did the same with his, and after pausing for a moment to listen, checking no one was coming, they got to work.

Once they were done, they each put their bags on their backs and retreated out of the tuck shop, Julian taking one last look at the shelves - you couldn't tell anything had been moved, not unless you were actively looking for signs of stealing - before locking the door behind them.

They crept back over to the kitchen door, moving slower now to try and hide the rustling sounds coming from their bags, and then let themselves out into the corridor. It was still deadly quiet out here - eerily quiet, in fact, and Julian tried even harder to move in a way so his bag wouldn't rustle.

Over the next ten minutes, they made their way along corridors, across hallways, up flights of stairs, and past endless doors (using their pass key when needed to open the fire doors), all the while hoping above hope that no one would catch them.

After what felt like an eternity the boys reached the third floor where Jane's dorm was located, and after taking a deep breath, Julian knocked lightly on the door, a very specific series of knocks and taps that he'd planned earlier with Jane. It had been fun, coming up with their very own 'secret knock', and he hoped that was just the start of all the fun they'd soon be having.

That was, if she ever answered.

At first nothing happened, and Julian was worried that perhaps Jane had fallen asleep, even after all their preparations and promises. Perhaps she was a heavy sleeper and the sound wouldn't wake her up? Perhaps they'd got the wrong room, and they were about to wake up a load of girls they didn't even know?

Perhaps. Perhaps. Perhaps.

Julian exchanged an anxious glance with Phil, and he was just about to pull out the map to Jane's dorm to check where they were when the door in front of them creaked open, just a little at first, then wider.

There was a small amount of light coming from the dorm, just enough to see Jane standing in the doorway, but not enough for them to see much beyond her svelte silhouette. Julian looked her up and down, trying not to get too aroused.

A moment later, Jane reached out, grabbing Julian by the front of his shirt and pulling him into the room. Phil followed behind.

The girls had placed all of their pillows and duvets on the floor space, creating a nice, if small, area to sit down on. Several of them were holding torches - the same kind that Julian had brought with him on his little quest - illuminating the room here and there in strange splotches of light.

Julian sat down next to Jane, with Phil on his other side, while the other girls sat down around them. He could tell Phil was nervous - his gaze kept darting around the circle of girls as though he didn't know if he should look them directly in the eyes or not - and to tell the truth, he was a little nervous too.

"So," said Jane, "what have you got for me?" She bit her lip a little after she asked the question, something that sent Julian crazy - and something that Julian thought Jane probably already knew.

"What have I got?" asked Julian, a little confused.

"She means the food," said Phil, shaking his head.

"Oh," said Julian, taking his bag off his back and pulling out the treats.

Phil did the same with his own bag, and soon there was a pretty impressive mountain of snacks piled in the middle of the little duvet island they'd made on the floor.

Their bags were now empty, though Julian had kept one item from his, and he handed the chocolate ice cream tub to Jane. "I got this for you," he whispered, not wanting anyone else to hear.

"Oh," said Jane, "thanks Julian, but I hate chocolate."

"I thought . . ."

"Only joking," she said, before ripping the top off the tub. "I just wanted to see your reaction - you're so cute when you're freaking out."

"Thanks for that, Jane."

"No problem. And thanks for the ice cream."

"You're Phil, right?" one of the other girls asked, pressing her hand on Phil's thigh. "Thanks for getting the food. I'm Vicky, by the way."

Phil smiled shyly. "It was nothing."

Julian watched this exchange with interest, then turned his attention back to Jane - they were staring at each other like . . . well, like a couple of love-sick teenagers.

"So," said Julian, still staring at Jane, "when are we going to find somewhere private to go?"

"Private?" asked Jane, frowning a little. "But I thought the whole point of tonight was to hang out and eat food. Why, what did *you* have in mind?" She was trying hard to keep a straight face, Julian could tell. "Look, Julian, I'm really impressed with you getting all this stuff for us. So, to show you my gratitude, how about I return the favour? Say, tomorrow night?"

This time it was Julian's turn to frown. "You want to raid the tuck shop?"

Jane rolled her eyes. "No. I want to come and visit you in *your* dorm." She glanced around the room. "Without all my friends."

"Oh," said Julian, trying very hard to seem not at all bothered with what she'd just said. "I guess that'd be OK."

Jane stared into his eyes, causing a thrilling shiver to dart up his spine. "It's a date. Tomorrow night, same time. Make sure you wait up for me."

"Oh, I will," he said, his voice suddenly raspy as he handed over a spare pass key to her. He didn't think he'd ever be able to sleep again after this.

Half an hour later, when the boys headed off back to their dorm, Phil asked, "Is Jane really going to come to the room tomorrow?"

"So she says," Julian replied. "I gave her the key, anyway. And I was thinking - that dorm bedroom across the hall from us is still empty, isn't it? They're getting it ready for redecorating?"

Phil nodded. "Empty, but probably locked."

"Only one way to find out," said Julian, and when they eventually got back to their corridor, he went over to the spare dorm bedroom and pushed on the door. It swung open immediately.

Julian turned to face Phil in the semi-darkness. "I know where *I'll* be spending tomorrow night."

CHAPTER 6

Somehow Julian got through the rest of the day, and when they climbed into their beds at 'lights out' time, he was almost shaking with expectation. Phil hadn't said much to him all day - he thought he was probably jealous that Julian was going to get some tonight - but he hadn't been angry with him or anything. Just quiet.

Julian waited, and waited, and waited. He was determined not to fall asleep, but even so, when the quiet yet distinctive knock sounded on the door, he found he'd been dozing.

Quietly getting out of bed, he crept over to the door, opening it just a crack as Jane had the night before.

There she was, looking as beautiful as ever, and he was just about to say so when he noticed someone standing behind her.

"Vicky?" he whispered.

She nodded. "Is Phil up?"

Julian grinned. If Phil had been jealous of him before, he wouldn't be now, and after telling the girls to wait a second, he ran over to Phil's bed and shook him gently awake.

"Wha? What is it?"

"Just come with me," said Julian. "Trust me; you want to get up and come and see who's here."

Bewildered, Phil got out of bed, following his friend to the door. When they were both out in the corridor with the door closed behind them, Phil turned his sleepy gaze to Vicky.

"Hi . . ." he whispered, unsure of what he was meant to say or do. He was pretty much still half asleep, after all.

"Hi yourself," replied Vicky, leaning forwards and kissing him on the cheek. "Why are we out in the hallway?"

Phil looked confused for a moment, but Julian answered for the both of them. "Come over here." He led them to the spare dorm bedroom, quickly opening the door and ushering them inside.

Julian closed the door behind them, and they all took a moment or so to get used to the darkness - there wasn't any form of light in here at all, which in a way made the whole thing much more thrilling.

"I thought this would be more private," said Julian, reaching out and finding Jane's hand in the darkness.

She leaned into Julian, pressing him against the wall and kissing him softly.

While Phil couldn't see exactly what they were doing, he soon got the gist of it, and after finding Vicky's hand and taking it gently in his, he led her over to the other side of the room, as far away from the others as possible.

Julian and Jane were already on the bed nearest the door, and neither of them were paying any attention to what Phil and Vicky were doing - as far as they were concerned, right now they didn't exist.

Julian was still kissing Jane as they writhed around awkwardly on the mattress, but Jane clearly wanted to move on. Taking his hand, she guided it under her skirt, Julian's whole body tingling as his fingers grasped her thigh. Slowly, he slid his palm along her leg, stopping only briefly when he got to her underwear before plunging his hand under the material, making her back arch and a loud gasp to escape from her lips.

Pulling away, she grabbed at the bottom of Julian's t-shirt, tugging it quickly over his head as though desperate to get to the next stage.

He didn't complain, and as soon as she'd got it over his head, he started pulling down his trousers. Julian felt gawky and uncoordinated, but he didn't much care in the moment - he just wanted to do it.

When he was just down to his underwear he turned his attention to Jane, pulling off her own t-shirt and her skirt until she was just in her pants and bra. She looked so vulnerable like that, and so unsure, but she nodded at him as though telling him to continue.

Shivering, he placed his hand over Jane's left breast, thinking back to that day next to the river, the moment he'd really started feeling something for her. She moaned quietly.

Sliding his fingers gently under her bra, he squeezed the soft flesh until Jane whispered, "Wait, stop. You're hurting me - not so hard!"

"Sorry." Embarrassed, Julian stopped, and after a moment or so Jane leaned forwards and unclasped her bra from the back.

"It's fine, just don't be so rough."

He couldn't see a great deal in the dark room, but his eyes had adjusted enough to get the vague outline of her shape, of all her curves, her perfect skin. He just sat and stared at her for a while, and he could almost sense her rolling her eyes at him.

"What are you waiting for?" she whispered, a definite desperate edge to her voice, causing his entire body to start tingling again.

He dove at her bare torso, knocking her down onto the bed with more force than he'd intended. He paused for a moment, worrying that he'd hurt her, but Jane just laughed. He leaned down until his face was just inches away from Jane's skin, breathing in her scent before kissing her between her breasts.

As he moved his mouth around her chest, kissing and teasing her, Jane groaned quietly, arching her back.

After a minute or so she reached down, placing her hand on Julian's underwear and grasping him through the material. She did it slowly, as if unsure whether to do so. It made him pause for a moment, his entire body stiffening under her touch, and for a second they just lay there, their hearts beating, their breathing getting faster and faster with every passing moment.

Julian could hear Phil and Vicky at the other end of the room, their own unique moans and groans floating over to them, and while he paid them little attention, there was something about the whole situation that thrilled him on a whole other level - something about doing it with other people in the room made it feel far more risqué.

Then, everything seemed to happen in a flash. Jane reached under the elastic waistband of Julian's underwear, grasping his flesh so hard he thought he might explode right there and then, and when he tried to pull his pants down, he was fumbling like . . . well, like an awkward teenage boy.

Luckily, Jane didn't seem to care; she was ready to go now, and after helping him wriggle out of his pants, she pulled her own down and off in one quick movement.

This was it, thought Julian: this was the moment. But at the back of his mind, something was niggling at him. "Jane," he whispered, "I don't have any . . . protection."

She shifted under him for a second before whispering back, "It's OK, I stole my older sister's pills."

Julian paused for a moment. "And those will work?"

"They do for her. I wouldn't be doing this otherwise, Julian, so let's just get on with it, shall we?" She sounded frustrated, something Julian could very much understand.

He didn't want to wait anymore, and by the way Jane was writhing under him, grasping him yet again and guiding him to where she wanted him, neither did she.

After kissing her once again - this time more deeply and passionately than before - he thrust into her, making her scream out in what he hoped was pleasure but which sounded a little like pain as well.

"Are you OK?" he whispered, stopping briefly while enjoying the sensation of their bodies coming together.

She moved underneath him a little, getting more comfortable before replying, her voice low and raspy, "I'll be fine. Don't you dare stop now."

He could feel her heart fluttering underneath him, could smell her anticipation in her sweat, could still taste her from when they'd kissed. It was a sensation overload, and he gave himself a split second to think how different this was to all those times he'd imagined it, before thrusting into her again.

This time he thought her cry was 100% pleasure, and as he moved in and out, she reached her legs up, wrapping them around his lower back. He wasn't sure if he was doing this correctly at all, and although the movements the two of them were making could never be called graceful, it felt good - and that was all that mattered, wasn't it?

Julian tried to keep it together, but it was so hard; *he* was so hard. He was about ready to burst, but he hung on, enjoying the feeling of Jane writhing underneath him, enjoying the way her legs wrapped around him, enjoying the sensation of them becoming one - finally, after all those months of wishing and daydreaming.

She moaned again, pushing her chest into his and making them closer still, her hands moving over his back, her fingernails digging into his skin. They'd probably leave a mark, Julian thought absently, but that was OK. That was good. Right now she could have scratched half of his skin clean off and he wouldn't care, he wouldn't stop.

So he carried on, their bodies moving in time, quicker and quicker as they headed towards their climax, and when Jane squeezed her legs around him as hard as she could, her hot breath in his ear as she clung on tightly, he exploded, all of his pent-up energy and desperate desires flowing out of his body at once, leaving him drained but satisfied. *Very* satisfied.

They lay there like that - still wrapped around each other - for another minute or so, waiting for their breathing to return to normal, and after a while, Julian listened out for his friend at the other side of the room. The moaning and the movement coming from their bed had stopped.

When they'd finally caught their breath, Jane extricated herself from Julian and started fumbling about in the dark for their discarded clothes, throwing him his t-shirt, his trousers, his pants. She dressed quickly and silently, and Julian followed suit.

A few seconds later, they heard Phil and Vicky moving over to them, and when Phil said, "Alright?" Julian could almost hear the grin in his friend's voice - so he'd done it too, then. Good on him, Julian thought.

The four of them ambled slowly over to the door, Julian opening it just enough to see if there were any signs of movement in the corridor. There was nothing, so he let them out, and when they were all standing under the dim ceiling lights, they gave each other the once-over.

They were all shining from sweat, their hair sticking out all over the place. It was pretty damn obvious what they'd been up to.

As Vicky said goodnight to Phil, Jane leaned into Julian, reaching her arms up around his neck and kissing him, slowly yet passionately.

By the time she pulled back, Julian was almost ready to go again, but Jane shook her head.

"We'll have to do this again sometime," she whispered, giving Julian's hand a brief squeeze before heading off down the corridor.

Vicky followed, both of the girls glancing back over their shoulders before heading round the corner, out of the boy's wing and back to their room.

There was a moment of silence as Julian stared after Jane, then he turned to face his friend, grinning from ear to ear. "Good night?" he asked casually, as if they'd all just been out on a double date to the cinema.

"The best," replied Phil, unable to stop himself from breaking into a massive smile.

Shaking his head, Julian was just about to walk over to their dorm room door when Phil grabbed his sleeve, pulling him back.

"Hey," he said, "what did you use?"

"Use?" Julian asked, his mind blank.

"You know, for protection," replied Phil, raising his eyebrows.

"Oh, we . . . didn't. Jane takes her sister's pills. She assured me it's fine. Why, what did you use?"

Phil shrugged, looking a little embarrassed. "Well, I didn't really have anything either, so . . ." He trailed off, clearly not wanting to say any more.

"So what?" asked Julian, intrigued now.

"I used my hankie."

Julian stared at him, trying not to laugh. "A *hankie?*"

Phil shook his head, and even in the dim lighting in the corridor, Julian could tell his cheeks were turning red. "I didn't know Vicky was going to come tonight, did I? I didn't exactly have much time to get prepared!"

Julian patted his friend on the shoulder. "I'm sure it's fine. Did it seem to . . . you know . . . work?"

Shrugging, Phil took his white handkerchief from his pocket and held it out towards Julian, who jumped back, letting out a disgusted shout.

"Get that thing away from me!" he whispered angrily, though he laughed when Phil jumped forward, dangling it in his face. "I swear to God, Phil . . ."

With that, Julian ran over to the dorm door and let himself in, a laughing Phil following in behind as he tucked the handkerchief back into his pyjama pocket. He loved riling his best friend up, and he was in such a good mood now that he couldn't help himself.

They ran over to their respective beds, not even trying to be quiet anymore - neither of them cared. What they cared about was what had just happened, something they couldn't quite believe actually *had* happened. Anything else just seemed small and unimportant in contrast.

"What's up with you two?" James hissed from one of the beds. He sounded groggy and annoyed.

"Wouldn't you like to know?" asked Julian as he slipped into his bed, not caring how happy he sounded.

CHAPTER 7

Over the next few weeks, Julian and Phil got to work, cutting more pass keys and selling them to other boys in their dorm, either for a cash amount or for something much more valuable: homework.

Things were going well. Julian and Phil were pretty much heroes to the rest of the boys on their wing, and not just because of the pass keys - rumours had been flying around that they'd done it with two of the girls from the third floor, rumours that neither Phil nor Julian would confirm. Of course, they didn't deny it either, and their friends guessed quite quickly that the rumours were true.

Yes, they were extremely popular at school - that was, until one day a few weeks into the term.

One morning, Julian was having breakfast in the dining room with Phil when one of the prefects walked in, yelling at everyone to be quiet.

This was a highly unusual occurrence, and Julian nudged Phil in the side. "Something's wrong."

"What?" asked Phil, looking up from his cereal. "What is it?"

Julian had the feeling he knew *exactly* what it was, and this was soon confirmed by the prefect - a girl a little older than Julian, but still in his year, who he'd seen lurking around the school corridors. She was well-built (but not fat by any stretch of the imagination), and she looked like she meant business. While she had attractive features, they were generally made slightly less attractive by her constant frown, as though she was suspicious of everyone and everything around her.

"I need everyone to stop eating," she announced as she glanced around the room, "and head over to the theatre. The headmaster needs to talk to you all about something very important. Come on, that's an order!"

"I knew it," said Julian, his heart sinking. "It's the tuck shop. He knows."

Phil rolled his eyes. "You don't know that, it could be anything - literally anything."

Julian, however, had a gut feeling, and his gut feelings were rarely wrong. He could feel his own pass key burning a hole in his pocket - he kept it on him at all times, just in case their rooms were ever searched - and as he stood up, he instinctively picked up Phil's banana from his plate.

As they all filed out of the kitchen, Julian glanced at Phil. "Try and cover me while I do this, OK?" he asked, indicating his pocket, where Phil knew the key was. His friend nodded, and as they headed into the corridor, Phil took the role of lookout.

As he went, he peeled the banana just enough to see the light yellow flesh beneath, then he slid the pass key carefully inside, the metal gliding easily into the soft fruit.

Squeezing the top of the banana peel until it closed again, he placed the whole thing in his pocket, upside down in case the key started to poke out.

He had no control over the other pass keys that were out there, but he tried not to think about that as they headed to the theatre - if he did, he thought he'd probably throw up.

When they got to the theatre, Julian could see the headmaster standing on the stage, staring at them all with a look that could only be described as contempt.

Julian groaned inwardly - this was it. He could feel it.

"It has come to my attention," the headmaster said, addressing the room, "that the stock in the tuck shop has been rapidly diminishing of late." He glared at everyone, clearly very angry - as if the stolen food was a personal attack on his own character. "It doesn't seem to occur to the students in this school that the snacks and drinks we provide - the snacks and drinks we don't *have* to provide, I should point out - cost money. And every time something goes missing, that's money we have to find from somewhere in the budget."

Julian was staring at the headmaster, making sure he didn't look away or do anything that might be construed as appearing guilty.

"We don't know how this has happened," the headmaster went on, "but we know that someone here got into the tuck shop last night and stole approximately fifty pounds' worth of goods. This is theft, pure and simple. It is illegal. And we're going to find out who the thief - or thieves - are. I can tell you that right now."

Julian's mind was all over the place, and when the headmaster started ordering the students to form a line in front of several members of staff, he started sweating.

"What are they doing?" whispered Phil, trying to see over people's heads. "Are they searching their pockets?"

"Yes," said Julian, who had a slightly better view from where he was standing. "And they're doing something with their hands too . . . they're checking their hands, I think." He shrugged at Phil, but as they joined the queue and got closer to the staff members, they realised that they were shining lights onto the students' hands.

But it wasn't a normal kind of light . . .

"Is that UV?" asked Phil, who was pretty sure it was, but couldn't for the life of him think why it would be so.

Julian shrugged, and as a couple of boys who'd already been inspected walked past on their way to leave the theatre, Julian grabbed one of them by the sleeve. "Hey," he whispered, lowering his voice even though he wasn't anywhere near the headmaster, "do you know what's happening?"

The boy - Trevor, if Julian remembered correctly - nodded. "They're checking hands for ink."

Phil nodded too. "Invisible ink, right? That's why they're using UV light."

"That's right," replied Trevor. "Seems like when they got wind of the food getting stolen, they put ink all over the shelves in there. They did it last night, right before someone raided it. Was it you?"

Both Julian and Phil shook their heads. "Not us," said Julian. At least not this time. The night before, both of them had taken a little visit to the hayloft in the grounds, a place they went sometimes to get away from everything. Julian had been hoping he'd be able to lure Jane there, but had so far been unsuccessful.

Trevor shrugged before leaving the theatre, and Julian turned to face Phil. "They can't trace the keys back to us, can they?"

Phil thought about this for a moment. "I don't think so, but that's not to say someone isn't going to mouth off about it - I wouldn't be surprised if they put us in the firing line to save their own arses."

Right then, there was a commotion at the front of the queue, and Julian could just about make out two boys - Tommy and Lee - talking loudly at once, obviously trying to explain the invisible ink that had just been made very much visible on their hands.

Julian's stomach churned, but he could hear everything they were saying, and they hadn't yet mentioned his name. Or Phil's. Tommy and Lee were good guys - hopefully they wouldn't dob them in.

"It's not what it looks like," Tommy was saying.

"We've been nowhere near the tuck shop! How would we get in?" asked Lee.

"It must be a prank."

"Yeah, someone must have come and put the ink on our hands while we slept."

"We'd never steal from the school, Sir!"

"Never in a million years!"

That was good, thought Julian. Deny everything. If they incriminated Julian and Phil, they'd be incriminating themselves too. Well, more than the invisible ink already had.

There was some shuffling around as the staff members searched the boys, and soon they were holding up two shiny pass keys. Julian's stomach lurched again.

"It's as I thought," shouted the headmaster, making Julian jump even from so far away. "If anyone else has a key on them, give it to me *right now*, or the consequences will be a hundred times worse for you."

There was silence for a moment - a silence during which Julian felt the banana in his pocket, making sure it was still intact - and then two more boys stepped forward, taking out their own keys and handing them over.

"Anyone else?" shouted the headmaster, now clearly furious.

Phil glanced at Julian, but Julian shook his head: he had no intention of just handing the key over.

"Prefects, if you wouldn't mind helping with the search, please?" the headmaster asked, and soon both boys and girls were heading up the line of students, searching them as if they were going through airport security. There seemed to be no concern for gender - girls were searching boys, and boys were searching girls.

Soon the female prefect who'd told everyone to leave the dining hall was standing in front of Julian, smiling at him - she was obviously enjoying this, enjoying having even more power than usual over the students. "You got any keys on you?" she asked. Julian suddenly remembered her name: Laura.

He shook his head, but she started searching him anyway - patting down his shirt, running her hands around his waist, then smoothing down his trousers first on one side and then the other. If Julian hadn't been so terrified of getting caught, he no doubt would have found the whole thing incredibly arousing.

When the prefect got to his pocket, she wrapped her hand around the banana, raising her eyebrows. Again, if he hadn't been so terrified . . .

"What's this?" she asked, the corner of her mouth turning up into a smirk.

"It's a . . . b-banana," Julian stammered, wondering just how guilty he must look.

He could imagine what was going to happen next: Laura reaching into his pocket, bringing out the fruit, seeing how it was open at the top. He could picture her delving into the soft flesh, bringing out the key and waving it in the air in triumph. He could imagine the headmaster coming over, shaking his head - both in anger and disappointment - then the look on his mum's face when she found out he'd been expelled.

But all Laura did was wink at him before moving onto the next person in the line.

Phil - who'd just had a rather less erotic search from one of the male prefects - let out the breath he'd been holding in. "You are one lucky bastard, you know that?"

Julian nodded, unable to speak, and soon the searches were over. They'd found another key on top of the others, but apparently no one so far had mentioned either of their names.

"Alright, alright," said the headmaster, raising his voice and causing everyone else to stop talking. "I think we've seen enough. You are to go on to your lessons without breakfast," - there was an audible moan at these words from pretty much everyone in the theatre - "and anyone caught lingering around the tuck shop without permission will be suspended immediately. Have I made myself clear?"

The boys responded with a reluctant, "Yes, Sir," and as soon as the headmaster had marched off the stage, Julian ran out of the theatre.

That had been a close call.

That evening, he climbed the tree outside Jane's dormitory and threw a stone at the window. He'd been stressing out about the keys all day, and he wanted - no, *needed* - to see her.

Moments later, Jane appeared, opening the window and leaning out towards him. "What are you doing?" she hissed.

"What do you think I'm doing? I'm here to see you."

Jane rolled her eyes, but Julian thought he could see a small smile start to grace her lips. "Well, I can't see much of you in that tree."

Julian grinned. "Which is why I suggest we go over to the hayloft. We can . . . talk . . . there."

Jane raised her eyebrows. "Talk? That's what you want to do?"

"You *know* what I want to do . . . but yeah, talking would be good too." He paused for a moment. "Today's been kind of rubbish. What do you say?"

Jane thought about this for a moment, then nodded. "Give me ten minutes. Meet me at the bottom of the dorm stairs."

"Ten minutes," he said, grinning again.

Julian couldn't believe it - she'd actually said yes! - and after climbing down from the tree, he waited in the darkness until five or so minutes had passed.

Then, being as quiet as he possibly could, he made his way inside. After moving over to the bottom of the staircase, he took a deep breath, trying to prepare himself for what was about to happen.

Moments later he saw movement at the top of the stairs, but when the girl came down, he saw that it wasn't Jane; it was Laura, the prefect. His stomach lurched.

"Julian, isn't it?" she asked as she headed down. "Banana boy. What are you up to?"

Julian shrugged. "Couldn't sleep. Thought I'd walk around for a bit."

"And climb a tree and wake up several girls in the dorm? Throwing stones against the window is vandalism, you know."

He closed his eyes, unable to believe his luck. How much worse could this day get?

"I know what you're up to," said Laura, "and I know what we're going to do about it."

"What?" asked Julian with a sigh, now resigned to the fact that he was going to get in trouble - big trouble. And a lot of it.

"The hayloft," Laura said, her words completely catching Julian off guard. "You know it."

"What? Yes . . ."

"Meet me there tomorrow night," she said, "after dinner. Once it's dark. We'll figure out a way for you to pay me back."

"Pay you back . . . for what?" asked Julian, who was beginning to feel a small but very real ray of hope in this whole mess of a situation.

"For not telling anyone about your little tree-climbing stunt," she said, shrugging. "I've heard Jane talk about you, you know, and I want to see what you've got. First hand."

For a moment, Julian was stumped. "Jane?"

"Just meet me at the hayloft. Come alone. And make sure you don't tell anyone." With that, she moved over to Julian, leaned into him, and kissed him right on the lips. He could smell her perfume, could taste her strawberry lip balm.

"Tomorrow," she said, and then she left.

CHAPTER 8

The next day, Julian couldn't concentrate on anything. His school classes went by in a blur, and he hardly even remembered having breakfast or lunch with Phil.

By dinnertime, Julian was looking at his watch every few minutes, willing the time to go by faster and wishing the sky would finally go dark so he could sneak out to the hayloft.

"So let me get this straight," said Phil, through a mouthful of chicken, "you went to meet Jane last night because you're so obsessed with her, and now you're going to go and meet this Laura girl in the hayloft?"

Julian shrugged. "I'm not *obsessed*. And anyway, it's not like I have a choice, mate."

Phil paused for a moment, his fork halfway to his mouth, his eyes locked on his friend's face. "You'll tell me what happens though, right? Like, all the details?"

Julian grinned. "*All* the details."

After dinner, Julian and Phil went to their allocated study room not far from their dorm to wait for darkness to fall.

They sat in that room for an hour or so, discussing Laura and what might happen as they gazed out of the single window, watching as the sun set. They couldn't see much out of that tiny window - just a narrow view of part of the school field - but it was enough to tell them what they needed to know. Soon, it was time.

"Good luck," said Phil as he watched his friend walk over to the study room door. "If anyone notices you're gone, I'll cover for you."

"Thanks," said Julian, grinning, before opening the door and peering out into the corridor. All was quiet; most people were probably either actually studying or hanging out in their dorm rooms.

He marched down the corridor as fast as he could, his heart hammering in his chest the whole time, absolutely sure that he'd turn a corner to find a teacher there, ready to yell at him.

At that thought, he stopped in his tracks. What if this was a trap? After all, he didn't really know her, and he had no reason to trust her.

On the other hand, this little meeting could be exactly what she'd said it was, and if he didn't go and see for himself, he knew he'd regret it.

Now feeling a bit less enthusiastic about the whole thing, Julian started walking again, letting himself out of a side door and running across the grass in the darkness. He went as fast as he could, hoping no one would see him and alert a teacher, and when he found himself outside the stable building, he breathed a sigh of relief.

He pushed hesitantly on the old door, which creaked open slightly, allowing him to enter the abandoned building. He knew that the school used to keep horses in there, but since that was no longer the case, hardly anyone ever went in there anymore - apart from a few unruly students.

Closing the door behind him, Julian paused for a moment to let his eyes adjust to the gloom of the stables - there were windows in here, but they were covered in a thick layer of dust, only letting in the smallest amount of light from the moon and the main school building in the distance.

There were a few old crates in here, a few black bags full of junk, a pile of rope in the corner . . . all ancient discarded things that didn't look like they'd seen the light of day in years. It was a little creepy.

Crossing the cold concrete floor, Julian made his way over to the corner, where an old rickety ladder lay propped up against the brick wall. It disappeared up into the shadows, and Julian shivered.

Placing first one foot and then the other on the ladder's rungs, he slowly ascended, pausing every so often as the ancient wood creaked under his shoes. There were cobwebs covering the ladder, and he was sure he saw a spider - really just a blob in the gloom - as it scuttled down the side and went past his feet.

As Julian got to the top, he peered over the opening to the hayloft, immediately able to see better - there was a large round window up there, and someone had wiped off all the grime, allowing a small but useful beam of light to illuminate the top of the barn.

Now he could clearly see the wooden beams and the hay on the ground, and in the middle of the space - sitting on what appeared to be a picnic blanket - there was Laura.

Julian sighed in relief. She was alone, and she was smiling - for once. It *couldn't* be a trap - if she'd set him up to get caught in the hayloft, she'd be in just as much trouble as he would be.

No, this was real. This was really happening. He shivered in anticipation.

"So you came," said Laura.

"I didn't have much choice, did I?" Julian replied, pulling himself up the last few feet and scrambling into the hayloft. He could just about stand up in there, though it was tight, and slowly, he walked over to the middle of the space where Laura was sitting.

"No," she said, "and you won't have much choice about what we do up here either. Does that worry you?" She was smiling, and now that he was closer, Julian could see a slight hint of seduction in that smile. It made his knees go weak.

"That doesn't bother me at all," he replied honestly. He was already getting aroused and they hadn't even done anything yet.

"Good," she said, reaching up and pulling him down to her level. "Undress me."

A thrill ran through him at those words, and he immediately reached out towards her top.

Laughing, Laura held her hand up, stopping him in his tracks. "Not so fast. Do it slowly."

Nodding his understanding, Julian took a deep breath before reaching out again, this time being careful not to come across as too eager. Laura shuffled closer to him, pushing out her chest as she did so, and Julian started undoing the buttons on the front of her shirt, his fingers trembling slightly as he tried to get himself under control.

When he pushed the shirt off her shoulders to reveal her simple white bra beneath - her nipples raised through the material - he felt another one of those shivers run through his entire body.

"Take my skirt off," she commanded, and he reached down and pulled at the thick fabric. She lifted herself so he could drag it down off her hips, then she raised her legs in the air so he could slip it off over her feet.

She was now lying just in her underwear, and he stared at her for a moment, taking her all in. The moonlight pouring in through the single window highlighted her pale skin, making her look ethereal and out of this world.

"Take off your clothes," Laura said next, her voice full of prefect authority. "All of them." She threw him a quick smile. "You can do this bit quickly if you like."

Julian didn't need to be told twice - he almost jumped out of his trousers and shirt, although he did hesitate slightly before taking his underwear off; it was cold up here, after all.

Laura watched all of this with great interest, and when he was done, she said, "Lie on top of me and kiss me."

Julian lowered himself over Laura, her cold skin touching his and making his entire body tingle. Then he leaned down and started kissing her as though his life depended on it.

"Woah, hold up," she said, yet again pushing him away. "Do it slowly. What's the rush? I want to feel every part of it." She licked her lips once she'd finished speaking, and Julian could feel himself getting harder and harder. "Now kiss me."

Not entirely sure if he was doing it how she wanted, Julian leaned down again and slowly pressed his lips to hers. He could taste her strawberry lip balm, and he basked in how soft and smooth her lips were.

Laura kissed him back, also slowly, wrapping her arms around his neck and raking her hands gently through his hair.

Going at this speed seemed to create an entirely different experience, and as Julian pressed his body harder against Laura, he thought how amazing it felt.

They kissed like that - softly and sweetly - for a few more seconds, and then, finally, Laura opened her mouth, pushing her tongue against Julian's lips and making him harder than ever.

After what felt like an eternity she plunged her tongue into his mouth, and Julian did the same, though they were still going at that wonderfully slow pace. Laura gripped his hair harder as Julian trailed his hands down the side of her body, revelling in her beautiful soft, cold skin.

Laura groaned - which Julian took as a signal to speed up - and soon they *were* kissing as if their lives depended on it, their increased movement making the wooden beams of the hayloft creak underneath their bodies.

After a minute or so Laura pulled away from the kiss, pushing on Julian's chest again and making him stop.

Julian immediately started positioning himself over her, but Laura grabbed his arm as she shook her head. "Tonight's all about me," she whispered, as she glanced down at herself. "Take it off."

Happy to oblige, Julian reached down and pulled off her under-wear, before reaching out for her bra. She leaned forwards so he could undo it from the back, and after a bit of fumbling, he managed to do it. Pulling the straps down off her shoulders and over her arms, he stared hungrily at her large, round breasts.

"Now," she said, pointing downwards. "You can use your tongue and your fingers, nothing else."

Julian stared at her as she glanced down at him, at how aroused he was; she could see he was ready to go, but she wasn't going to let him off that easily.

"Go on," she said. "I'm waiting." With that, she spread her legs wide open, inviting him in, and he didn't hesitate.

Reaching down, he pushed two fingers inside her, immediately feeling the warmth and the wetness. He didn't really know what he was doing, but he'd rather die than admit that to Laura, so he just pushed them in as far as they would go, immediately causing Laura to shout out.

"Be gentle!" she yelled, for the first time sounding angry, and Julian immediately brought his fingers out.

"Sorry," he mumbled, leaning down and kissing her just as gently as before.

"It's OK, just not so rough." She paused, thinking about that for a moment. "At least, not tonight."

The thought of this happening again sent another thrill through him, and he kissed her again on the lips before moving his mouth slowly down her body, kissing her here and there as he went. Laura shivered wonderfully at his touch.

After - gently, this time - pushing two fingers into her, he moved them around until Laura suddenly shuddered beneath him. Realising he'd found the sweet spot, he continued to massage that area, pushing his fingers in and out at a tantalisingly slow pace.

"Get faster," Laura moaned, and he obliged, moving his fingers more quickly now and watching in fascination as she writhed and moaned on the blanket.

"Now do it with your tongue!" she demanded, and Julian leaned down, breathing in her sweet scent before slowly starting to lick her, making her shiver all over again.

"More!" she shouted, and he pushed his tongue in further, trying to locate that same sweet spot from before. When he found it, she screamed in pleasure, and as she started to shudder again he grabbed hold of her hips, pinning her to the ground as he thrust his tongue further inside her.

She moaned again, and this time he reached out further, grabbing a breast in each hand and squeezing them as he pleasured her.

She screamed his name, sending another thrill through his entire body, and he sped up, writhing along with her now as she moaned and groaned.

He could feel her about to climax, and he felt ready too, despite her not even touching him down there yet.

Just as he'd had that thought, Laura reached out either side of her, grabbing the blanket in her hands and scrunching it up in her ecstasy as she let out one last scream.

Julian watched her, enthralled, taking in every inch of her body, every ounce of her pleasure. It was almost too much.

He pulled back as she started to relax her body, waiting for her to open her eyes and look at him. He was throbbing down there now; he knew he needed to get some relief -and soon.

"That wasn't half bad," she said eventually as she sat up, the sight of her naked body in that pose doing nothing to hinder his excitement.

He watched in despair as she gathered up her clothes and got dressed - ignoring him the whole time - and when she stood up, ready to leave, he grabbed her hands in his.

"Laura," he said. "What about . . .?"

She looked down at him - as if suddenly remembering he was naked - and let out a little giggle. "Oh right." She paused for a moment, thinking. "Well, I was going to leave you to sort that out yourself, but as you've been so good to me . . ."

She strolled right up to him, staring at him straight in the eyes as she grabbed him down there. Then she started moving her hand up and down his length, all the while maintaining eye contact, all the while smiling that seductive little smile she'd been wearing when he'd first got up there.

It was his turn to moan now, and as he felt his legs start to buckle, he reached out and held onto her shoulders. She didn't seem to mind.

She sped up, moving closer and closer to him until her shirt was touching his bare skin, and just as Julian had expected, it didn't take long until he was shouting out in his climax.

Laura stepped to the side at the last moment, and as soon as he'd finished, she leaned over and kissed him briefly on the lips. "I'll see you tomorrow night. Same time? Otherwise, you'll know what'll happen."

Julian nodded. Honestly, at that moment, she could have told the headmaster whatever she wanted to and he wouldn't have cared. All he could think about was what had just happened, and how amazing it had felt.

CHAPTER 9

The rest of the term passed by in a blur; what with classes, exams, and his frequent visits to the hayloft, time seemed to be speeding by faster than ever.

Things had been awkward with Jane for a while - as she knew what he was doing with Laura in the hayloft - but after explaining the whole blackmail thing to her, Julian managed to get her back on side.

Soon it was the last few days of not only the school year, but Julian's last ever school year, and he couldn't wait.

He couldn't wait to leave those classrooms and teachers behind, but he was also looking forward to the big leaving party that was thrown every year.

The party itself didn't sound too thrilling, but Julian had several plans to liven things up a bit, and he'd managed to rope Phil in to help him achieve them.

There was the time honoured spiking of the punch, which Phil was happy to sort out - paying someone to go into a shop for him, then pouring the newly acquired vodka into several smaller pop bottles.

Julian told Phil to save some of the alcohol for them and the other boys in their dorm - they could have a bit each before the dance started, to get them 'warmed up'. Phil was glad - he felt nervous about the dance.

Julian, on the other hand, was having a ball; as well as livening up the party with the contents of the pop bottles, he also had some other plans for his last few days at school. For one thing, there was the contest.

'The contest' was something Julian had come up with as a way of truly ending the school year in style, but Phil wasn't quite so enthusiastic about the whole thing.

He was too busy thinking ahead to life after school, and so was Vicky. It turned out she had an on-again off-again thing with a guy who lived near her parents, and she'd told Phil she would probably go back to him again once they'd finished the school year.

Phil was a little disappointed at this, but Julian told him to be realistic; they never would have seen each other after school anyway, whether that other guy was involved or not.

"Plus," Julian said, "that means you can take part in the contest with me."

Phil groaned. "Are you still going on about that?"

"Why not?" asked Julian. "It's going to be one of the last chances we get with any of the girls in this school."

Phil sighed. "OK, I'm in. So what are the rules?"

Julian went and sat next to Phil on his bed. They were in their otherwise empty dorm, the others having gone off to do some last-minute studying. "We'll do it on a points system. Five points for kissing someone . . . ten points if there's any touching going on . . . twenty points if any clothing is removed . . . and fifty points if you go all the way."

So with that, the contest was planned, and that night they started getting ready in their dorm room, putting on their suits and passing around a couple of glasses of vodka.

Phil took a swig, shuddered, and passed it on to Julian.

"Here's to a great night!" he said before downing rather a lot of vodka, causing the other boys to clap and whoop.

Half an hour later, Julian, Phil, and the other guys from their dorm entered the dining room, which had been completely transformed for the night - the chairs and tables had been put away, a DJ stand had been set up at one end of the room, and the walls were covered in balloons and streamers. The room was in semi-darkness, with the main source of illumination coming from the DJ booth, with its flashing multi-coloured lights. There was a huge mirrorball hanging down from the middle of the ceiling, casting weird and wonderful shapes on the floor and the walls, and the DJ was currently playing some cheesy pop song.

Julian walked over to the food and drink tables, which were lined up on one side of the dining room. Phil and the others followed.

The food was pretty standard buffet fare, with crisps and sandwiches and tiny cakes, but what Julian was looking for was right at the end of the table - a huge bowl of punch, like they always seemed to have in American movies when students go to their high school prom. It was completely unguarded - there were no teachers or prefects standing anywhere near it - so it was asking to be spiked, really.

"I'll go first," Julian whispered to the others, bringing his bottle of 'pop' out of his pocket and unscrewing the lid. "Cover me."

His friends did as they were told, gathering around Julian and looking out on the room, as casually as they could, to make sure no one was going to come over and see what they were doing.

"Now," said Julian, once he was finished, "shall we begin?"

Phil groaned as his friend grinned at him. "You still going on about the contest?"

"Hell yes!" said Julian, downing his drink.

Rather reluctantly, Phil did the same.

"OK. Meet me back here in an hour and we'll see how far we've got." Julian was still grinning, clearly exhilarated by the whole prospect.

"Fine," said Phil, shaking his head. "An hour."

Julian took a moment to look around the room, which by now was a lot more full, and he soon spotted Laura the prefect.

After catching her eye, she strolled over to him. She was wearing a long black dress and black high heels - she was stunning.

"You scrub up well," she said, smiling. "You want to dance or something?"

Julian shrugged. "Dancing isn't really my thing . . . I was hoping we could go somewhere . . . I don't know . . . a little more private?"

"I told you those hayloft lessons are over now. You're on your own."

"No, I don't want another lesson . . ." He paused for a moment, embarrassed all of a sudden. "OK, let me be honest. I've got a bet on with Phil, and some of the other lads too."

"Ah," said Laura, nodding. "I see. So you want to use me to win some stupid competition you've got going with your mates?" She raised her eyebrows.

Julian sighed. "Basically, yeah. Help a friend out?"

"I suppose I could help you out this one last time."

Relieved, Julian followed her across the temporary dance floor, only vaguely noticing a not very impressed-looking Jane glaring at him as they left.

"Where shall we go?" asked Julian as they headed into the corridor, trying not to think about Jane.

Laura thought for a moment, then after a brief pause, she moved over to one of the doors going off the corridor, turning the handle to see if it would open. It did, and she stood back triumphantly.

After entering the closet - which was pretty big really, for a closet - Julian pulled the door shut behind them before anyone could see what they were doing.

"So," Laura said, her voice somehow sounding far away in the darkness, "what are we doing? What's the competition?"

Julian explained the points system to her.

"Right. Well, in that case . . ." She reached out in the gloom, finding his face and leaning into him. She kissed him on the lips, slowly and gently, then pulled back. "Five points to Julian! Now, if you want, you can take off one item of my clothing."

Julian frowned, even though Laura couldn't see his facial expressions in the darkness. "But you're only wearing a dress."

"And what about what's underneath?" asked Laura.

"Oh, right," said Julian, suddenly feeling incredibly nervous, but excited as well. The fact they were right near the dining hall where the dance was taking place added a whole other level to their little rendezvous.

Julian sensed Laura moving in the darkness, and after taking his hand in hers, she placed it on her thigh as she raised her leg up, her high heels banging against the shelf next to Julian as her dress rode up. Then she leaned into him again - her leg resting against his side - and kissed him, this time more deeply and passionately, before bringing her leg back down.

She moved her hands to hold her dress up, then said, "pull them down now."

Julian was happy to help, and as he leaned down to tug on her underwear - which felt amazingly silky and smooth - he had to stop himself from doing anything more. He knew how Laura liked him to obey instructions, but also how she hated him doing anything she hadn't told him.

The silk pants slid easily down her long, smooth legs, landing on the floor next to her heels. She daintily stepped out of them, picked them up, then leaned into him again, shoving them into one of his trouser pockets. "A little keepsake," she whispered into his ear, making him shiver.

"OK," he said, trying to calm himself down. "So that's another twenty points . . . though we missed out the touching . . ."

Laura took his hand in hers again and pushed it up against her left breast. She was leaning into him again, and she let his hand linger there for a few seconds before she guided it down to below her navel. "You know what to do."

Julian certainly did, and as he pushed his fingers inside her, she let out a loud groan, seemingly not caring if anyone outside heard them.

She leaned in to kiss him again, this time giggling as she pulled away. "You've been drinking, haven't you? So have I." She giggled again, showing him a different side to her; in the hayloft she was always so cold, so in control.

She leaned into him again, whispered, "ten points," then kissed him with far more enthusiasm than she ever had before.

"Want to go for the full fifty?" he said, half joking, and not at all expecting the response he got.

Laura grabbed his shoulders, slamming him into the shelves and causing several unidentified objects to fall off and crash to the floor. His fingers were still inside her, and she pushed against him as hard as she could before leaning back briefly then doing the same thing again.

"I'm going to miss this," she said, and before Julian even knew what was happening, she unbuckled his belt, making his trousers drop to the floor. Then she unbuttoned his shirt, placing her hands on his chest as she continued to gyrate against him. Without wasting another second, she pulled down his underwear before grabbing his hands and slamming them against one of the shelves. She then lifted her leg like she'd done before, leaning into him, and him into her.

She let go of his hands, allowing him to grab her hips as she moved up and down, more things falling off the shelves around them as they got faster and faster, rougher and rougher.

Julian could tell Laura was about to scream, and just as she opened her mouth, he clamped his hand over her lips, muffling her shout. She bit down on one of his fingers, but in his climax, he didn't much care; he hardly even felt it.

Just then they heard noises outside - people talking - and both of them immediately stopped moving. Still pressed together, they waited in silence, their hearts beating fast, their bodies still very much aroused.

There was laughter out in the corridor, and a second later, the door swung slowly open.

This is it, thought Julian, this is when the headmaster catches me having sex in the cleaning cupboard . . . but it wasn't the headmaster at all.

Next to the door stood two girls - two of Laura's friends - and they were both gawping at the sight before them.

"You don't waste any time, do you?" asked a girl called Emily, though Julian wasn't sure if she was talking to him or Laura. She was Canadian, and he had to admit, her accent alone made him ready for more.

The other girl just laughed, then turned and fled - the sight of them in the closet was obviously too much for her.

"Julian," said Emily, "your friend Phil tried it on with me. So this is part of your little competition, is it?"

Julian nodded, unable to say anything. He hadn't thought Phil would bring up the competition when trying to get with a girl, but if the other lads were being loudmouths, she could have heard it from them. Hell, the whole school could have heard about it by now.

"Well, I felt kind of sorry for him so we had a bit of a kiss and a feel." She grinned. "Although I have to say, it looks a whole lot more interesting in here."

"Emily, you're so bad!" She turned to face Julian. "She doesn't care who she gets it on with. Boy, girl, you name it."

Julian suddenly felt himself get extremely aroused again, and Laura giggled at his reaction.

"Get in here, Emily, before the whole student body sees Little Julian."

Emily let herself into the closet and closed the door behind her. Julian couldn't believe his luck.

Without saying anything, Laura backed off from Julian, allowing Emily to lean forwards and kiss him. When she pulled away, Laura moved in next to her, also leaning in to kiss Julian. There was a brief pause then, and Julian could only assume they were kissing each other.

He could feel himself getting harder and harder by the second.

He could feel Emily's hands on his chest, and just as she was trailing her fingers down his torso, the door opened again.

Julian gasped as he saw Jane standing there, hands on her hips, staring at the three of them, but Laura and Emily just laughed.

"You're disgusting," she spat at Julian, before running off and leaving the door wide open.

As much as it pained him to do it, Julian pushed Emily and Jane away, quickly pulling up his pants and trousers and doing up his shirt as he ran out into the corridor.

Jane's surprise appearance had shaken him, and he no longer felt at all excited, which he thought was just as well considering he was now running after her into the dining hall.

"Jane, wait!" he yelled, as she ran over to the food table.

He followed behind her, hoping he'd be able to talk to her and calm her down, but when he got there she turned to face him, her face red, her eyes full of tears.

"I knew you'd go off with Laura tonight," she shouted, "but another girl as well? Do you not care about me *at all*?"

She was slurring her words a little, and Julian suddenly found himself wishing that he'd never spiked the punch in the first place. It seemed that vodka was very fast-acting.

"Jane . . . it's not what you think."

"Oh really?" she spat, leaning forwards and pulling something out of his pocket. "So what are these then?" She held up Laura's silk pants, shaking them at him angrily.

He was just about to open his mouth to apologise when Jane threw the underwear on the floor and leaned over the table, grasping the now half-empty bowl of punch and just about managing to hold it up in front of her.

"Jane . . . what are you . . ."

By now the music had stopped, the DJ evidently wanting to see - and hear - how this would pan out, and Julian had just realised the entire room was now watching them as Jane lunged forwards, throwing the remains of the punch at him and soaking him through.

It was embarrassing, sure, but that wasn't the worst part - not by a mile. The vodka in the punch had gone all over his face, and it was now stinging his eyes as he staggered around, half-blind.

He could just about see a chair next to the food table, and although he tried heading towards it, at the last moment Jane pushed him, causing him to go crashing into the table and pulling down not only the tablecloth, but plates and plates of food as well.

It was as he was lying on the floor, surrounded by food and napkins and plastic cutlery, that he realised the room had gone deadly silent. If he'd seen anything like this happen, he would be howling his head off with laughter, so why was no one even gasping at his stupid stunt?

A second later, he knew why, and as the headmaster leaned down to be in his field of - blurry - vision, he closed his eyes, hoping the stinging would stop.

"Julian, I think the dance is over for you." He turned to the rest of the room, taking in the drinks the people were holding and the slightly glazed look on many of their faces. "And I think it's over for everyone else too."

There was a lot of moaning and gasping at *that*, but Julian tried not to listen. What a disaster.

He spent the rest of the evening in the main office, cleaning himself up and getting the alcohol out of his eyes as the headmaster watched on from his desk.

Fortunately, it seemed that he hadn't got wind of the contest or what had been happening in the closet, but he was more than aware of the spiked punch.

"I've got no proof that you put alcohol in that drink," said the headmaster, "so count yourself lucky. If I did . . ." He trailed off, shaking his head.

Julian actually shuddered.

"Right," he said, sitting up straighter in his chair and staring at him, "you've got two more days at this school. Try not to screw everything up, will you?"

Julian couldn't help it - he laughed. "Yes sir."

CHAPTER 10

On the night before their last day, Julian and Phil made their way onto the roof - where some workers had left behind some ladders and paint pots from a recent job - armed with a paintbrush and a torch each. After doing a thorough search of the area and peering out at the grounds to check they were alone - it was 2 a.m. so they hoped no one would be around - they got down to business.

Each grabbing a tin of white paint, Phil and Julian took the lids off the tubs and dipped in their brushes.

Then, slowly and carefully, they started painting the huge clock tower that looked down over the quad, whitewashing the entire thing, clock face and all - it looked pretty spooky in the moonlight. Next, they painted several large letters on the roof, spelling out the words 'GOOD BYE'.

When they were done, they stood back and admired their handiwork, grinning at each other in the darkness. Julian was satisfied - he'd finally left his mark on the school.

"You happy with that?" Phil asked, hoping they could go back to the dorm before anyone saw them.

Julian nodded. "I'm very happy, Phil. *Very* happy."

The next morning, Phil woke to find Julian leaning over his bed, grinning. "Get up, Phil - you're missing all the fun!"

Phil sat up slowly, rubbing the sleep from his eyes. He was exhausted, but Julian seemed fine. In fact, Julian seemed *great*. "What?" was about all he could manage.

"Come on - you've got to see this."

Groaning, Phil dragged himself out of bed and quickly pulled on the nearest clothes he could find. He'd literally just got his shoes on when Julian dragged him over to the door, pushing him out into the corridor.

Despite the early hour, the school was buzzing - some people making the most of their last few hours with their friends, while others rushed around and packed, making sure they could leave as soon as humanly possible.

Julian and Phil made their way through the manic students and even more manic-looking teachers, and finally they emerged outside, where things were even crazier.

There was a whole crowd of people - consisting of students of all ages, not to mention staff members from every area of the school - and they were all glancing up with wide eyes, taking in the most recent 'changes' to the clock tower.

The whitewashed tower and clock face looked pretty spectacular, Phil had to admit, and the 'GOOD BYE' in large white letters was the finishing touch. The students seemed to be thinking the same, and Phil noticed that even a few of the teachers were trying hard not to laugh.

Suddenly, a voice from the edge of the crowd roared, "What is the meaning of this?" and when Julian and Phil turned around, they saw the headmaster. He didn't look happy.

"Who did this?" he roared, turning around to glare at everyone. "This is disrespect at its absolute worst!"

This only made the students in the crowd laugh, though Julian and Phil managed to stay remarkably straight-faced.

This lack of laughter on their part immediately got the headmaster's attention, and he glared at Julian for a good few seconds before striding off, shouting, "The Final Address is in twenty minutes in the main hall. Don't be late!" over his shoulder as he went.

"I think we got away with that!" whispered Julian.

Twenty minutes later, the whole of the final year were gathered in the main hall, watching as the headmaster took to the little stage at the front of the room.

"It's that time of year again," he said, "when we have to say good-bye to some of you - to the next generation. It's always emotional, so I'll keep my speech brief." He paused, clearing his throat. "Over the years we've had some exceptional people walk our halls and take our classes - people who've gone on to do incredible things with their lives - and this year is no exception. In ten or twenty years' time, I expect to be hearing great things about each and every one of you." His eyes flickered to Julian then as he said, "Even the ones who don't think they're capable."

Julian swallowed, and Phil turned to him, his eyes wide.

The headmaster carried on. "To whomever it was who painted the clock tower, I have to say: you are not the first to do something like this on the last day of term, and you certainly won't be the last. I just hope that, going into the future, you will have more respect for the property of others, and for the institutions where you will be further educated. Life isn't a joke, and at some point, you just have to grow up."

Julian lowered his eyes then, for the first time feeling a little regretful of his actions. Only a little, though.

"Anyway," continued the headmaster, "let's not leave on a sour note. I am very proud of what this year has achieved, and I very much look forward to seeing what you'll accomplish in the future. Good luck, and remember - your life is what you make it. Goodbye!"

Everyone in the room started clapping then, and despite the headmaster's earlier words, Phil and Julian joined in - it was kind of contagious.

"Well, that's it!" said Phil to his friend.

Julian nodded. "That's it."

Soon it was time to leave, and Julian and Phil joined the rest of the leaving students on the quad, dragging their cases and bags out of the main building.

Julian stared at the clock tower again, a feeling of pure sadness washing over him as he looked at the words they'd painted there.

"Well, this is it," Phil said, clapping Julian on the back. "We sure had some good times, didn't we?"

Julian grinned. "We sure did."

"And you know the best thing?" asked Phil, as the two turned and started strolling away from the school grounds.

"What?"

"We get to do it all over again in college."

Julian grinned, and suddenly, he felt a little better.

CHAPTER 11

The summer seemed both long and short for Julian. Being back at home was difficult after spending so much time with the boys in the dorm, but he managed OK - his mum often worked late, and he had more than enough opportunities to show the local girls what he'd learnt at school.

He enjoyed having no responsibilities for a while - no homework, no job, nothing to take up his time other than hanging out with friends and adding up his conquests - and while he wasn't looking forward to all the work he'd have to do when he got to college, he *was* looking forward to all the new people he'd meet.

By 'people' he meant 'girls'.

He'd decided to attend a technical college where he could take a catering course. After all, he'd enjoyed his cooking classes at school and he thought he was pretty good at it - it was something he could actually turn into a career. He'd meet a hell of a lot *more* women in the process.

He'd spoken to Phil a few times since leaving school, and was happy to hear he was having some fun too - he'd had a couple of summer flings, and Julian liked to think that the passing on of his knowledge had helped his friend, just as Laura's little hayloft lessons had helped him.

He was definitely feeling a lot more self-assured around girls now; knowing what he was actually doing had got rid of his nerves, allowing him to just go for it. The confidence oozed off him, and the girls had come flocking.

The first day of his catering course went well. He'd moved into his new room the night before and the next morning, he turned up for his orientation bright and early.

As he waited for the class to start, he caught a glimpse of his reflection in a mirror, marvelling at what he saw.

Julian's appearance had changed drastically over the summer, the most notable difference being his hair - it was long, as was the fashion these days.

People were slowly learning to loosen up - both in terms of what they wore and how they acted - and Julian thought it was the perfect time to be starting college. Some of the people at school had been so stuck-up and frigid, and he couldn't wait to become acquainted with the more laid-back college girls.

He'd found he could now grow facial hair, and the bit of stubble he was currently sporting made him look a good few years older than he was - or at least, that's what Julian hoped.

During his orientation session he checked out his new classmates, taking in the appearance of each one in turn. There were around thirty girls in the class, and his teacher - who was perhaps in her mid-thirties - was female too.

Julian looked back at the rest of the class. College, he decided, was already a million times better than school; he could certainly get used to this kind of male: female ratio.

As he swept his eyes over the girls in his class, he found that they too were staring at him, seemingly checking *him* out; several of the girls smiled at him, making sure they made good eye contact.

They all looked pretty good. Not one of them looked as though they'd be stuck-up, or like they'd be horrible to talk to, and most of them clearly took pride in their appearance. He'd struck gold.

He thought of Phil - who'd gone to an engineering college and who right now would no doubt be surrounded by big, burly boys - and tried not to laugh.

"Right," said his teacher, Mrs Matthews, bringing Julian out of his little daydream. "I want you to split up into groups and introduce yourselves to each other. You will be spending a *lot* of time with the people in this room, and the more you get on, the better this year will be for both you and for your grades. OK, let's get into groups of five to six. Come on!"

Julian immediately headed off to two blondes he'd seen in the corner of the room - one with long straight hair and one with long wavy hair. They were both slim and petite.

"Hi," he said, "I'm Julian."

The straight-haired girl nodded. "I'm Rosie. This is Clara."

Three others joined them. There was a slim redhead, a tall girl with dirty blonde hair, and a black-haired girl with green eyes who was so stunningly beautiful he had to do a double-take - how he'd not noticed her originally, he had no idea.

They introduced themselves - Sally, Harriet, and Jenny - and then all five of them just stood there, staring at him.

"So, how come you decided to go to catering school?" asked Jenny, the black-haired beauty. "You don't usually get a lot of men who are into cooking." She raised her eyebrows, and Julian immediately pictured them together in bed, her silky black hair cascading down her bare shoulders.

He managed to pull himself out of that particular daydream after a couple of seconds, and he hoped he wasn't blushing as he answered, "It was either this or engineering school with my friend . . . what can I say? I'd take a class full of beautiful women over a group of dirty guys any day."

Rosie, one of the blondes, pretended to fan her face with her hand. "We've got a live one here, girls," she said, raising her eyebrows. "I think there's going to be some competition for Julian's affections this year, am I right?"

The other girls nodded, looking him up and down and then smiling at each other.

"You *are* single, aren't you?" asked Clara, the other platinum blonde. "If you say no, you just might break my heart." She placed her hand on her chest dramatically.

"Oh, I'm single," replied Julian, grinning despite his best efforts to play it cool. "I am very, very single."

"Right," said Mrs Matthews again, "the groups you're standing in now are the groups you're going to be in for the next term." This announcement was met with a few rather rude groans from some of the girls, but Julian couldn't have been happier.

And fortunately, the girls in his group looked happy with this announcement as well.

The rest of the orientation continued smoothly, and Julian even started to look forward to the actual content of the classes. After not being very academic all the way through high school, this was a new feeling for Julian.

Of course, he'd have to put the effort in to get a good grade.

As he left the room, he thought he caught Mrs Matthews looking at him, and later on - when he was back in his room - his thoughts returned to her. To her womanly figure and the sexy glasses she wore. He'd noticed how her long red hair fell around her shoulders, down to her impressive cleavage. Usually, whenever he pictured female teachers, he thought of the ones at his old school - horrible strict beings, with their hair pulled tightly back against their skulls and not an inch of makeup in sight. Mrs Matthews was different. Very different.

CHAPTER 12

The next morning at breakfast, Julian ran into Jenny in the college canteen, she of the long dark hair and bright green eyes.

"Morning," he said cheerfully, trying to act normal in the face of such intense beauty.

"Hey," she answered, "You know, I was going to ask if you wanted to get together tonight for some food? I'm thinking of going for some pizza, and maybe even some ice cream. We can hang out in my room a bit first. What do you say?"

Julian grinned. "That sounds great," he said, really meaning it.

"Cool, come and find me after the last class - we'll go straight there if you want?"

He nodded, grateful, and when they took their trays of food over to the table area, they sat down together without even discussing it.

Julian smiled; the day was getting off to a great start. And it was only going to get better.

That evening, after a long day of classes - which Julian just about managed to keep up with - he followed Jenny back to her room, trying not to look at her body as she walked ahead of him; she was wearing an exceptionally figure-hugging dress, and despite his resolution to become friends with her, he couldn't help but wonder . . . and daydream . . . and fantasise . . .

When they got to her room she let him in, gesturing at one of the two beds. "I'm rooming with Clara but she said she's going to be out for most of the night."

Julian nodded as he sat down. "Great . . . so, when are we eating?"

"Straight to the point, aren't you? I thought we could eat later."

Julian tried not to look too disappointed - the truth was, after a whole day talking about and cooking food, he was ravenous. It was one of the biggest problems with catering school so far, he'd found.

Yes, he was hungry for food, but when Jenny reached over and put her hand on his leg, all thoughts of dinner completely left his mind. "I mean, I thought we could eat *after*."

Julian gulped.

"I've seen the way you look at me, Julian," she said, moving closer to him on the bed. "The way you stare at me, at my body. Or have I been imagining it?"

He just about managed to shake his head. "Not imagining it, no."

"So, what's the problem?" she asked, leaning in even closer.

She was still waiting for him to reply, so clearing his throat, he said, "There's no problem . . . I just . . . you're absolutely stunning, and I'm . . ."

She pressed her hand against his chest briefly, as though about to push him away. Teasing him. "You're someone I'd like to get to know a little better."

"Really?" he asked, mentally kicking himself for acting so insecure despite knowing that he could handle this situation pretty well if needed.

"Really," she said. "And you're not so bad-looking yourself, you know - for the record."

The way she was looking at him, he actually believed her, as amazing as that seemed.

Now, with his confidence well and truly boosted, he leaned into her, putting his own hand on her thigh, just underneath the soft fabric of her dress.

"That's more like it," she said, and before he knew what was happening, she was moving her beautiful long legs, positioning herself over him, with one leg either side of his.

Then, as she leaned over to kiss him, she pushed him against the wall - rather aggressively - making him stiffer by the second. He kissed her back, wrapping his arms around her waist and pulling her in closer.

Her lips were soft, but everything else about the situation was hard and rough as she moved on top of him, gasping in between their fast, passionate kisses.

Still not quite believing this was happening to him - with a girl like Jenny, and on only the second night of college - it took Julian a few moments to notice when the door to the room opened, letting in a slant of bright light from the corridor outside.

"Well," said Clara from the doorway, "what have we got here?"

Julian's entire body stiffened, his mind going back to that night at the school leaving party, when Jane had caught him in the closet with Laura and Emily. This was a completely different situation, but his reaction was pretty much the same. He felt caught out, like he'd been up to something he shouldn't have. Which was ridiculous.

Jenny, however, just shook her head. "Clara, I thought you knew Julian was coming over."

"I did. But my plans fell through. I'm afraid you're not kicking me out of my own room, even if it *is* for Julian." She winked at him, and he could feel his cheeks getting even redder.

Sighing, Jenny rolled over, back onto the bed, before quickly giving Julian a cushion to place over his trousers, for which he was incredibly grateful.

"Maybe we can pick this up tomorrow?" she whispered, while Clara started taking books out of her bag and spreading them on her bed on the other side of the room. "I'm babysitting for a family friend . . . and they have a nice house. A nice, private house," she added, throwing a pointed look over at Clara.

Julian nodded immediately before asking, "Who are you babysitting?" If it was several teenage kids it might ruin the mood slightly, but even then, he probably wouldn't say no.

"Just this boy, Charlie. He's pretty young but he's not a handful. And he goes to bed *early*."

"OK," said Julian, feeling a little more comfortable now, "I'm in."

"So," said Jenny, her green eyes sparkling in the light from a nearby lamp, "what should we do now?"

Julian shrugged. They were at the house of Jeremy and Linda Bishop, who had been gone for just over an hour. Charlie - the kid they were babysitting - was upstairs, safe and sound in his own bed, and for the first time since their passionate kiss in Jenny's room, they were both alone with each other.

"Oh, I don't know," he replied, raising his eyebrows. "I mean, I could come up with a few ideas if you want me to?"

"Oh," she said, her voice suddenly low and husky, "I think I could come up with some ideas myself."

Julian swallowed, glancing quickly up at the ceiling. "What if the kid hears?" he asked, half of him genuinely worried while the other half of him screamed at himself to stop stalling.

Jenny thought about this for a moment. "You're right; the walls *are* quite thin in here."

Julian's face dropped, making Jenny laugh, and after a moment or two she said, "What do you think about taking this outside?"

Julian looked over at the patio doors, at the darkness beyond. He'd never done it outside before - oh, he'd fantasised about it, sure, but it had never actually happened. The hayloft was the closest he'd come.

"Won't it be a bit cold?" he asked, yet again kicking himself for giving her reasons not to go ahead with the whole thing.

Jenny leaned forwards, placing her hand gently on his trousers as she whispered, "Don't worry - I'll keep you warm."

With that, she leaned into him, kissing him lightly and slowly on the mouth. He wanted more - he wanted her to press her lips against his in a passionate rage like she'd done the night before - but she was apparently having far too much fun teasing him to do that. He supposed he couldn't really complain.

"So?" she asked, after pulling back.

"Let's do it," Julian replied, this time with absolutely no hesitation whatsoever.

Jenny took his hand, standing up from the sofa and leading him over to the patio doors. They were unlocked, and after sliding one of them open - and letting in a brief gust of cold night air - she pulled him into the space between them, pressing him against the side of the door as she kissed him again, this time in a much more satisfying manner.

Once she'd stopped - and once Julian had got his breath back again - he peered out at the patio and the garden beyond. "Where shall we do it?" he asked.

"Well, this garden's a little small . . . I was thinking about heading next door instead."

"Next door?" asked Julian, a bit lost. "Do you know those people too?"

"I do, as it happens," she replied, "and I happen to know they're away tonight." She paused, her eyes twinkling in the light still coming from the living room. "I also happen to know they have a swimming pool."

At that word, Julian became a hell of a lot more interested. "A pool?" he asked. "Is it heated?"

Jenny laughed at that - long and loud - and Julian had to kiss her just to shut her up; the last thing they needed was the child waking up upstairs.

They stopped kissing, and Jenny took Julian's hand in hers. "We won't be long, and don't worry - I know Charlie. Once he's down, he sleeps like the dead. He won't know we've gone."

Julian didn't feel that great about leaving the kid all alone in the house, but he really didn't want to miss this opportunity, and knowing that they'd only be next door, he nodded in agreement.

Jenny quietly closed the patio doors behind them before leading Julian across the garden to a small door in the fence - one Julian wouldn't have noticed at all if she hadn't pointed it out to him. Leaning down, she grabbed the handle and pulled it open.

When she'd said the word 'pool', Julian had been thinking of a tiny thing - no bigger than a hot tub, perhaps - but the view that greeted him in the next-door neighbour's garden was anything but tiny. Their house was huge and grand, and they had a swimming pool to match.

Not only was it large, but it also looked beautiful in the evening light: it was lit up with hundreds of twinkling lights that were dotted all around the garden, and Jenny sighed in contentment as she stood and admired it.

"Pretty great, huh?" she asked.

Julian just nodded in agreement, then watched as Jenny took off her shoes, standing at the edge of the pool and dipping one of her toes in the bright turquoise water. "Mmm, lovely."

Julian had to agree, especially when Jenny pulled her dress off to expose a matching set of black lace underwear. They even went with her long, dark hair, which cascaded around her shoulders exactly as it had done in all of his daydreams and fantasies.

"You're beautiful," Julian breathed, the words coming out of his mouth before he even knew he was going to say them.

Jenny turned to face him, her smile lighting up her entire face. "Thank you," she said, as though she wasn't used to getting compliments - which was ridiculous. She looked like a goddess, and especially right now with all the tiny lights dancing across her skin.

She walked up to him, leaning in for another kiss before pulling down her knickers and delicately stepping out of them. Then she put her hands behind her back, expertly undoing her bra before dropping it onto the ground.

Within seconds she was standing in front of Julian completely naked, smiling at him in that own special way of hers - it was as if she was constantly ever so slightly intoxicated, and that was exactly how she made him feel.

He continued to stare at her, taking in her beautiful curves and her flawless skin, a shiver passing through him as he caught the scent of her hair on the breeze - it smelled of a delicious strawberry shampoo, and he had an almost incontrollable urge to reach out and run his hands through her long locks.

"Well?" she asked, staring at him expectantly. "Are you going to join me or not?"

Julian didn't need to be asked twice, and it only took him ten seconds to get out of his clothes. When he was ready, she put her arms around his torso, pulling him into her as she kissed him deeply, her tongue in his mouth, her hands in his hair. He could smell the strawberry shampoo more strongly now, and in that moment, he didn't think he'd ever smelled anything so sweet in his entire life.

Then, before he knew it, he and Jenny were crashing into the water; he'd been so focused on that wonderful scent of hers, he hadn't even realised she'd been leaning over, pulling him in.

He wasn't a huge fan of water, but right now, as the warm liquid rushed over their naked bodies, he thought he'd never felt anything quite so wonderful in his entire life.

They were submerged for a few seconds - still kissing, still entwined around each other - and then they broke through the surface, Julian gasping in the cool night air as he pulled himself away from Jenny for a moment to get his breath back.

They swam together in a little circle for a minute or so, neither of them taking their eyes off the other one as they drank in each other's naked - and slightly distorted - forms beneath the water as they moved.

Julian was completely mesmerised by the way Jenny's hair was floating in the water, looking silky smooth and longer than ever as it drifted around her shoulders, as if in a dream.

Then, just when he thought he couldn't wait any longer, Jenny moved towards him, grabbing his arms and pushing him against the side of the pool. It hurt a bit as his body collided with the tiles, but he paid it no attention - in fact, it added to the whole mood somehow. A little pleasure, a little pain . . .

The feel of Jenny's large, round breasts pressing against his chest made him immediately stiff, and he caressed them as they rose above and dipped below the water level. He could both smell and taste the chlorine, thinking that the chemical scent would never smell the same to him after this - instead of horrible swimming lessons in primary school, it would remind him of Jenny, of her lovely hair and alluring eyes, of her smooth skin and incredible figure.

As he was thinking these thoughts, she wrapped her legs around him, squeezing him so hard he wondered where she was getting the strength from. Then she kissed him hard on the lips before sliding her mouth up to his ear and nibbling gently on the lobe.

With her breasts still pressed against his chest, he had to gasp to stop himself from climaxing too early - he needed to get some air into his lungs, needed to keep himself under control.

That was easier said than done, however, as at the next moment, Jenny reached beneath the surface of the water, grabbing him and making him jump. She smiled at his reaction, then started - ever so slowly - to run her hand up and down his length, all the while pressing her breasts into his chest.

As she continued, she pushed herself upwards in the water, and moving forwards, he closed his mouth around her left breast, his arms creeping around her back and pulling her towards him so he could get a better hold.

She carried on - getting quicker and quicker - and after moving his mouth over to her right breast, licking the skin and tasting the chlorine on her, he moved his own hands under the water, pulling her hand off him and manoeuvring her perfect body until he was entering her, making her entire body spasm as she screamed out loud.

With his hands on her hips, he pumped her body up and down in the water, his excitement growing as he watched her arch her back, her long, luscious hair reaching down almost to her lower back.

He dug his hands deeper into her sides - knowing he was probably hurting her but realising, like him, that she was actually enjoying the pain - and as they moved up and down in the pool, the water splashing their faces and naked torsos, he felt like he was thrusting deeper into her than he ever had with Jane or Laura.

It was excruciating, but wonderful, and as they came together, a shot of pain jolted through his entire body, giving him the most unexpected and amazing climax of his entire life.

After they'd both yelled out into the night, he held Jenny close to him, not wanting to let her go, not wanting this moment to end. She wrapped her arms around his neck, panting as her beautiful body rested against his, and sighed.

He thought he could stay like this, with Jenny, here in this stranger's pool, forever.

Right now, he could die happy.

And that's when he heard it - a quiet but very real clearing of a throat, coming from someone standing at the edge of the swimming pool.

They'd been caught, which was bad - very bad - but that was the least of his problems, as when he looked up at the person who'd caught them, he was mortified to see it was their teacher, Mrs Matthews.

Feeling all of the blood drain out of his face, he turned to Jenny. She had her hand clamped over her mouth in surprise, but she was trying not to laugh.

At least *someone* was finding this funny - Mrs Matthews just stared at him, her face completely unreadable.

"I think you'd better get back to your babysitting duties, Jenny," she said eventually, gesturing at the heap of clothes they'd both left at the side of the pool. "Jeremy and Linda will be home soon."

Julian couldn't believe what was happening, and as he stared at Jenny, he hissed, "this is Mrs Matthew's house? And you *knew*?"

Jenny shrugged, seemingly unaware - or not caring - that as she did so, her breasts broke above the surface of the water. "Sorry Julian, I should have told you - but I knew that if I *did*, there'd be no way I'd get you in this pool."

Mrs Matthews cleared her throat again. "And now it's time you both left. Don't you agree?"

Julian nodded, not wanting to piss off his teacher any more than he already had done. This was just too much.

Although, at the same time, he couldn't help but notice how amazing she looked. She'd clearly got dressed up for her big night out, and was wearing a very low-cut black sparkly dress, with one slit up the side that showed off her smooth, bare leg. Her long red hair was piled on top of her head, a few ringlets hanging down around her perfectly made-up face. She looked ten years younger than she did in class, and even then she didn't exactly look *old*.

Julian shook his head, trying to bring his thoughts back to his incredibly embarrassing present.

"If you leave in the next three minutes, I won't tell my husband about this, OK?" she said, and in the twinkling lights surrounding the pool, Julian noticed that her cheeks were red.

She took one last look at them before leaving, and once he and Jenny were safely out of the pool and back in the house next door, he grabbed her - gently - by the arm. "Are you insane?" he asked, as she shrugged him off and handed him a towel. "Our teacher?"

"Do you regret it?" she asked. "The sex, I mean."

Julian paused for a moment before shaking his head. "No. Of course not. It was . . . it was incredible."

"Well, then, what's the problem?" she asked.

Julian shrugged, and as he got dressed, he tried not to think of the next day at school - how would he ever look Mrs Matthews in the eye ever again?

CHAPTER 13

As it turned out, his morning class at school wasn't quite as embarrassing as he'd thought it would be - and he'd spent the entire night coming up with all kinds of humiliating scenarios in his head, unable to sleep a wink.

No, it was as if somehow, overnight, Mrs Matthews and Jenny had come to some kind of understanding - either that, or they were both just very good at avoiding confrontation.

Either way, it was far better than what Julian had been expecting and obsessing over, so he decided to just get on with the class, trying not to make eye contact with Mrs Matthews, or Jenny, or anyone really.

Jenny, however, did make actual contact with him a few times throughout the lesson, brushing her hand against his or squeezing his shoulder as she passed, but she didn't try and talk to him, and for that Julian was grateful - if he started reliving the events of the previous night in a roomful of young, gorgeous girls, he might find himself in a bit of a sticky situation.

He thought he'd got lucky with Mrs Matthews, who he pictured in that sparkly black dress more than a few times during the lesson, and he was hoping she had just decided to forget the entire thing.

He'd been so close to getting through the entire lesson without anything being said, but then, as he was leaving, she shouted out, "Julian, will you stay behind for a moment, please? I'd like a word." She'd said this without looking up from the papers she was reviewing, and as he moved over to her desk (as everyone else - including Jenny - left the room), he had no idea how this was going to go.

Reluctantly, he sat down in the chair in front of Mrs Matthew's desk, waiting while she finished reading whatever it was she was reading. Then, when the last student had left the room and closed the door behind them, she glanced up, fixing him with her steely gaze.

"Is there anything you'd like to say to me?" she asked, her face straight, giving nothing away.

"No . . . yes . . ." he stammered. "I . . . I just want to say I'm sorry," he eventually spat out, fidgeting nervously in his seat. "I had no idea it was your pool, but even so, we shouldn't have broken in like that. I'm sorry you had to . . . had to see that."

There were a few seconds of silence - *agonising* seconds of silence - before she spoke, and as Julian listened, he couldn't believe it; the words that came out of his teacher's mouth were probably the last ones he would have ever expected.

"Well, *I'm* not sorry I had to see that."

Julian let the words linger in the air for a moment, unsure he'd heard correctly. "What?" he whispered, after realising she wasn't going to say any more without at least some kind of input from him.

She smiled at him - only a brief one, that was gone in an instant, but it was definitely there. "For someone so young, you sure seemed to know what you were doing. I was impressed."

Julian could feel his heart thumping madly in his chest, and suddenly his throat had gone very, very dry. Was this a test? Was she trying to see how he'd react? He had literally no idea what was going on, and again, all he could say in response was, "What?"

Mrs Matthews stared at him for a moment - as if *she* were the one who was trying to figure *him* out - then she stood up from her chair, strolling around her desk and perching on the edge of it, right in front of him. "Tell me, how many women have you been with?"

Julian nearly choked on his own saliva.

"Go on," she said, "it's OK to answer. I won't tell anyone."

He paused for a few moments, then mumbled, "a few."

"No," she said, without hesitation, "how many *women* have you been with? I assume they were all girls, like Jenny."

Julian shook his head, now more confused than ever. "I'm sorry," he said eventually, "but am I in trouble?"

Mrs Matthews smiled at him. "Last night has nothing to do with school. You weren't in a cooking class at the time, were you?"

"No, but, I mean . . . aren't you going to punish me or something?"

At those words, her smile - a grin, really - widened. "Interesting you should say that, Julian," she said, reaching out her leg and propping her high heeled shoe on his lap. "Because that's exactly what I was going to suggest. What *punishment* would you like?"

Julian could feel himself sweating, but he could also feel something else - something happening to his own body just below the shoe she was now digging into his trousers.

"W-what?" he stammered, now looking completely bewildered. "What's going on?"

His teacher took her shoe off his lap. "I'm sorry," she said. "I know I shouldn't be doing this, and if we *did* do this, no one could ever, ever know . . . but I have to say, when I found you and Jenny in my pool, I wasn't angry. I was jealous."

Julian couldn't believe what he was hearing. "Jealous?"

She nodded. "It was so passionate, so erotic, so sensual . . . Do you know how long it's been since my husband and I . . ." she trailed off, shaking her head. "Never mind. But seeing you in my pool like that, it was just hard to believe how young you are. If you were a couple of years older, and not my student . . ." she trailed off, looking into the distance as she bit on her lip. "But no matter." She shook her head, as though trying to get back to her normal, teacher-like self. "Please, forget I ever said anything." She took a deep breath as she stood up. "It was a momentary slip, a moment of madness . . ."

Julian realised she was flustered, and for the first time since she'd started their extremely odd conversation, he believed she was telling the truth - she wanted him. Mrs Matthews, his older, sexy teacher, actually wanted *him*. He didn't know what was happening in this class - perhaps someone had spiked all the ingredients they were using - but he knew one thing: he wasn't complaining.

Although he knew it was against *all* the rules, and although he knew she was married, he couldn't quite help himself; he just kept thinking of the look that would be on Phil's face when he told him of what had been happening at college. There was also the thought of Mrs Matthews herself, and not for the first time he wondered what those curves of hers would look like out of their clothes. Or how her vivid red hair would look spread out over some crisp white bed sheets.

The fact that she was *so* off-limits - being a teacher and a wife to someone - just made things all the more tantalising, and before he'd even given it a second thought, he stood up, grabbing her by the waist and pushing her back against the desk.

"Julian," she whispered, all her confidence and authority now seemingly gone, "we can't . . . I wish we could, but we can't. I could lose my job, my husband . . . you could get expelled . . ."

Julian hesitated for a moment then, prepared to back off if she absolutely wanted him to, but the look in her eyes said otherwise, and the next moment, they were kissing each other as if their lives depended on it.

He did spare a brief thought for Jenny - the beautiful, stunning Jenny - but then he thought of her laughing in the face of their teacher, and he didn't worry so much; to say she seemed laid-back about things was a vast understatement.

Kissing someone almost double his age was an experience, and one he was quite enjoying - she moved her tongue in a different way to the girls he was used to, held him in a different way, gasped in a different way.

Julian could feel himself getting extremely aroused. If this was what she was like just kissing, who knew what the sex would be like?

Still knowing it was wrong but now completely unable to stop himself, Julian reached down and grabbed her thigh. It felt good under his skin, more solid than the waif-like girls he'd been with but just as smooth, just as inviting. Mrs Matthews had womanly curves, she had the experience, she had everything.

She didn't flinch at his touch, and encouraged, Julian slid his hand slowly up her leg until he reached her knickers - a tiny lace thong. The thought that she'd been wearing this kind of underwear under her normal teaching clothes blew Julian's mind, and he tugged on it hungrily, eager to get inside.

"We can't," she moaned, though by the sound she made, she very much wanted to. "Someone might walk in."

That thought should have made Julian want to stop, but it only made him more hungry for her - the fact that this was forbidden on so many levels, and the idea that absolutely anyone could walk in on them at any moment - made the whole thing a hell of a lot more erotic.

And to think, he was about to do it with a teacher! The thought made him incredibly stiff, and as he placed his fingers under the band of her underwear, he pushed into her, making her moan again.

She was staring at the door, afraid someone might open it and see them, but just as with Julian, the urge to continue what they were doing seemed to win out; she couldn't stop now even if she wanted to, which apparently, she didn't.

With Julian's hand still between her legs, she leaned back on her desk, knocking all kinds of things to the floor without a care in the world. Julian leaned over her, now more ready then ever, and when he unbuckled his belt and pulled down his trousers, she didn't tell him to stop.

The next moment, he was entering her, quickly and urgently, and she leaned into Julian, pressing her mouth against his neck as she silently screamed into his hot skin.

He reached out for her breasts, sliding his hands under her smooth silk shirt and squeezing them as he moved back and forth on top of her. The idea that he was having sex with a teacher, in *his* classroom, on *her* desk, was almost too much to handle, and he felt the same thrill he'd experienced the night before with Jenny in the swimming pool - knowing they were doing something wrong, but doing it anyway. As he thrust into his teacher again, Julian thought that feeling was quite possibly the best, most effective aphrodisiac available.

She was gripping his back - her long nails digging into his shirt - and just as he was about to climax he heard voices outside, in the corridor. Just beyond the door to the classroom.

They both stopped immediately, and he was reminded yet again of being caught in the closet at school with Laura and Emily.

"This here is one of our main cooking classrooms," came the voice, and Mrs Matthews immediately sat up, pushing Julian off her as she fumbled with her shirt.

Reluctantly - but knowing he had no choice - he pulled up his trousers, did up his belt, and was just helping her put the stationery and papers back on her desk when the door opened.

It was the head of the college, and he showed in a happy, smiling couple - possibly the parents of some potential new student.

"Ah," he said. "Helen. I was hoping you'd be here." He paused, his gaze switching from her messy hair to Julian's red face. "Are you OK? You look a little flustered."

Julian hid a smile as she replied, "I'm fine, thank you. Julian was just helping me with something." She turned to face him. "I'll see you tomorrow. We can finish this up then?"

Julian grinned in response before almost running out of the room, nodding at the head and the couple as he went. Yes, finishing up was exactly what he wanted. And he was looking forward to it already.

And now, Julian thought to himself as he left, he knew her name - her *real* name. Helen. He thought it suited her perfectly.

As soon as he was out of the classroom, he ran off to find the nearest payphone. He just had to tell Phil about this!

CHAPTER 14

Phil was, as expected, incredibly jealous of Julian's recent antics, although it took him a while to truly believe what his best friend was telling him.

Julian loved keeping Phil up to date with his conquests, although his and Helen's relationship had been more flirty than anything else since that one time in the classroom. He thought she was just trying to keep things low key for now - worried that someone might find out - but after a few months, he started to think that nothing would ever happen between them again. She'd put things on hold, and he wanted them to very much start up again - the sooner the better.

The truth was, this wasn't just a student and teacher fantasy for Julian anymore; he was well and truly smitten with Mrs Helen Matthews. He'd even stopped hooking up with Jenny - amazing, beautiful, sexually-ready Jenny - because he couldn't stop thinking about his teacher.

Every class was pure agony as he watched her move around the room, leaning over and talking to the girls, knowing full well that he was looking at her, especially at her cleavage that seemed to be getting more and more enticing with every class - he was sure she was wearing lower cut tops and shorter, tighter skirts for his benefit, even though she wouldn't let him touch her or even really talk to her. It was as if she got off on making him all hot and bothered, like some kind of weird power trip.

Julian didn't give up that easily, and with every class he had with Mrs Matthews, he would wait around once it had finished, hoping to be the last one left so he could get some alone time with her. This didn't always work, and Julian became more and more frustrated as the months went on.

One day, as soon as the last person left the room, Julian went over to Helen, determined to make himself heard. "Do you want to do something tonight?" he asked casually, hoping his plan would work.

This question made Mrs Matthews - who was in the process of marching away from Julian - stop mid-stride, and she turned back to look at him. "What?"

Julian cleared his throat, suddenly nervous now that he'd - finally - got her attention. "I heard you earlier, telling that other teacher that your husband was away. So, do you want to do something tonight?"

Helen's cheeks turned red as she took a step away from him. "You realise this is incredibly inappropriate, Julian," she said after a while. "You know I'm your teacher."

Julian pretended to think about this for a couple of seconds before replying, "Hmm . . . well it's probably not as inappropriate as us having sex in your classroom." He looked pointedly at the desk, his eyebrows raised.

Helen's eyes flashed in anger, and she took a step towards him again, this time getting even closer to him than before. "Are you trying to blackmail me?"

Julian let out a quiet laugh; blackmail was the last thing he had on his mind. He supposed his nerves had just made everything come out sounding all wrong and jumbled up. "No, no . . . of course not. I just . . ." He took a deep breath, psyching himself up to say the words. "I can't stop thinking about you, *at all*. I can't concentrate in class - especially with you looking so incredible all the time - and I just want to be with you again. But properly, this time. What do you say?"

Helen's expression softened. "You know we can't, Julian. I want to as well - believe me - but if anyone ever found out . . ."

"Well, we'll just have to make sure no one finds out then," said Julian, hoping he was sounding as reasonable as possible.

"I don't know . . ." replied Helen, frowning and biting her lip.

She looked so sexy that before he knew what he was doing, Julian leaned into her, placing his hands gently around her waist as he kissed her deeply. She resisted for a couple of seconds, and Julian was convinced she was about to pull away when she actually leaned into him instead, kissing him back just as passionately. She wrapped her arms around his back, her hands slowly lowering until they were grasping his buttocks.

After a while she *did* pull back, managing to whisper, "We shouldn't be doing this," before going straight back to kissing him again.

After what felt like an eternity - a very nice eternity, Julian thought - they stopped the kiss, holding each other close as they both got their breath back.

Julian couldn't believe what he was feeling. Usually by this point he couldn't wait to get straight to the sex - although if that *did* happen right now, he'd be very happy indeed - but somehow, the kissing was enough.

Helen hadn't said anything else since they'd started kissing, and just as the silence between them was threatening to become monumental, Julian whispered, "Look, I'd really like to be with you tonight, if that's what you want too. I don't want to put you in an awkward position, but I think you know there's something between us. And . . ." he trailed off, turning a little shy all of a sudden.

"And what?" she asked.

"And . . . well . . . it's my birthday tomorrow, and I don't have any plans. I'm away from my family and most of my friends . . . and I just wanted to do something to celebrate it." He grinned. "Honestly, I couldn't think of a better way than celebrating with you."

Helen leaned forwards for another quick kiss. "OK. But not at my house and not in your dorm room." She wrinkled her nose at that, as if she couldn't think of a worse place to get together with someone. "Let me rent a hotel room for us."

Julian shrugged. "I can't ask you to do that."

"You're not," she replied, squeezing his arm gently. "It'll be your birthday treat from me."

Right then, Julian felt closer to Helen than ever before. No one had ever really made much of a fuss about his birthday, and now he was going to spend his 'birthday eve' in the company of this incredible woman. He couldn't quite believe it. "OK," he said eventually, "that would be nice. Thank you."

Helen kissed him again before pulling away. "I'll phone the hotel this afternoon and we can meet there at eight. Do you know the Green Deer Guesthouse?"

Julian nodded. This birthday was turning out to be a pretty good one after all.

CHAPTER 15

It was eight o'clock and Julian was standing outside the Green Deer Guesthouse, trying not to look too conspicuous. He'd put on his suit - the only one he owned - in an attempt to look at least vaguely respectable, and he'd carefully brushed and gelled his hair, making it slightly sleeker and less frizzy than usual.

Just then, as if appearing out of the shadows like some mystic goddess, there she was: Helen Matthews. Even in her long trench style coat she looked incredible, with her sexy high heels and her lovely red hair cascading down around her shoulders.

"Helen," he said, standing up straight and hoping he looked suave and sophisticated, or at least more manly than usual.

She smiled at Julian before taking his arm and leading him inside, out of view of whoever may be passing by outside the hotel. Once they were in the foyer, she leaned over and gave him a quick kiss on the cheek. "It's good to see you, darling. Did you have a good day at work?" She moved her gaze over to the concierge at the check-in desk, as if trying to give Julian a message.

He grasped her meaning immediately, and as they walked over to the desk, he tried to act as 'husbandly' as possible, although he wasn't really sure how on earth he was supposed to do that. After all, he'd never been married, and he couldn't even begin to imagine what that would be like.

"Welcome to the Green Deer Guesthouse," said the man at the desk, smiling even though he was clearly exhausted and probably just wanted to get home. "How can I help you this evening?"

"We're Mr and Mrs Bold," replied Helen quickly, before Julian could say anything to blow their cover. "We booked a room for the night."

The concierge looked down at his large booking sheet, running his finger over the pages until he got to the name 'Bold'. "Ah yes," he said, reaching under the desk to grab a key. "You're in room 103. If you'd like to follow me."

As he stood up from behind the desk, he glanced briefly at the two of them - no luggage between them, no wedding ring on Julian's finger - but he didn't say anything.

They followed him along a corridor, up some stairs, and along another corridor, and then he opened the door to room 103 before handing the key over to Julian. "Please do let me know if I can help in any way."

"Actually," said Helen, "please could you bring up a bottle of your finest champagne? It's my husband's birthday."

Julian tried not to laugh - being called 'husband' was just too weird - as the concierge nodded.

"Yes, of course, madam. I'll bring it right up." He turned to Julian, holding out his hand. "May I offer you many happy returns, Sir."

Julian shook his head - as if he was being called 'Sir'! "Thank you," he just about managed to say in response.

Helen thanked him too, and after they watched him head off along the corridor and down the stairs, Julian led Helen inside the room.

Not that you could really call it a 'room' - it was *huge*, the biggest hotel room Julian had ever seen. He supposed it was what you'd call a 'suite', with its own bathroom, bedroom, and seating area, though he didn't really know, never having been anywhere near a hotel suite before in his life.

As Helen closed and locked the door behind them, Julian turned to face her, his expression one of awe. "This must be costing a fortune! And the champagne . . . you didn't have to . . ."

"Don't worry about it; it's your birthday!" She leaned in and kissed him, slowly and sensually. "And I'm going to give you a birthday you won't forget."

Julian's heart started thumping at those words, and after kissing her again, he said, "You look amazing, by the way."

"You look pretty good yourself," she replied, before placing her rather large handbag on the little side table. "Now, I'm afraid I haven't got you a physical present, but I've got something I think you might like a little more."

Julian raised his eyebrows, his nerves suddenly gone now that they'd successfully got into their room without anyone spotting them or raising the alarm. "I can't wait," he said honestly.

Taking his hand, Helen led him over to the seating area. She kissed him again - a little more fiercely this time - and then pushed him down rather roughly onto the sofa. "Wait here. I'll be right back," she breathed, leaning over him and kissing him again. Julian caught some of her perfume as she leaned into him, the scent enveloping his entire body and simultaneously making him feel incredibly relaxed and completely aroused.

He watched Helen as she sauntered back over to her handbag, picked it up, and slipped into the bathroom, closing the door behind her.

As Julian waited, he started picturing what her body would be like. After all, he'd had sex with her once before, but they'd been - more or less - fully clothed, and despite her increasingly tight outfits in class, he hadn't seen her in her underwear, let alone naked. Though he'd seen it in his mind hundreds of times.

He took several deep breaths, trying to calm himself down in preparation for when Helen appeared again. He wanted to prove to her that he could be just as much of a man as her husband - more so, in fact. It was clear she wasn't happy with him, after all. She'd probably be a lot happier with Julian, whether she realised it or not.

He had just started to imagine what her husband looked like - partly to keep himself from getting too prematurely excited, partly because he was just curious - when there was a knock on the door.

He froze, thinking that her husband had somehow found out where they were, and then he remembered the concierge. Sighing with relief, he went over to the door, unlocking it and opening it to see the man from the front desk standing in the corridor. He had a little trolley with him, and as Julian stepped aside, he wheeled it into the suite and over to the seating area.

"Birthday champagne!" he said, placing the little trolley next to the table. "I've also put a few chocolates for you both, on the house," he added. "Happy birthday."

Julian thanked him again and then saw him to the door, which he locked as soon as he'd left; the scare he'd got thinking about Helen's husband finding them hadn't quite gone away yet.

Walking back over to the seating area, he looked at the trolley. There was a bottle of champagne in a large silver ice bucket, two champagne flutes, and a small dish of rather posh-looking chocolates. Truffles, perhaps.

He was just about to grab the champagne bottle when the door to the bathroom opened, and Helen stepped out.

Julian's building anticipation suddenly burst like a bubble; she was still in her coat, looking exactly the same as before.

Helen smiled - a teasing, seductive kind of smile. "Are you ready for your birthday surprise?" she asked as she sauntered over to him, slowly, as if even though she knew he was raring to go, she wanted to remain in control. She glanced briefly at the champagne and chocolates, nodded, then looked back at him.

"Oh, I'm ready."

He walked back over to the sofa, where he sat down and placed his hand on the seat next to him. "Why don't you come over here?" he asked.

She held out her right hand, wagging her finger at him as she frowned dramatically. "Now, now, don't be so impatient . . . I'm the teacher here, aren't I?"

Julian nodded. "Sure. I'm just the student, ready and willing to learn. So . . . what are you going to teach me?"

She smiled seductively at him again. "What *aren't* I going to teach you?" She paused, looking around the room. "But first, you need to sit like a student. Move to that chair." She pointed at a wooden chair that had been put against a table to create a makeshift desk.

It looked pretty uncomfortable but Julian did as he was told, amused at the realisation that he was still responding to her as if she was his teacher, not his lover.

Once he was seated - Helen having turned the chair around to face the main seating area - she reached into her bag and pulled out a pair of shiny silver handcuffs.

"Wait," said Julian, starting to stand up. "This isn't some kind of prank, is it? You're not going to handcuff me down and then escape, leaving me here to rot?"

"It's just so you don't get tempted to do anything you shouldn't . . . not yet. This part is strictly viewing only. You can look but you can't touch, got it?"

He sat back down in the chair without any further complaints, and Helen handcuffed one of his hands to the armrest.

"There, that's better," she said when she was done. "Now, sit back and enjoy the show."

At the word 'show' Julian's arousal grew, and even more so when Helen went over to the radio on the side table, turning the dial until she got to what sounded like a rock and roll station.

She started dancing then - swaying to the beat - and suddenly Julian realised what was happening: she was going to do a striptease. His gorgeous, amazing teacher was going to do a striptease. For him. He grinned; he bet her husband rarely got stripteases from her.

As she danced, Helen reached down to grab the buckle on her coat belt, undoing the clasp and slowly pulling the belt out away from her. Her movements were so smooth, so sexy, and she did everything in time with the music.

"Are you ready for your lesson?" she asked, a twinkle in her eye. Julian just nodded in response - he wasn't sure any actual words would come out if he opened his mouth. "OK then," she said, undoing each button on her coat as slowly as possible.

Julian just sat on the chair, waiting hungrily.

Raising her eyebrows, she pouted at him as she danced, and Julian could feel himself getting hard. He already appreciated the way she walked around her classroom, but he'd had no idea she could move like this. He watched her every move, studied her every step. He didn't want to miss even a single moment of this.

Once she'd undone all of the buttons on her coat, she took it off, throwing it at Julian.

Now he could see what she'd been wearing under her long coat - a typical 'teacher' outfit if ever he saw one, but one that was completely sexed up. As well as her high heels, she was wearing a tight black pencil skirt, a crisp white shirt, and a deep red cardigan. The shirt and cardigan were tucked into the skirt, and the shirt looked at least two sizes too small for her - the top few buttons wouldn't close, meaning that he could see a hint of her underwear underneath. With her dark red lipstick and thick black eyeliner, she looked every inch the man-eater.

Julian gulped, unable to take his eyes off her as she continued to dance to the music. She unbuttoned her cardigan, pulling it off as slowly as she possibly could, before flinging it around her shoulders. She took the end of each sleeve in either hand, then tugged it back and forth like some makeshift feather boa. She winked at Julian.

After throwing the cardigan at him, Helen started dancing around his chair, getting tantalisingly close to him and then jumping out of reach again whenever he tried to touch her. She was definitely enjoying this, and although it was driving him crazy, Julian had to admit he was enjoying it too.

Next, Helen slowly unzipped her skirt, which fell to her ankles in an instant. Julian was excited to see what this would reveal, but the shirt she was wearing was so long, it covered up everything down there. Not that he could really complain - he thought that the sight of his teacher, standing there in nothing but a white shirt and stilettos, would stay in his mind forever.

"What shall I do now?" she asked him, teasing, as she continued to dance.

"I think you should take off the shirt," Julian replied, clearing his throat when he heard how croaky it sounded.

"Hmm," Helen said, as if trying to decide whether this would be the best course of action or not. She undid a couple more of the buttons, allowing him to catch glimpses of underwear - flashes of black and silver - and when she unbuttoned the rest and let her top fall to the floor, he gulped audibly at the sight before him.

Mrs Helen Matthews was *incredible*. She wasn't the tallest woman in the world, but the sexy black stilettos she was wearing added to her height, accenting her curves even more than usual and making her look even more amazing than she generally did.

The stockings she was wearing finished halfway up her thigh, and they were held up by a lace garter belt, the sight of which sent shivers down Julian's spine. Her knickers were the same black lace, though they had silky silver edges. Julian had expected to see her in some kind of skimpy bra, but the corset she was wearing - black with silver ribbon - was far sexier than any lone bra could ever be. It cinched in her waist, going out at the top where her voluptuous breasts almost spilled over the edge of the corset, giving her the most gorgeous hourglass figure Julian had ever seen. The girls he'd been with had been sexy, sure, but they'd mostly been slim or 'skinny', and even Jenny - with her large, round breasts - had been built like a stick insect in comparison to his teacher. Helen's curves were mesmerising.

He made a move to get up - he wanted to be close to her, to feel her skin on his, to run his hands up and down that silky black and silver lingerie - but the handcuff soon put a stop to that.

Helen whispered, "Not yet." Then, delving into the top of her corset, she brought out a shiny silver key, which she threw over to him. Luckily, he managed to catch it with his spare hand. "Free yourself, then join me over on the sofa," she commanded.

He didn't need to be told twice - he fumbled with the key in the handcuffs, eventually getting out of them before almost running over to the sofa. It was good to be sitting on something soft after the cold, hard chair, but he found that he sort of missed the feel of the handcuffs on his skin. He placed the key and the cuffs carefully on the side table, then focused back on Helen.

Smiling at him, she moved over to the ice bucket on the trolley, picking up the champagne bottle and untwisting the metal wire that held the top on. Next, she walked over to the sofa, draping herself over Julian and kissing him intensely. With her legs either side of his, she dug her knees into his thighs as she popped the cork off the champagne bottle, the bubbly liquid spurting out of the top.

Laughing, Helen held the bottle over her chest, Julian watching as the champagne poured over her breasts, down her corset and between her thighs. She arched her back, pushing into his crotch as the liquid ran over her soft skin.

Julian couldn't take it anymore - he had to touch her. Leaning forwards, he grabbed her round her waist, feeling the silk and the lace under his fingertips as he pressed his face into her chest. He licked the champagne off her breasts while she dug her knees even harder into his thighs. The drink was sweet and fruity, and he greedily licked up every last drop from her skin as she watched him intently.

Smiling, she took a sip from the champagne bottle - which had now stopped erupting - before handing it to Julian, who did the same.

After they'd each had a few sips of champagne, Helen stood up and went back over to the trolley, putting down the bottle and picking up the little dish of chocolates. She then sauntered back over to the sofa, again lowering herself down over Julian's lap. Holding out the dish, she raised her eyebrows at him, and he took it without hesitation.

Moving closer to him, she opened her mouth while Julian picked up one of the chocolates. He raised it to her lips, and she took a small, delicate bite out of its soft brown exterior. She moaned in delight, taking the rest of the chocolate from him, and before he could take his hand away, she licked his fingers while shifting on top of him to get more comfortable.

When she was done, she took the dish out of Julian's hand, feeding him one of the chocolates while he stared back at her, never taking his eyes off hers. It tasted good, but Julian thought Helen tasted a whole lot better.

Placing the dish with the remaining chocolates on the side table next to the sofa, Helen raised one of her hands to the top of her corset, letting her fingers play almost idly with the small zip there.

Julian hadn't even noticed the zip, and after looking at her beautiful face, he leaned forwards, reaching out his hand towards her breasts.

"I think you can do better than that," Helen said, pinning both of his hands back against the sofa. Challenging him.

The corset was now right in front of his face, and realising what she wanted him to do, he leaned forwards again, this time using only his teeth to pull on the zip. It made a satisfying sound as it opened, but even more satisfying was the way Helen's breasts seemed to spring out of their bindings, as if they'd just been waiting to burst free.

Helen moaned as Julian finished unzipping her, and when the corset dropped to the floor behind her, he launched himself at her naked torso, hungrily closing his mouth over each breast while he pulled her towards him.

He wanted to kiss every inch of her skin, to savour her scent, to relish her taste - he wanted to remember this moment forever.

But Helen wanted to move on, and when he finally came up for air, she tugged at his jacket, pulling it off him before quickly and efficiently unbuttoning his shirt. She was moving at a much faster pace now, and it was clear that she wanted this just as much as he did.

Soon he was as topless as she was, and after a bit of manoeuvring on the sofa, she took his shoes, socks, and trousers off as well.

She was still in her knickers and stockings, and while Julian had no intention of removing the latter - they were just so sexy to look at - he couldn't wait to get her panties off.

So he reached out, running his fingers under the delicate silk edge - which made him shiver yet again - but before he could do anything else, she put her hand on his, stopping him. "Let's take this over to the bed," she whispered, "and bring the champagne. The handcuffs too." She paused, considering. "And the ice."

With that she stood up, sauntering over to the bed area while Julian watched her go. He dashed over to the trolley as quickly as possible, grabbing the ice bucket with the half-full champagne bottle in and taking it over to the bed, along with the cuffs from the table.

By the time he got there, Helen was lying on top of the covers, her legs spread open as she propped herself up on her elbows. She was smiling at him, and again Julian wondered how the hell this had even happened - not that he was complaining.

Placing the ice bucket on one of the bedside tables, Julian then lowered himself over Helen, who wrapped her arms around his shoulders as they kissed.

After a few seconds he pulled back, her arms falling down onto the bed as he continued to kiss her, this time on her neck, then her chest, then her stomach, until he was right where he wanted to be.

He glanced up at her from his position, looking past her beautiful breasts to her gorgeous face. Now more excited than ever, he started pulling her knickers down.

As her pubic area was revealed to him, he paused, looking at it in astonishment. Obviously he knew she was a redhead, but it hadn't really occurred to him that she might be ginger down there too.

"Is there a problem, Julian?" she asked, to which he shook his head in response.

"No problem whatsoever," he replied, before continuing to pull her knickers down. He left the garter belt on, and when her underwear reached the tops of her stockings, he undid the delicate little clips so he could pull them all the way down her legs. When her knickers were off, he redid the clips.

She was now in her stockings, heels, garter belt, and nothing else. Julian stared at her in adoration.

Then, not wanting to hesitate any longer, he spread her legs wide again, pushing her hips down into the covers as he thrust his head at her ginger pubic area. He pushed his tongue inside her, still tasting the champagne in his mouth as he licked her - it tasted wonderful, and he made a mental note to combine bubbly alcohol with sex more in the future. It added a whole new element to things.

Helen writhed around on the bed, moaning, but just as he was finding her sweet spot, she reached out, pushing his head away. "Wait," she groaned, "the handcuffs."

Julian hesitated. "I'm not sure I'll be able to do anything if I'm handcuffed again . . ."

"Not for you, for *me*. Handcuff me to the bed . . . then you can do whatever you want with me. And I mean *anything*." She raised her eyebrows as she licked her lips.

That was an offer Julian simply couldn't refuse, and as fast as he could - although he tried to be gentle - he took the handcuffs and placed them around her right wrist, with the other one going around the bedpost.

"There's another set in my handbag," Helen whispered, and Julian went and retrieved it. He pulled out the second set of cuffs, but not before he'd seen what else was in her bag.

"What's all this?" he asked, bringing out several random items - candles, a lighter, some rope . . . the list went on.

"Just some things I thought we could experiment with a little," she breathed, her voice husky. That twinkle was back in her eye, and Julian grinned in response. His birthday really had come early! "Cuff my other hand, then you can decide what you want to use on me."

Julian cuffed her left hand to the other bedpost, then sat back and looked at the woman in front of him. She was staring at him, that half-smile on her face, and she was his to do with as he wished.

After peering into her bag at the other objects she had in there, he decided to go with the candles, and after lighting a match, he held it against the wick of a chunky red one. It soon started to burn, and Julian looked over at Helen, suddenly hesitant. "Are you sure about this? I don't want to hurt you."

"You've obviously got a lot to learn about pain and pleasure, Julian, but don't worry - I'll teach you. While we wait for the candle, how about starting with some of the ice?" She glanced at the ice bucket next to her.

Thinking that ice sounded safer than fire, Julian placed the candle carefully on the bedside table before picking up the ice bucket. Then, taking the bottle of champagne out, he took a few sips before leaning over Helen. She opened her mouth, and he poured the fizzy liquid between her lips, being careful not to let it all gush out at once. She drank a few mouthfuls then he pulled away, looking longingly at her body.

Putting the ice to one side for a minute, he positioned himself over her and poured the rest of the champagne onto her now warm skin, starting at the base of her neck. He watched, mesmerised, as it trickled down her body, making its way around her curves and heading down towards her thighs. She writhed as the cool liquid flowed over her, and Julian watched for just one second longer before leaning down to lick it all up.

He started at her breasts, then made his way down her torso before eventually stopping at her pubic area. He kissed the little ginger hairs, then started licking and sucking the liquid. He desperately wanted to be inside her, but he knew that the foreplay hadn't finished yet, and he wanted to make her happy. So, he licked at her some more, making her groan, before reaching out for the ice bucket.

Taking a couple of cubes in his hand, he placed them on her stomach, making her shudder. Then he moved them around her skin, up around each breast and back down below, where he hovered them just above her ginger pubic hairs. She shivered, and he bent down, taking the ice cubes into his mouth before pushing his tongue back inside her.

This time she shuddered - almost violently - and he had to reach out and clamp her legs to the bed to steady her. She was moaning more and more now, and he suddenly wondered if there was anyone staying in the hotel room next to them. If there were, they'd probably be able to hear all of this. They might even complain to the concierge.

The thought made him want to do this even more than ever, before anything went wrong and stopped them in their tracks.

By now the candle had started to melt, and after swallowing what remained of the ice cubes, Julian reached out for it, again hesitating before bringing it over to Helen's body.

"Do it," she whispered, her eyes alight with desire. "Make me scream."

Julian didn't want to hurt her, but he had to admit, this was one of the sexiest things he'd ever done, and taking one more look at his teacher - handcuffed to the bed like something out of a school boy's fantasy - he bent over her chest and tipped the candle.

The wax fell in a little pool between her breasts, and Helen bit her lip as she tried not to yell. Once she'd got her breath back, she whispered, "More!"

Julian tipped the candle over again, this time over her stomach, watching in fascination as the wax fell onto her skin. It sizzled a little where it met the remains of the ice cubes, and Helen's entire body spasmed beneath him. She groaned again, louder this time.

Julian was just about to reach out to grab the ice bucket - thinking he could cool her down before she got too hot or before the wax did any permanent damage to her skin - when she wrapped her legs around his waist, dragging him down again. "I'm ready," she said breathlessly. "I'm ready now!"

After manoeuvring his body into the right place, Julian thrust into Helen, crying out when his skin made contact with hers, the melted wax between them heating up his body instantly.

She was right - it hurt, but damn did it feel good!

Pressing further into her, he inhaled the scent of her skin - candle wax mixed with champagne and perfume - as he screamed out loud. He wasn't thinking about anyone hearing them anymore; he couldn't care less. The concierge could barge into the room right now and still he wouldn't be able to stop.

Helen screamed too, clenching her legs even harder around his body as he writhed on top of her. The heel of her stilettos dug into his skin, making him shout out again - both in pain and in pleasure. He certainly *could* learn a thing or two about that from her, he thought to himself as he pulled out and then thrust back into her.

This time she screamed at the top of her lungs, the shocking sound making Julian harder than ever. He increased his speed, and as he thrust in and out of her, sweat trickled down his back in a single stream.

She seemed to like the way things were progressing, and Julian just had enough time to think that he'd never done it like this ever before - so raw, so fierce - when Helen dug her heels so deep into his skin that he thought she must have drawn blood by now.

He thrust into her again - one last long, deep thrust that hurt both her and him, but pleasured them both too - and then he was done, collapsing into her, his head resting between her breasts.

They were both still panting, and it was a while before either of them could say anything.

When Julian had finally got his breath back, he pulled away, looking up at Helen's face. "Did I hurt you? Was that . . . too much?"

"You *did* hurt me, and it was perfect. Did I hurt you?" She glanced down at her stilettos.

"You did, and it was perfect." He moved up along her body so he could kiss her, then he started sitting up. "I'll get you out of those cuffs in just one second."

He started moving towards the table, but she put her stockinged leg up against him, acting like a barrier.

"What do you think you're doing?" She was smiling seductively again. "We're not done yet."

Julian couldn't believe it - he was absolutely exhausted, and he thought she must have been too. "What?" was all he could ask.

"We have this hotel room for the entire evening," she replied, glancing at the clock on the bedside table. "And it's still three whole hours before your official birthday. I'd say we've got a whole lot more celebrating to do. Don't we?"

Julian didn't know what to say, but as it turned out, he didn't have to try and think of anything, as at that moment, the phone on the bedside table started ringing.

Helen and Julian looked at each other, and as Helen's hands were somewhat occupied already, Julian reached out to pick up the receiver.

"Hello?" he asked, not really knowing what to expect. Perhaps there *had* been a complaint, he thought absently.

"Yes, hello," said a man's voice, which Julian immediately recognised as belonging to the concierge downstairs. "I have just received a message from a Miss Kelly Bolton. She has asked me to inform Mrs Bold that her . . . er . . . husband has just arrived home."

Julian moved his gaze over to Helen, and looking at his expression, her own immediately clouded over. She sat up straighter, or as much as she could do with being handcuffed to either side of the bed.

"Right, thank you," said Julian, before placing the receiver down. He relayed the message, and Helen swore under her breath.

"Get me out of these cuffs," she commanded.

"What's going on? Who's Kelly Bolton?"

"She's my best friend, and she lives right across the road from me," Helen explained. "I tell her everything - she knows all about you. I trust her with my life, so I know she'd never say anything. I asked her to keep a look out in case my husband came home early." She groaned, but not in the way she'd been groaning a couple of minutes ago.

"Which he obviously has. I'm sorry, Julian, but I've got to go. I can't risk him getting suspicious, and the later I am, the more questions he's going to have for me."

Julian nodded, standing up and getting the keys to the cuffs in a daze. He was bitterly disappointed that they wouldn't be spending the night together, but at least the phone call had come *after* their little experiment in the bedroom. He had to be thankful for that.

He freed Helen, then watched as she jumped up and ran into the seating area, picking up items of clothing and dressing as quickly as she could. Then she grabbed her bag and ran over to the bed, where Julian was still sitting.

"I'm sorry," she said, "but stay here, make the most of the room. It's all paid for - the guy downstairs has my details. And I *promise*, one night soon, we'll spend the entire night together." She leaned down and kissed him gently. "Happy birthday, Julian."

And then she was gone.

CHAPTER 16

As it turned out, Helen Matthews kept her promise, and their night together happened far sooner than Julian could have hoped for. In all honesty, he thought their time in the hotel room would be their last - after all, she was still so worried about her husband finding out - but just a week later, Mrs Matthews asked Julian to stay behind after class.

Julian immediately started getting his hopes up, and once everyone had left the room, Helen went over to him, pulling on his shirt until he was close enough to place her lips on his.

"You seem like you're in a good mood," he said, after pulling back from what was an incredibly passionate kiss.

"I should be," Helen replied. "My husband's gone away for the weekend on business. *Far* away - I saw him get on the plane this morning and everything. There's no chance of him turning up again without any notice. So I'm free tonight, if you are?"

Julian grinned. "I think I can find some time for you," he joked. "Where are we going? Back to the hotel?" He thought about the concierge and the awkward phone call he'd received. Maybe not.

Helen pondered this for a minute. "Not anywhere around here. I think even with the Guesthouse we were risking someone local seeing us . . . no, let's take a drive, somewhere out in the countryside. We can find a nice pub somewhere, have a nice meal, see where the evening takes us . . . how's that sound?"

"That sounds perfect." And it honestly did - while the hotel room had been great, and while the sneaking around had been kind of erotic, the thought of going on an actual meal with Helen sounded wonderful. They could pretend they were a real couple, on a real date - not just two people who occasionally got together to have sex. He'd fantasised about that almost as much as he'd fantasised about Helen in that corset and those stockings.

"OK, then it's settled," she said. "Can you drive?"

Julian nodded, eager as ever to please.

"Great. Pick me up at seven from . . ." she thought again for a moment, obviously pondering where she wouldn't be seen by anyone, "the corner of Meadow Road and Virginia Street? Do you know where that is?"

Julian did, and he said so before kissing her again. "I'm looking forward to it," he breathed, wrapping his arms around her.

She smiled, then pushed him away as she glanced at the door. "Until tonight."

That evening, Julian drove down Virginia Street at exactly seven o'clock. He couldn't let anything about this night go wrong, and he wanted to start by making sure he was there to pick her up at the right time.

As he turned into Meadow Road, he breathed a sigh of relief - she was there, in her long trench coat and sunglasses, looking like someone out of an old spy film. She wasn't wearing her heels today, he noticed - which he was slightly disappointed about - but she still looked great. Of course, in his opinion she could wear a sack and she'd still look absolutely gorgeous.

He pulled over to the side of the road just long enough for her to jump into the passenger side, and then he carried on driving. Now he *felt* like someone in an old spy film, both of them looking in the car's mirrors to check no one had seen them.

"I think we're OK."

Helen just nodded. It was clear she was nervous about being spotted; she even lowered herself slightly in her seat, despite her large sunglasses covering most of her face anyway.

"So where should we go?" Julian asked eventually. He was driving out of town, but other than that, he had no idea where he was going.

Helen gave him directions to a large country pub - The Black Lion - and as Julian drove there, neither of them spoke. You could have cut the tension in the car with a knife.

As soon as they were out of the car and into the pub, however, things got less awkward. Well, they were talking now at least.

"Are you OK?" asked Julian, genuinely concerned.

Helen was looking far more relieved now they were off the road. "Yes, thank you. I'll be even better after a large glass of wine though."

They took a seat at the back of the pub - Helen thought sitting in the middle of the large space would rather be asking for it - and ordered their drinks, and then their food.

Helen looked lovely in a black and white floral dress, and Julian complimented her as she took a sip of wine.

"Thank you," she said, before looking over her shoulder for about the hundredth time. It was ridiculous; every time the large pub door opened, letting in a cold breeze of outside air, Helen would jump as though she'd just been electrocuted. She was making Julian nervous too, and even he started glancing at the door every time someone came in.

"Do you want to go back home?" Julian asked, even though that was the last thing in the world he wanted to do. "You seem . . . tense."

Helen sighed, downing the remains of her glass before ordering another one. "I thought it would be easier out here, where there's less chance of running into someone you know . . . but there's always a *slight* chance, isn't there? We're not *that* far from home. What if someone from the college comes in here? What if one of my husband's friends sees me? Someone I don't even recognise? How would I know?"

Julian sighed too. So much for a lovely, normal date! "I'll take you back. There's no point being here if we can't relax, and I don't like seeing you all anxious like this. We can do this another time. Maybe?"

Helen's expression softened. "I'm sorry. I really wanted this to work out, but I don't think we should go home just yet. We just need to go somewhere . . . less public."

Julian frowned. "Where do you mean?" he asked as the waiter brought over her wine. He had another beer. "Where's less public than a pub in the middle of nowhere?"

"I don't think we need a specific place," she said after a while. "I mean, we have your car . . ."

Julian grinned, liking the sound of where this was going. Perhaps the night wouldn't end so badly after all. "Well, you tell me where to drive and I'll drive there."

Helen nodded, seemingly a lot more relaxed now that she'd made a decision. Or perhaps it was the wine that was relaxing her - before they left, she ordered a couple of more glasses. Julian had one more beer then stopped, wanting to remain at least a little level-headed for the drive.

When they were back in the car, Helen navigated Julian off the main road and up a long, winding country lane. Julian had no idea where they were, which he supposed was good - if *they* didn't even know where they were, how was anyone else going to find them?

It was dark by now, and seemingly endless green hedges - looking almost black in the moonlight - flashed by as they went past. Helen was a *lot* more relaxed than she had been, the wine having done its thing, and she kept nuzzling into Julian as he drove, kissing his neck and nibbling on his ear. It was driving him crazy, and it was all he could do to keep control of the car.

At one point she started fumbling with his fly, and he immediately called out, "Woah, wait! If you do that while I'm driving, I'll end up killing us both!"

Pouting, Helen looked out of the windshield, pointing at a gate up ahead. It was open. "Head into that field. But turn the headlights off first - the last thing we want is a nosy farmer coming to see what we're up to."

Julian did as he was told, and after turning into the large expanse of grass, he drove slowly over to the left, where there was a long wall running along the side of the field. He brought the car to a stop behind it, killed the engine, and turned to Helen.

He could just about see her face by the moonlight coming in through the car windows, and in the slight shadow she looked more beautiful than ever. He was a lucky man, that was for sure.

"So," he said, "what shall we do now?"

She smiled at Julian as she leaned towards him, gently caressing his hand. "I can probably think of something."

Grinning, Julian pulled her into him, kissing her eagerly. It was cold now that the engine was off, but Julian knew a pretty good way to heat things up. As if in anticipation of this, Helen wriggled out of her coat and threw it onto the floor of the car.

She kissed him back, and Julian was just about to suggest that they move to the back of the car when she leaned down, pulling on the lever of his seat and forcing him backwards. Now that there was more room between him and the steering wheel, she climbed over the gear stick and the handbrake until she was sitting on top of him, her legs resting on either side of his thighs.

Julian immediately felt himself get hard - doing it in a car with a teacher? Now *this* was hot.

As she kissed him, Helen fumbled at his belt, as if she couldn't wait to get this going, and in turn, Julian slid his hand under her dress, caressing the tops of her thighs as she writhed around on top of him. A thrill - like a jolt of electricity - ran through him as he realised she wasn't wearing any underwear.

Once she'd undone his belt, she tugged at his jeans, forcing him to lift his whole body - and therefore hers, too - upwards so she could pull his trousers down, at the same time pulling down his underwear just enough to uncover him without making him freeze to death in the car. He ran his hand along her thigh again, feeling the goose pimples on her cool flesh. She was shivering.

"Are you ready?" whispered Helen, in between some long, passionate kisses.

"Always," replied Julian.

She moved herself into position, the contrast between the cold air in the car and her inside warmth making Julian shiver and gasp.

As she moved up and down on top of him, the air in the car started to change, and soon they were both sweating as the windows steamed up around them.

Reaching out, Julian pulled at the halter neck of Helen's dress, gasping again as the ends unravelled, falling away to reveal her breasts, her nipples raised and hard.

He grabbed onto them as they rocked together, squeezing them so hard he thought she was going to scream out in pain, but instead she just kept on going, leaning back every so often to breathe in some fresh air.

As they were getting ready to climax, both Helen and Julian raised their arms, pressing against the roof of the car with their hands as though trying to keep their passion within the vehicle instead of exploding outside of it. Julian yelled out Helen's name as she bit her lip, and then it was over, Helen leaning over him and panting, resting her head against his neck.

They stayed that way for a few minutes, and then Helen manoeuvred herself just enough to help Julian pull up his underwear and his jeans. She tied her halter neck back up, then leaned against him again, seemingly too exhausted to move.

Reaching over to the passenger seat, Julian just about managed to grab her jacket, which he draped around her body before putting his own arms around her, underneath the large trench coat. She nuzzled her head into his neck again, and the next thing he knew, she was breathing deeply, having fallen asleep against him.

He smiled, wishing every night could end this way, and then Julian too closed his eyes, letting himself drift off.

He awoke some time later - going by the early morning light, several hours had gone by - his neck stiff and his entire body shivering, despite the nice and warm Helen who was still curled up on his lap. Upon his movement, she woke up as well, stretching out as much as she could in the small space.

"Morning," she said, kissing him briefly before opening the door and climbing out of the car. It was a cold and frosty day, and the car was covered by small dots of early morning dew. "I'll be right back. Nature calls."

Julian nodded before getting out of the car himself, where he stretched his arms out and yawned loudly.

He was about to go off and find somewhere to relieve himself, but before he could move away from the car, Helen came running back, her expression a mixture of amusement and alarm.

"We have to go," she said, grabbing his arm and almost pushing him back into the car before running around to the passenger side.

"Why?" he asked, bewildered, as he started up the engine.

"Well . . . you know this field? The one we thought was empty?"

"Yeah . . ." replied Julian slowly.

"It's not empty," she said, trying not to laugh. "We're in the middle of a scouts' outing!"

Well, that was the *last* thing he expected her to say. Julian put the pedal to the metal and drove out of there as though his life depended on it.

As they went, a group of young scouts watched them go, confused.

CHAPTER 17

The weeks went on - with Julian and Helen meeting up whenever they could (which wasn't very often) - and eventually, Julian moved out of the college campus so he could help his mum, who'd opened a new pub. He was sad not to be so close to the school all the time, but glad to get some of his own space back, so he didn't resent it too much.

He helped out behind the bar, which was a bit of a pain, but it did bring with it some advantages. For one thing, it was far enough away from the college that Helen could visit him without being worried about any of her colleagues or students seeing her.

Which was exactly what she did one night in the middle of term, when Julian was yet again helping behind the bar.

He was staring into space, absentmindedly cleaning a pint glass, when she walked in, the few regulars turning to look at this goddess of a woman as she self-consciously headed towards the bar.

Julian was so surprised he nearly dropped the glass, but he just about managed to keep his cool. He did, however, cough loudly as he flickered his gaze over to his mum, who was watching Helen from the other end of the bar, immediately curious. Julian hadn't exactly mentioned their little relationship to her.

"Mrs Matthews!" Julian shouted, a little too loudly, as Helen perched on one of the bar stools in front of him. "I've not seen you around here before."

"I was just visiting a friend and I remembered you saying that your mum's pub was near here." She glanced at Julian's mum, who walked over to her son.

"You know Julian?" she asked, frowning.

"I'm sorry," said Helen, holding out her hand. "Let me introduce myself. I'm Helen Matthews, I'm one of your son's catering teachers at the college."

Julian's mum shook her hand, never once taking her eyes off this glamorous woman who, to her, looked nothing like any teacher she'd ever had at school. "Nice to meet you," she said eventually. "What can I get you to drink?"

"Oh no, sorry," replied Helen apologetically, "I'm afraid I can't stay. But there was something I needed to talk to Julian about." She lowered her voice, as though he wouldn't be able to hear her. "There's a problem with Julian's coursework, and I don't want him to fail just because of a few technicalities." She glanced at Julian, speaking louder this time as she said, "I have a spare few hours and the classroom will be empty right now. If you'd like to come in and try again, I can give you a new grade before the marks come out officially."

Julian's mum narrowed her eyes. "Do you give up this much of your free time to your other students, Miss Matthews?"

"It's Mrs . . . and I do what I can to help them out, yes. As you can imagine, being the only boy in the class can be a bit overwhelming sometimes, so I just want to make sure he's getting graded at the same level as the girls. Would you be able to spare him for a few hours?"

Julian's mum seemed to think about this for a while. "I suppose so." She looked over at the other end of the bar, where Gerald - one of the regulars - was raising his empty pint glass at her. "Well, I have to get back to it." She turned to Julian. "Good luck with your work, darling."

And then she was gone, off serving Gerald his fifth or sixth drink of the night.

Julian - who had been holding his breath this entire time - started laughing nervously as he let himself out from behind the bar. "I can't believe you just did that," he whispered at Helen as they left the pub.

"Would you rather I didn't come at all?" she asked.

"No," Julian replied, "but next time - maybe give me a bit of a warning?"

They took Julian's car, and after he'd been driving for about five minutes, he looked into the rear view mirror, frowning.

Helen noticed straight away. "What is it?"

"It might be nothing . . ." Julian replied, "but I think that car's following us. It's been right behind me ever since we left the pub."

Helen immediately went on high alert. "Oh god," she said, leaning forwards and squinting in the mirror. "That's my husband's car!"

Julian's heart skipped a beat. "Are you sure?" he asked. "You're not just being paranoid?"

Helen glared at him. "I'm sure! He must have followed me to the pub." She closed her eyes, her hand resting on her chest. "And I thought I'd been so careful! I got two different buses to get to you."

"Why would he have followed you?" asked Julian, clearly panicking. "Does he know about us?"

Helen shook her head. "No, but I think he's been suspecting something . . . he was asking me all these weird questions last night. Oh god . . ."

"What do we do?" yelled Julian, completely losing his cool. This thing with Helen was fun, but he didn't want to get beaten up because of it. Suddenly, the whole stupid affair seemed very, very real. *Too* real.

"Just keep driving," Helen said, glancing nervously into the mirror. "Maybe we can lose him, and then he'll have no proof. I can just deny everything."

Julian raised his eyebrows. "You really think that'll work? If he's seen you, he's seen you."

Helen took a deep breath. "He's seen me get in a car with a student, that's all."

"So we should go to the college? Keep to our story?"

Helen immediately started shaking her head. "No, the last thing I need is to get my colleagues involved in this. Just keep going - you can lose him, can't you?"

In all honesty Julian had no idea, but he supposed they didn't really have much of a choice, so after glancing at Helen again, he put his foot down as hard as he could.

The engine roared loudly as Julian's car jumped forwards, but as they were on a main road with lots of traffic, they only got so far before having to slow down again.

"We need to get out into the country," Helen hissed. "An open road."

"Give me a chance," retorted Julian. He carried on, turning into roads without indicating and rushing through red lights whenever he could - he just hoped that no one would get hurt, and that no police were watching any of his illegal moves.

Whatever he did, however, the car behind him did the exact same thing. If they'd had any doubts that it was Helen's husband before, they certainly didn't now.

At one point the car behind them came so close to the back of Julian's vehicle, he was sure that her husband was trying to run them off the road, but Helen didn't believe it. "It was probably just an accident," she said, slipping down into her seat in the hope that he wouldn't see her.

By now the car behind was beeping at them, the sound piercing through Julian's already jumpy heart as he carried on driving. He was becoming more and more reckless - even driving up onto the curb at one point - and more than anything in the world, he wanted this to end.

Julian was just thinking that it never would when he saw his chance: a large van swerved into their lane at the last minute, pushing in between Julian's car and Helen's husband behind and creating a much needed gap.

Julian didn't waste any time - he increased his speed as much as he could, overtaking the car in front of him and then racing along the street until he came to a side road.

He turned into it - which was thankfully empty of any moving vehicles or pedestrians - and immediately killed the lights. He then quickly and quietly manoeuvred in between two parked cars on the side of the road, before staring intently at the rear view mirror. Helen did the same.

A moment later, a car passed by the entrance to the side road, going fast. It was out of sight a second later.

"Was that him?" asked Julian, his heart still pounding. "Did we lose him?"

Helen nodded. "That was him. And yes."

After sitting there in the darkness for what felt like forever, Helen turned to face Julian. "I'm sorry," she breathed, her voice barely audible, "but that was far too close."

"What are you saying?" asked Julian, his own voice quiet as well. He knew what she was saying, but he didn't want to believe it.

"This has to end. Right now. It's just not worth it anymore - I don't want to lose my husband." She put her hand on the door handle, getting ready to open it.

"Hey!" cried Julian, reaching out and grabbing her arm. "At least let me give you a ride home."

Helen shook her head, and in the dim light, Julian could just about see what he thought were tears in her eyes. "It's too risky. I'm sorry Julian, but this can never happen again." She paused - Julian thought she was pondering whether to kiss him goodbye or not - and then she let herself out of the car without another word, slamming the door shut behind her.

Julian stared ahead of him into the night, numb, the thought of never being with Helen again leaving him with an odd empty feeling in the pit of his stomach. What was he going to do now?

What was he going to do without her?

CHAPTER 18

1977

It was that time of year - the dreaded exam period - and Julian was anything but ready for his City and Guilds catering exam.

The only good thing about this exam was that it was multiple choice - meaning he had a one in four chance of getting the answer right each time - and it was this thought he was clinging onto as he headed into the large exam hall.

There were rows after rows of tables - the entire catering class was taking the exam at the same time - and as he walked down a row to find his place, he caught Jenny's eye from across the room. She hadn't really been talking to him, but it seemed that exam season had pushed all her other worries out of her mind, and she smiled at him nervously from her own table as he passed by.

Julian eventually found his seat, and as he sat down and looked around him, he tried to come up with a plan.

If only he'd done some - *any* - revision, he thought to himself, and that was when he looked across at the student sitting next to him.

The girl hadn't been in any of his classes, but he recognised her from around the college - it was hard *not* to, as she had such a distinctive appearance. With her large, black-framed glasses and her two long pigtails, she looked the very stereotype of a clever, well-prepared student - a nerd, pretty much.

And, as Julian looked quickly down at her table, he realised some-thing: he could read her name on the front of her exam paper. Josie Williams. And if he could read her name from this distance, he'd be able to see her answers as well . . .

Not wanting to be too obvious, Julian pulled his gaze away from her paper, looking down at his own as he waited for the exam to start.

As Josie Williams turned her sheet over, he did the same, and every so often he would lift his face up and stare into the distance, dropping his gaze quickly before looking down at his paper and seeing which letters Josie had gone for. She was working quickly, and that was good - she obviously knew what she was doing.

A, D, B, B, A, C, A . . . Julian filled in the letters accordingly, putting a different answer every so often so it wouldn't look *too* suspicious if someone were to compare his answer sheet with Josie's.

By the end of the hour, he was confident that he had most of the right answers down, and that his paper wouldn't raise any red flags with any of the markers.

As everyone filed out of the room, he found himself walking directly behind Josie Williams as she talked to one of her friends.

"How'd you find it?" a brunette girl asked her.

"Pretty much as I expected," Josie replied confidently. "You?"

The girl shrugged. "It was pretty hard. And I'm really not looking forward to the City and Guilds catering exam tomorrow."

Julian stopped mid-stride as Josie said, "Yeah, that's going to be the tough one. Today's was just a warm-up, I reckon."

Josie and the brunette girl carried on walking, but Julian found he couldn't get his feet to move. Not after what he'd just heard.

"What's up with you?" Jenny asked, seemingly appearing from nowhere. "You look like you've seen a ghost."

Julian turned to face her, the smile slipping off her face as she took in his expression.

"What is it?"

He cleared his throat, eventually asking, "Were we all doing the same exam in there?"

Jenny frowned. "No, there were about four or five different papers I think. Why, you didn't have the wrong paper, did you?"

Julian put his hand up to his head, massaging his temples - he suddenly felt very, very nauseous. "I had the right one," he sighed, "but with all the wrong answers."

Jenny sighed, shook her head, and then was gone. She'd obviously had enough of his drama, and honestly, Julian had too - why could he never do anything right? Why did he always have to screw everything up?

As it turned out, he did - by some miracle - manage to get a few questions right on his exam paper, but it was by no means enough to save his skin, and while he still hoped he wouldn't come bottom of his class, that hope was rather short-lived.

Not only that, but things were made so much worse when they handed out the work experience placements. He knew that with his marks he wouldn't have been given a top hotel or a fancy restaurant to work in, but he was hoping for something perhaps not *too* bad - a small café or a farm shop, maybe. Somewhere he could flirt with female customers and have a bit of fun.

But that wasn't meant to be, and what he actually got was a canteen. In a tractor factory. Full of dirty, greasy men.

He wasn't even allowed to do any actual cooking in the kitchen - his main jobs were cleaning, washing up, and dishing out food to the factory workers. Yes, he was the one who had to stand there in an apron, handing out spuds to sweaty, middle-aged men.

And, on top of all that, he had to wear a hairnet. Yes, a hairnet, like a high school dinner lady.

The hours were long and the 'experience' he was getting was minimal. After all, how much skill did it take to place a potato on a plate? But he knew he had no one to blame but himself, so he sucked it up and spent his days daydreaming about as many girls as possible. Mrs Matthews even made a few appearances in his preoccupied mind.

Somehow he made it through his placement, and as he hung up his apron and his hairnet on his last day, he sighed in relief, not caring who heard him. No one particularly liked him there anyway - in fact, most people didn't even seem to notice he was there. They saw the food, but not the person giving it to them. Typical.

He felt so good as he walked out of that factory for what he very much hoped would be the very last time, and that good feeling lasted as he got in his car and started driving off, away from the factory, away from the men, away from that whole horrible experience.

His good mood didn't, however, manage to last.

Ten minutes later, his car's engine started making rather worrying clunking sounds, and a couple of minutes after that, he pulled over to the side of the road just as it spluttered and died.

He tried the key in the ignition - once, twice, three times - but there was nothing. It was dead. Just like the vague dreams he'd had of being a caterer.

Slamming his hand on the dashboard, Julian swore loudly before getting out of the car and leaning against the door.

It was a nice day, but somehow that seemed to make things worse - he was sweating as he stood there in the sun, wondering what to do next, and soon he had a full-on headache. So much for his good mood.

He stood there like that for ten minutes or so, holding his thumb out and watching several cars go by, and he was just about to start walking off to try and find a garage when a car pulled up at the side of the road.

The car was unlike anything he'd ever seen; to say it was 'flash' was an understatement. It was one of those big classic American cars - a Cadillac, by the looks of it - and it was painted an eye-watering shimmering gold colour.

As the car pulled over, Julian approached it a little nervously; he was more than intrigued to see who on earth was behind the wheel of such a vehicle, but he was pretty anxious too. After all, this clearly wasn't just any old person.

He leaned down to look inside the passenger side window, half expecting to see someone famous.

The man in the passenger seat wasn't famous - as far as Julian knew, anyway - but he sure wasn't 'regular', either, and he stared at Julian intently, making him feel even more nervous than before. He had a rather blank expression on his face, though somehow he managed to look pissed off at the same time, as though Julian had *made* him stop his car and come to his rescue.

His most distinguishing feature, however, wasn't his face at all but his huge mop of thick, curly black hair. Julian had never seen anything quite like it. He was wearing a rather ratty-looking blue vest top, which showed off his muscly arms; this guy was clearly strong and could definitely take care of himself. His tattooed arm rested on the passenger door, his fist clenched as though he was ready for a fight. Julian gulped.

After what felt like forever, Julian managed to pull his gaze away from this fascinating man enough to look over at the driver's seat. Sitting there was another man, this one looking a bit more respectable, in black trousers and a white shirt. The way he sat and the way he looked at Julian made him think he was on the clock - perhaps a driver employed to chauffeur this strange man around? By now, Julian was more intrigued than ever; you didn't get many people with their own drivers around these parts. Most people didn't even have their own cars.

"Having a bit of trouble?" the man with the hair asked, his voice so low and quiet Julian could barely make out his words over the sound of the car engine, though he *could* just about make out a Brummy accent.

Julian nodded. "The engine's completely dead."

"I've been there," he replied, nodding too. "Where you heading?"

After hesitating for a second or two Julian told him where he lived, and the man gestured at the back door. "Get in. I'll give you a lift."

"Thanks," he said, opening the door and sliding in.

As he entered the vehicle he noticed a strange smell, but it wasn't one he could easily put his finger on. His first thought was that it smelled a little like when you go to the zoo, but why would this man or his car smell like that?

At the other end of the back seat there was a rather large oblong-shaped object, covered over with a blanket. He must have a dog in there or something, thought Julian. A large, smelly dog. Well, as long as it stayed put in the cage . . .

As the driver started off, the man in the passenger seat turned around to talk to him. "So what's your name, friend?"

"Julian," he replied automatically. "And you?"

"The name's Reggie," he said. "You coming back from your job? School? What?"

"Last day of work experience," Julian explained, before going on to tell Reggie all about his rubbish placement and how he'd come to find himself there.

Reggie laughed. "You remind me of myself at your age. Good lad."

"So what do you do?" he asked eventually, not wanting them to lapse into an awkward silence.

Reggie blew some air out of his mouth as he shook his head. "What *don't* I do? That's the real question."

His vagueness and the fact he was unwilling to answer him properly immediately made Julian suspicious, and again he got a waft of that same strong animal smell. He glanced at the object on the back seat, wondering if he really wanted to find out what was under there, or if in this case, ignorance was bliss.

He was just about to ask Reggie about it when he heard a sound coming from beneath the blanket - like something was moving around in the cage. Whatever the 'something' was, it sounded pretty big.

"Reggie?" Julian finally managed to stammer, after a moment or two of silence. "What's in the back with me?"

Reggie laughed, loudly and heartily. "Ah, you noticed that, did you? I'm so used to him, I forget he's there most of the time. That, my friend, is a lion cub."

At those words, Julian turned away from the blanket and the object - cage, it was definitely a cage - underneath, his entire body suddenly stiffening in fright. It may have only been a baby lion, but it still had teeth and claws . . . it was still *wild*. What on earth was it doing in this car? Who were these people?

"But don't worry," Reggie added, "he only escapes every now and then."

Julian slid down in his seat, closing his eyes and taking a long, deep breath. How on earth did he get himself into these situations?

"So," said Reggie, as though nothing strange was going on at all, "the address you gave me . . . that's a pub, right?"

Julian nodded, trying not to look over at the cage on the seat. "It's my mum's place."

He noticed Reggie and the driver exchanging a look.

"Always good to make new friends, isn't it?" asked Reggie before carrying on, "Me and Johnny here, we like a good pint now and then. Maybe you could give us a couple on the house, for saving you from the side of the road?"

Julian nodded again. He didn't care if they wanted ten pints, as long as they could have them in the pub and not in a car with a wild animal. "Sure, no problem."

"That's my man," said Reggie, grinning again. "Look, I've only just moved into the area - I haven't really found my local yet. Let's see if your pub is up to scratch!"

Julian nodded again, then - as the silence stretched out in the car - he thought he'd try asking Reggie about his job for a second time. "You've just moved here? Was that for work?"

"Yeah, I work in the construction industry, and by the way, I know a *lot* of people. If you need a job, I'm your man. You know, if you ever get bored of helping out your mum."

Julian still wasn't sure about this guy, but it was always good to know people who could get you work, he supposed - he mentally filed the information away for later.

Just then, a loud ringing sound filled the vehicle, and when Julian shifted in his seat he could see a large car phone in the centre console. He'd never seen one before, and he watched in fascination as Reggie picked up the receiver, his voice suddenly changing as he spoke to the person on the other end - it was more authoritative, less jokey than the way he'd been speaking to Julian. This phone call was obviously business-related, but it didn't sound like much to do with the construction industry, and the whole thing was just a little bit odd - every other sentence ended with Reggie saying, "Over," like he was talking to someone on a walkie talkie.

As they pulled up outside the pub, Reggie turned around to face Julian in the back of the car. "Looks like we'll have to have those pints another time. You working tomorrow?"

Julian nodded as he replied, "All day." Then, giving one last hesitant glance at the cage on the seat, he undid his seatbelt and let himself out of the car. "Thanks again for the ride."

CHAPTER 19

Julian had just opened the glass washer - expelling a cloud of steam into the bar as he did so - when he heard a couple of loud voices coming down the entrance corridor.

He knew who they were before they even entered the bar - he'd recognise that loud, brash Brummy accent anywhere.

Sure enough, Reggie came into the room, looking around and taking in his surroundings. He was with Johnny, his driver, and a beautiful, tall, dark-haired woman. Reggie had his hand on her waist and she too glanced around the place, looking vaguely bored.

Reggie and the others headed over to the bar.

"I thought we'd have that drink now, Julian," he said, grinning. "You remember Johnny? And this here is Lucy." He squeezed her around the waist, making her roll her eyes.

Julian said hello, suddenly a little nervous, then asked what drinks they'd be wanting.

"Wine for the lady - red, a shandy for Johnny, and I'll have half a bitter and a Bacardi."

Julian started getting out the glasses. "What would you like in the Bacardi?"

"Nothing," replied Reggie, as if that should have been obvious.

Once they all had their drinks - on the house, as promised - Julian introduced the three of them to some of the locals and then to his mum. She looked a little confused as to where Julian knew these people from, but she didn't say anything; she just welcomed them to the pub and said she hoped they enjoyed their drinks.

As the place was pretty dead, Julian was able to go and sit with Reggie, Johnny, and Lucy, drinking lemonade while he listened to all of Reggie's wild stories.

As the drinks flowed, Reggie got louder and louder, while his tongue got looser and looser. He told Julian all about the animals he kept - and he didn't mean dogs or domestic cats. He had several lions, all of which he had many stories about, with the lion cub that Julian had met in the car being his newest addition. He said not only did he sleep with the cub to try and bond with it, but he also took it everywhere with him, and that the next time he came into the pub, he'd bring it along.

Reggie also told Julian of his friend down south, who owned a zoo and who trained animals for TV adverts and shows. He relayed tale after tale about his experiences with wild creatures, and honestly, Julian didn't quite know what to believe. As for the others, Johnny wasn't saying much, and Lucy seemed more interested in the wine than in what her 'date' was talking about. She was on her fourth glass already.

"What are you doing tomorrow?" Reggie asked eventually, after downing his most recent drink.

"Nothing . . ." said Julian, wondering why on earth he was asking.

"We're going to Birmingham, Johnny and me," Reggie carried on. "Back to my place. Come with us, see what we get up to. What do you say?"

Julian didn't really know *what* to say - or what to think in general about his new acquaintances - but there was just something about Reggie; whether his stories were true or not, it couldn't be denied that he was absolutely fascinating. And, as Julian decided right then, he wanted to find out more about this man. As much as he could.

He nodded, and Reggie smiled. "Great! We'll pick you up in the morning. 9 a.m."

It took Julian a while to get to sleep that night, wondering what the hell he'd managed to get himself involved with, but when he got into Reggie's car the next morning, he was buzzing.

He was in the back again, and although there was still a lingering smell of wild animal in the air, this time there was no covered-up cage on the backseat. He immediately relaxed, and then he heard the noise: there was something on the back windowsill.

Turning slowly to look behind him, Julian almost jumped when he saw it. The lion cub was now loose, roaming around on the ledge and peering out of the rear window. He clenched his fists together then took a deep breath, trying to get his fear under control.

"Don't mind him," Reggie said, turning around to look at Julian. "You'll be fine."

Even with Reggie's reassurance, Julian spent most of the journey keeping an eye on the lion cub, just in case it got it into its head to suddenly pounce on the new passenger. Julian had no idea how much damage a cub could do, but he guessed it still had sharp teeth and claws. Sharper than his, anyway.

Johnny drove Reggie and Julian to Reggie's house, and it looked like a pretty normal home, but as Julian got out of the car - very pleased not to be sharing a vehicle with a lion cub any longer - he heard a loud, low roar coming from somewhere in the garden.

Julian froze on the spot, halfway out of the car. That was no lion cub. That sounded like a giant, full-grown lion.

Reggie appeared next to him, patting him on the shoulder. "That's Leo. Don't worry, he's in his cage at the moment."

Julian nodded, trying not to think of the words 'at the moment' - when was he *out* of the cage?

A man emerged from the house then, and as he moved closer to the car, Julian could see that he only had one eye - there was a rather nasty-looking scar covering the flesh where one of them should have been, and Julian thought of the lion again. Was this an animal's doing? He shuddered.

"Ah," said Reggie, "this is One-eyed Mick. Mick, this is Julian - the guy I was telling you about."

"The one with the pub," said Mick, holding out his hand.

Julian shook it, trying to avoid looking at his bad eye. "That's the one."

"Mick here looks after my lions," explained Reggie, as they all headed towards the house.

"You're a lion tamer?" asked Julian, suddenly impressed.

Mick grinned. "Damn straight!"

Julian spent the day hanging around Reggie's place, and that evening, Reggie declared that he wanted to take the lions for a walk.

Julian stared at him, sure he must have misheard. "Sorry? A walk?"

Reggie nodded, as if it were the most normal thing to say in the world. "Yeah. I mean, I have to be careful - Leo recently escaped into the town, so they say they're going to revoke my licence. But we can still go for a little stroll."

Julian couldn't believe what he was hearing, but sure enough, he soon found himself heading out with Reggie, Leo, and the lion cub. Reggie had them each on a lead: one in his left hand, one in his right. It was the most bizarre sight Julian had ever seen - a man out walking his two pet lions as if they were dogs - and he just wished he had a camera with him to capture the moment.

They took the lions over the moors - which was windy and chilly and not at all very pleasant - and on the way back (this time Julian was driving, which was just as well as Leo took up the entire back seat - the lion cub was on the back ledge again, watching out the window), Reggie asked him to pull over at one of the local takeaways.

"I'm ravenous," he said as he got out the car. "Stay here while I get some food."

Before Julian could say a word Reggie was gone, and looking hesitantly in the rear view mirror, his gaze came into contact with Leo's huge, black eyes - he was watching him from the back seat. His lead was tied to one of the back headrests, but Julian feared that it wouldn't really stop Leo if he got it into his head to suddenly pounce. If he decided to do that, Julian was done for.

More than anything in the world Julian wanted to undo his seatbelt, open the driver's door, and get out, but he was worried that any movement might cause Leo to *actually* pounce, so he just sat there, in silence, completely terrified.

After what felt like an eternity, the passenger side door opened and Reggie got in, a large carrier bag full of food in his hand. The smell of chicken and chips filled the car, and he placed it on the centre console before telling Julian to drive on.

By the time they got back to Reggie's house, the enticing smell of the food mingling with the wild stench of the animals was starting to make Julian feel a little sick, and he'd just undone his seatbelt so he could get the hell out of that car when a loud roar came from just behind him. In all honesty, he nearly wet himself.

Turning very slowly to face Reggie, he saw that his hand was halfway to the carrier bag of food. Leo's large paw was on the package, right next to Reggie's palm. The roar was evidently Leo's way of telling Reggie who the food belonged to now.

"Have it!" shouted Reggie, for once sounding a little scared, "fucking have it, Leo!"

The lion roared again, and when he raised his huge paw and brought it down in a fast swipe, Reggie screamed out in pain.

Julian screamed too, thinking that this was it: this was how he was going to die. At the hands - or paws - of a lion who wanted his chicken and chips. What a ludicrous way to go.

Feeling very much on the verge of fainting, Julian stared at Reggie's arm, where his sleeve had now been ripped to shreds. Beneath it Julian could see torn flesh and blood, blood dribbling out and down onto the console . . .

Leo roared again.

With that, Reggie was out of the car, and after desperately fumbling with the door handle, Julian let himself out too. They both slammed the doors shut and then ran for the house, only stopping to look back when they'd got to the relative safety of the porch.

They could see the huge, terrifying shape of Leo in the car, ripping at the bag of food and destroying the leather centre console at the same time.

Reggie looked at Julian and shrugged. "Guess he was more hungry than I was."

CHAPTER 20

That crazy night was only the start of Julian's adventures with Reggie, though to begin with Julian pretty much just followed him around like a little lost puppy. He still didn't know what he was doing with this frightening yet fascinating man, but he found that he wanted to spend more and more time with him.

He looked up to Reggie, but he wasn't really sure how Reggie felt about him, and sometimes he thought he got on his nerves. One day, however, that all changed.

They'd gone to London, stopping off on the way to return the lion cub to one of Reggie's friends who owned a private animal studio, providing animals for the stage and TV. Reggie told Julian that his friend owned the chimps used for the PG Tips adverts, as well as the black panther that was used in various chocolate ads.

They were taken through to a backstage area, where there were some animals in cages, and Reggie headed over to one of them, gesturing at Julian to follow.

In this cage was a large lioness, who upon seeing Reggie, immediately stalked over to the edge of the cage, staring at him intently through the bars.

"Now, this is a very special animal," said Reggie. "We've got quite the strong bond, me and her."

Julian nodded, thinking about Leo. He wondered if this lioness had ever stolen Reggie's dinner or wrecked his car interior.

Before he could even think of saying anything in response, he watched in horror as Reggie opened the cage and proceeded to get inside. Not only that, however, but he then walked up to the lioness, opened her jaws, and stuck his head inside her large, terrifying mouth.

Julian could feel his heart pumping madly in his chest - honestly believing he was about to watch a man get eaten alive - but moments later, Reggie pulled his head out and reversed back out of the cage.

"Woah, you OK, Julian?" he asked, locking the cage door behind him. "You look like you've seen a ghost."

Julian found that he couldn't say anything, and Reggie smiled as he strolled over to another cage.

"Now this, my friend, is Ben the chimp. We get on pretty well too."

Julian's mind was still on the little stint Reggie had pulled with the lioness, so when Ben the chimp reached out through the bars and grabbed Reggie's scarf, banging him into the side of the cage, it took Julian a moment to realise what was happening.

By the time he *did* realise and had run over to the cage, Reggie's face was turning a rather alarming shade of purple - Ben the chimp was choking him.

Even though his fingers were trembling, Julian pulled the scarf away from Ben, trying to get Reggie free. The chimp, however, was having none of it, and he pulled back on the scarf with even more force than before, making Reggie whimper as his face slammed against the steel bars. Ben jumped up and down in response; he clearly thought this was some kind of hilarious game.

After a few more seconds of fumbling, Julian managed to undo the scarf at the knot, and Reggie fell to the ground, gasping.

Ben the chimp stared at him for a moment, then wandered off to the other end of the cage as though nothing had happened.

Crouching down to Reggie, Julian asked, "Are you OK?"

Reggie - who was still trying to catch his breath - nodded. "You," he eventually managed to say, "are the man. Thanks, mate."

Julian breathed a sigh of relief, too shaken up to say anything.

That was the afternoon that changed everything; from that day on, he and Reggie were thick as thieves - as Julian found out, saving someone's life will have that effect.

It wasn't long before Julian left his mum's pub, and soon he was both staying with and working for Reggie full-time.

He'd do odd jobs, drive him places when Johnny wasn't available, and pretty much try his hand at anything that needed doing.

One day, Reggie announced that they'd be staying in London for a bit at his friend's place - Terry, who lived there with his actress wife, Tina. They had quite a large flat and Julian had his own room. They stayed there for a while before moving into an empty flat nearby, although whose the flat was and why it was empty, Julian had no idea.

After driving Reggie to a business meeting one day, Julian (who'd been hired to drive him around for the afternoon) waited for his boss to return. When he did, Reggie informed Julian that he would be going out to Libya on the next possible flight.

"Libya?" asked Julian, surprised. "What's in Libya?"

"A construction job," Reggie explained, though Julian noted he didn't look at him as he said it. Not that Reggie was much for eye contact in general. "I need to price up the job and I have to be there myself to do it."

"OK," said Julian, who all of a sudden felt a bit lost. "And what do I do? Can I stay at the flat while you're gone?"

Reggie nodded. "I need you there to look after some deliveries for me - I just need you and Titch to check them off twice a week. Think you can handle that?"

Julian nodded too. "Sure."

"Just, you know," added Reggie, shrugging, "if anyone asks who you are, say you're the decorators."

"The decorators . . ." repeated Julian, before deciding he didn't want to know - obviously they *weren't* supposed to be staying there after all. "Sure," he said again. In all honesty, he didn't really know *what* to say.

So, just 24 hours later, Julian found himself alone in the flat, save for Titch (or Big Brian as he was also known).

It was pretty damn amazing to be staying in London. Before now, Julian hadn't even set foot in the capital, and as soon as he had, he loved it immediately; he loved the glitzy parts that Reggie often made him drive through, but he also loved the more gritty parts, away from the centre.

Home - and his mum's pub - seemed like a million lifetimes ago.

That night, Julian and Big Brian met up with a man called Adam in the local pub. Brian was friends with him and his wife, who turned out to be Deborah, a movie star.

A movie star! Julian couldn't believe how different his life was compared to even just two months ago. Hanging out with lions and celebrities, living in London . . . sometimes it rather felt like a dream.

And, if that wasn't enough, Deborah invited Julian and Big Brian to the film studios she worked at, which Julian agreed to immediately. This flashy lifestyle was pulling him in further and further, and he loved it; he wanted to experience as much of it as possible.

So, one day they all went down to the film studios, and it was at those studios that - to his complete surprise - Julian met Marjorie Smith, who was more popularly known as being a top beauty queen.

Julian had never met a beauty contestant winner before, and he was immediately hooked. She was radiant, with her long blonde hair and her big brilliant smile, and the floor-length sparkly black dress she was wearing didn't hurt much, either - it clung to each curve like it had been made just for her. Who knew? It probably had been.

He talked to Marjorie for a while, and just as he was about to leave, she turned towards him, smiling.

"Don't forget about me now," she said, before standing on her tiptoes and kissing him on the cheek.

There wasn't much chance of that happening, Julian thought to himself.

It was official: London was *amazing*.

A few days later, Reggie turned up at the flat, having just returned from Libya.

"How'd it go?" Julian asked as Reggie took the clothes out of his case. "Did you get the job?"

Reggie grinned, that little twinkle back in his eye again. "It's more or less in the bag, but . . ."

"But?" asked Julian, wondering where this was going.

"Let's just say I need to . . . 'persuade' . . . the officials to come round to my way of thinking. If I can butter them up enough, they'll accept the tender no problem."

Julian sighed. "Butter them up how?"

Reggie laughed, a loud and hearty sound that echoed around the large space of the flat. "Don't look so glum, Julian! I'm only going to throw them a party."

"A party," Julian repeated, nodding. "That doesn't sound too bad."

"You have no idea," Reggie said, the grin still on his face. "It's going to be the best damn party London's ever seen!"

The party was a lot bigger than Julian had expected; he'd been imagining quite a small gathering in the flat, or maybe at one of the local pubs, but Reggie went all out - he hired all of the function rooms at a nearby hotel.

Reggie had invited pretty much everyone he knew - Adam and his wife were there, along with Marjorie Smith, as well as several of Reggie's 'business associates', whatever 'business' that was.

As Julian (who for once was dressed up in a rather smart tux) glanced around the room, he noticed several women, all of whom looked like something out of a glossy magazine: perfect hair, perfect nails, perfect makeup . . . not to mention their glamorous clothes and amazing bodies. They wandered around the place as though they were floating, smiling at all the men and making them go weak at the knees. It was as if that was their sole purpose at the party.

"Reggie," Julian said after dragging his boss to the side of the main reception room, "who are all these women? How the hell do you know so many knockouts?"

Reggie stared at Julian for a moment - as though trying to figure out if he was being serious or not - before laughing in his face. It started off as a low, grumbling sort of chuckle, but ended up being so loud that several people turned to face them, intrigued as to what was so funny.

"Sorry mate," Reggie said, patting Julian on the shoulder, "sometimes I forget just how naïve you are."

Julian held up his hands in protest. "Hey, I'm *not* naïve . . ."

"Sure, sure," said Reggie, yet again patting him on the shoulder. "Don't worry, it's not a bad thing - it amuses me." He pointed at a few of the women at the other end of the room, lowering his voice as he said, "Those women are the whole reason for this party. They're my bribes."

Julian frowned for a moment. "You're bribing the people who have the power to accept your tender with . . . what? Prostitutes?"

"They're not prostitutes," said Reggie, lowering his voice even more, "and don't let them hear you say that word, OK? These are high class escorts. Very classy."

"And you think that'll work?" Julian asked, still frowning.

Reggie grinned. "If I know these men like I think I do, then yes - it'll definitely work. Throw in some free drinks and some good food, not to mention this great party, and the job's in the bag. One hundred percent guaranteed."

Reggie went off to get another drink, and Julian started making the rounds, mingling with people and trying to memorise their names - after all, they could be useful as future contacts. At one point he saw Johnny walk over to a tall, dark-haired man, whisper something to him, and then hand him a white envelope. It was bulging, absolutely stuffed full. The man tucked it into his inside jacket pocket, nodded, and marched off.

"What are you looking at?" a voice asked him, and turning around, Julian found himself face to face with Marjorie.

"Well, if it isn't the beauty queen," Julian said. "It's nice to see you again."

It was, as well - he thought Marjorie had looked stunning before, but tonight she looked completely out of this world. Her long, shimmery, golden dress turned heads wherever she went in the hotel, and not just for its colour - the slit in the side went up almost to her hip, showing off her shapely leg. She was also wearing incredibly high heels, and Julian had a hard time trying to stop himself from imagining those heels digging into him as the two of them had sex.

"So," said Marjorie, "when are you going to ask me to dinner?"

Julian couldn't believe it - the most stunning woman at the party had just suggested they go to dinner together. In truth, her beauty pretty much intimidated the hell out of him.

"How about tomorrow?" he shot back. "There's this little place on the Thames I've been meaning to check out."

"That sounds lovely. Pick me up at seven?"

Julian nodded, and was just about to lean in for a kiss when Johnny appeared by his side. "Sorry mate," he said, "but the boss wants Marjorie to meet someone. Don't worry, I'll bring her back soon."

Julian could have punched Johnny right then, but instead he just nodded, smiling politely as Marjorie got whisked away to meet some 'important people'. Julian vaguely wondered if one day he too would be an 'important person'. Maybe, if he kept in with Reggie; the guy seemed to know *everyone*.

After putting his empty glass down on a nearby table, Julian made his way over to the toilets and was just finishing up at the urinal when he saw two men come in. They were both wearing quite 'out there' cream tuxes and they both headed into the same toilet cubicle.

At first Julian wasn't sure where to look, or what to do. He also didn't know if they'd seen him or not, and if he started washing his hands, they'd *definitely* know he was there. The last thing he wanted to do was to interrupt . . . well . . . whatever they were doing in there.

As he slowly made his way over to the sinks, Julian was expecting to hear moans and groans starting to come from the cubicle, but as he gently turned on the tap and started washing his hands, he realised they hadn't completely closed the cubicle door - there was a gap of a few inches, and through it, he could see the two men, crouched down and leaning over the toilet.

OK, so perhaps they weren't having a sexual encounter after all, thought Julian, as he crept a little closer.

"That's the good stuff," said one of the men to the other, lifting his head up and wiping his nose. As he did so, he noticed Julian lurking just outside the door, and standing up, he pushed on it until it opened. "You alright there, mate?"

Julian nodded, not sure what to say, and when he glanced at the toilet seat he saw a couple of lines of white powder spread out on the black plastic. In his hand, the man had a rolled up bank note.

The other man - who was still crouched on the floor - looked up at him, a cloud of anger on his face, and Julian took a step backwards.

He hadn't meant for them to see him, and now he was very much concerned that they were about to get into a fistfight. The last thing he wanted was for Marjorie to see him with a black eye and a split lip - that was never a good look.

There were a few seconds of tense silence in the bathroom, and then the man with the banknote started laughing. "Alright, well don't just stand there. You want a bump or not?"

Julian hesitated, still not sure what to say. He'd never done any hard drugs - his drug of choice was usually alcohol - and he wasn't sure he wanted to start now.

"Thanks, but I think I'd better pass," Julian said, desperately not wanting to offend the two men in front of him.

The guy with the banknote frowned, taking a step closer, out of the cubicle. "You're not a grass, are you?"

Julian held his hands out in front of him, shaking his head. "No, no . . . I just . . . I'm on the clock. I work for Reggie," he stammered, hoping the people here knew who that was.

The man's face immediately cleared of all suspicion, and he whacked Julian playfully on the back as he said, "Good old Reg, known the bloke for years. Alright, well if you change your mind, we've got a load of the stuff in our room. Tell Reggie too."

Julian nodded - having no intention of mentioning this encounter to Reggie at all - and walked out of the bathroom as quickly as he could.

As soon as he was back in the corridor, Johnny appeared seemingly out of nowhere. Even though he was on the clock too, he was clearly drunk. "Julian!" he called. "You gonna try it on with the beauty queen then? Because I'm telling you, if *you* don't, *I* will!"

Julian shook his head, suddenly feeling very awkward indeed. When Johnny got drunk he got overly friendly, not to mention loud-mouthed, and he really couldn't be bothered to deal with that right now. "Just dinner," he said, walking away from Johnny as soon as possible.

After his encounter in the bathroom, Julian was feeling more than a little out of place, and now, glancing around the room again, he started seeing things in a whole different light.

As he moved through the different rooms, he noticed just how out of it most of the people looked. He knew this was a party and everything, but was absolutely everyone here either completely wasted or hopped up on drugs?

He saw several of the escorts already starting with their evening's work, draped over men on the sofas or leading them off down dark corridors. One of the officials looked like he was ready to get it on right there and then in the corner of one of the reception rooms, the escort giggling so drunkenly that Julian thought it might actually happen. She was sitting on the guy's lap, drinking champagne in between several long, slow kisses, the man's hands roaming over her body as though unaware anyone could see them.

As much as Julian hated to admit it, the sight was turning him on. Where was Marjorie?

He continued through the hotel, passing people laughing raucously or dancing with each other seductively, all the while looking out for Marjorie, or Reggie, or anyone he knew.

He narrowly missed getting in the way of a disagreement between two businessmen, who in their alcoholic haze wanted to work out their problem with their fists rather than their tongues. After nearly getting punched in the face, Julian decided to grab another drink himself and head outside for some air. Perhaps Marjorie was out there, he thought.

When he got outside, he saw a couple of people standing on the pavement, smoking, but apart from that, the road was pretty dead.

He could still hear the party raging inside, however, and turning to look up at the windows (which were glowing pink then yellow then blue then red with the disco lights), he tried to make out the shapes moving within. Of course, it was pretty useless - they were all just a blur of drunken bodies.

Sighing, Julian sat down on the cold stone step, still staring up at the hotel windows as he reflected on how much - and how quickly - his entire life had changed.

He sat there for another fifteen minutes or so, slowly finishing his drink, and when he started to realise just how cold he was becoming, he stood up, getting ready to head back inside.

Before he even made it up the steps to the front of the hotel, however, a huge crashing noise sounded on his right, making him jump.

When he looked up at the window just above him, he could hardly believe what he was seeing. The entire windowpane had smashed outwards as two men had seemingly fallen through it. It was only a drop of a few feet to the ground below, but it was enough to knock the wind out of them, and they both lay there, writhing around and groaning in pain, for a good ten seconds or so.

By now a whole group of people had appeared at the window, peering down, including an extremely drunk-looking Johnny and a rather red-faced Reggie, who spotted Julian and waved before turning his attention to the men on the ground.

Julian did the same, soon realising who they were - the two men from the bathroom who'd offered him coke.

He was just wondering if he should go into the hotel lobby and call for an ambulance when one of the men stood up, towering over the other and shouting, "Come on then! Let's finish this!"

The man on the ground groaned as he got to his feet, only just regaining his balance before the other man punched him on the jaw, sending him reeling backwards.

While the first man was celebrating his little victory, bowing to the people in the window, the man he'd just punched came up behind him, jumping onto his back and trying to hit him wherever he could. The people in the window cheered, clearly enjoying the show.

"Can you believe this?" asked a well-known voice from next to him, and when Julian turned to face Marjorie, he shook his head.

"I've been looking everywhere for you," he said. "Do you want to get out of here?"

Marjorie looked past Julian at the two men - who were now both on the ground again, but still trying to hit each other - and nodded. "I really, really do."

CHAPTER 21

The next night Julian had a shower, got ready, and went out to pick up Marjorie.

She was staying not too far from the Thames, so they walked down to the restaurant in the early evening darkness, looking every inch the sophisticated couple.

She was wearing another long dress - this one red and skin-tight - and he was wearing a suit and tie, with his best leather shoes. Her long blonde hair was tied up in an elegant ponytail, and a glittering silver necklace guided the eye to her enviable cleavage.

"So, tell me where we're going again," said Marjorie, as they strolled along the river. The moonlight was reflecting off its dark surface, the vast array of city lights on the opposite bank shimmering in the background.

"It's this new floating restaurant," Julian explained. "I hear the food's amazing."

"Sounds posh!"

"What, you don't think I'm posh?" asked Julian, pretending to be offended.

Marjorie let out a high, melodic laugh. "I think we're both about as posh as each other! It sounds lovely. Really."

A few minutes later they arrived at the restaurant, the waiter greeting them at the edge of the boat platform and checking their names on his list of reservations.

"Ah yes, here we are. Please, follow me," he said, before walking off among the sea of tables and chairs.

Julian and Marjorie followed, thanking the waiter as they sat down at a table right next to the water. As it was still relatively early, it wasn't too busy yet, although it was clear that these seats were the most coveted in the whole place - the people already having dinner had taken up most of the tables at the edge of the boat. Julian didn't blame them - from here, they had an absolutely stunning view of the river.

Another couple were sitting on the table next to them, and they were having a bit of an argument. The woman was very glamorous, but the man looked a little . . . well, rough around the edges. His thick cockney accent didn't help matters much, and Julian found the whole pairing incredibly odd.

"I wonder what they're arguing about," whispered Marjorie, leaning forwards so they wouldn't hear her.

Julian shrugged, annoyed. He was spending a lot of money on this meal, and he hadn't dressed up and brought Marjorie to a nice restaurant just so he could hear a couple arguing on the table next to them.

He tried to ignore it as they ordered their drinks and their starters, and they managed to make it through most of their main meal before it got too loud to ignore any longer.

"Just who the fuck do you think you are?" roared the man, banging his fork on the table in frustration. "I don't have to put up with this shit, you know!"

The woman laughed in response - a dirty, bitter kind of laugh - before screeching back, "Oh, really? And you think *I* should have to put up with this shit?"

"I think you *will* put up with it if it means me buying you all your pretty dresses and jewellery!"

With that, the woman stood up, grabbing the necklace she was wearing and pulling on it until the clasp broke. She then proceeded to throw it at the man opposite her as she yelled, "Fuck you and fuck your jewellery!"

That was it. Julian had been watching Marjorie's face throughout this whole exchange - had looked at her as she got more and more uncomfortable - and now he was more angry than ever.

Standing up himself, he turned around to face the couple. "Excuse me, but do you mind? We're trying to have a nice meal here and all we can hear is you two fighting! Do you have to use that kind of language?"

He realised how lame he sounded as he said it, but what was he meant to do with Marjorie here? The waiters were doing nothing about the situation, and he couldn't exactly swear back at them with his date watching.

There were a few seconds of silence - with seemingly everyone in the restaurant now staring at the four of them - and then the cockney guy gently placed his fork down, scraped his chair back, and stood up. He moved over to Julian without saying a word, towering over him as Julian realised just how large this guy was - he hadn't been able to tell when he was sitting down.

"What did you say?" the man asked, his voice so low it was barely audible.

Julian peered up at his face, at his red cheeks, his furrowed brow, his stubbly chin. Suddenly, he didn't feel so brave. If he wanted to, this guy could beat him up in an instant.

Unfortunately, it wasn't the guy's fists Julian had to be worried about, as just at that moment, the man pulled open his leather jacket, gesturing at what was in his waistband.

Julian gulped as he saw the dark but obvious outline of a handgun. This guy clearly wasn't just a loud-mouthed idiot; now Julian was thinking he must have been some kind of gangster. Suddenly, he wanted to be anywhere other than London.

"I asked you what you said, alright!" the man roared, and this time his voice was very much audible.

Julian shook his head, taking a step back. "I didn't say anything. I'll just . . . I'll let you get back to your meal."

"I don't think so mate," he growled back, his hand slowly making its way down to the gun, caressing it like he would caress a woman. "You see, I'm here trying to have a nice meal, same as you, and now I have to deal with you yelling at me? In front of my wife?"

Julian shook his head, unsure of what to say. He was very aware that all eyes were on him, but the only person he cared about was Marjorie; he'd been worried about this man ruining their date, but he seemed to be doing a bang-up job of that himself right now.

"So, are you going to apologise to me or what?"

Julian looked down at the gun again, at the man's hand running along its smooth surface. He could feel the sweat trickling down his back, could sense it appearing on his upper lip too. This guy was for real. "N-no," he stammered.

"No?" he roared. "You're not going to apologise?" He pulled at the gun, bringing it out of his waistband.

"No!" shouted Julian, his voice cracking. "I mean, I didn't mean to . . . I . . ." Words failed him as he watched the man bring the gun up to his face, and a second later, he found himself staring down the barrel.

All thoughts left his head then. He didn't care where he was or who was watching - he could have wet his pants and not cared - and he certainly didn't care about London or Reggie or his job. All he wanted was to be back home, working in the pub with his mum and being bored out of his mind. Right about now, that sounded like heaven.

He was still staring at the gun when he felt a tugging on his sleeve, and after what felt like forever, he was able to pull his gaze away from the deadly weapon.

It was Marjorie, her face as white as a sheet. "We have to go," she said. "*Now.*"

Julian was just about to open his mouth to say that in case she hadn't noticed, he was kind of in the middle of something right now, when the cockney man lowered his gun. Julian realised there was someone standing next to him. He was dressed all in white and was wearing a chef's hat.

"Now," he was saying, in a low, smooth, calming voice, "I'm sure the gentleman didn't mean any harm. We'll give you your meal for free if you just put the gun away. There's no need to call the police . . . we'll just pretend this never happened. What do you say?"

"Come on, Julian," Marjorie whispered, and while the cockney man was distracted by the chef, Julian followed her away from the scene, their food left half-eaten on the table.

When they were far enough away that he knew the cockney man wouldn't hear him, Julian asked, "Where are we going?" He was still in a bit of a daze, and it took him a while to realise that they weren't heading back the way they'd come in.

"There's another way out, further down the boat. The chef's friend said it would be better to go out that way - it's the service entrance for the kitchen."

"The chef's friend?" Julian repeated, still not entirely sure what had just happened. The sight of the gun had really messed him up.

"Yes," Marjorie replied, and this time she smiled a little. "You'll never guess who he is."

Julian had no idea how to respond to that - after everything that had gone on, he didn't much care *who* the chef's friend was, or what he had to do with anything - even so, when a man with long, dark hair and a beard popped up in the doorway of the kitchen, Julian gasped.

"Is that . . ." Julian trailed off as the man grabbed his arm, manoeuvring him into the kitchen.

"I'm George," he said, as if he had to explain who he was, "I hear you've had a spot of bother . . ."

"You could say that."

George nodded. "I came to see when I heard all the shouting. Right in the middle of my meal, I was."

"Sorry for interrupting," Julian replied automatically.

"It's not you who has to apologise, mate! I just hope Roger knows what he's doing. I'm sure he'll be fine - he's used to dealing with crazy customers."

Julian nodded, glancing briefly at Marjorie as they all rushed through the kitchen, waiters and chefs alike looking up as they went through.

Finally they were back outside again, hopping off the edge of the boat.

"Alright, if I were you I'd get out of here sharpish, in case that guy decides to follow you."

Julian nodded, before remembering the meal. "We haven't paid . . ."

"Don't worry about that," said George, looking at him as if he was mad. "The man pulled a gun on you; Roger will sort out the bill. He's a good guy. Now, may I suggest the lady comes with me?"

Julian did a double-take, unsure if he'd heard the man properly. "Sorry?"

George shook his head. "Look, the guy's after *you*, not her. Do you want to put her in danger any longer? You should split up." With that, he walked out into the road, flagging down a black cab. It came to a stop, the driver clearly recognising the famous footballer who'd pulled him over.

"Now get in," said George. "I'll make sure she's safe."

Julian didn't like this - Marjorie was meant to go home with him, not another guy, no matter how famous he might be - but he supposed he didn't have much choice. And besides, if the guy *did* try and come after him and Marjorie ended up getting hurt, he'd never forgive himself.

So, kissing Marjorie briefly on the lips, Julian said goodbye and jumped into the taxi.

"Just get me away from this restaurant, please," said Julian, still very much shaken from everything that had just happened.

The taxi driver nodded, and as he pulled away from the kerb, Julian watched Marjorie and George stroll off down the road.

"Was that George, that footballer?" asked the taxi driver, glancing at Julian in the rear view mirror.

"It certainly was," Julian replied, shaking his head.

Life was never boring around here, was it?

Julian was just relaxing into the seat, glad that the nightmare of an evening was finally over, when he heard a sound that made his entire stomach churn.

A gun shot.

That maniac was actually shooting at the cab!

The driver yelled out in surprise, then glared at Julian in the rear view mirror. "This your doing?"

Julian shook his head, unable to speak - he was just so grateful Marjorie wasn't still with him.

Another shot was fired - though from where, Julian had no idea, as he'd now slid down into the seat as far as he could go and couldn't see out the windows - and the taxi driver slammed his foot on the

147

accelerator, speeding along the road as if . . . well, as if he was being chased by a madman with a gun.

Julian kept thinking back to the cockney man holding the hand-gun in front of his face, and when one of the rear windows in the taxi shattered into a thousand pieces, he let out a loud, high-pitched, incredibly girlish scream.

Just then, however, the driver sped up even more, and risking a quick glance behind him, Julian saw the crazy cockney running along the street. By now he was clearly getting tired, and he slowed his pace until he had to stop and catch his breath. The driver took the car around a corner, and the man disappeared from Julian's sight.

Glancing in the rear view mirror, the taxi driver - who seemed remarkably unruffled by the whole situation - glared at Julian again. "You're paying for that window, mate," was all he said.

Julian nodded. His entire body was shaking, and he had no idea when it was going to stop.

When he finally got back to the flat that night, exhausted and embarrassed about what had happened, he got another shock: three extra people had seemingly moved in during the hour or two he'd been out. Mick was there, as well as some guy named Paul and a man named Old Arthur, who wasn't really that old. Apparently he was Reggie's 'financial guru' but Julian didn't much care either way - all he wanted to do was go to bed and pretend this horrible, awful, terrible evening had never happened.

That night, he dreamed of guns.

CHAPTER 22

As if this week couldn't get any worse.

As the light loomed up in front of the car, Julian slammed on the brakes, the screeching of the tyres almost deafening him as he tried to regain control of the vehicle.

He felt his entire body jolt in the seat as he was flung forwards, the seatbelt cutting into his flesh as it tightened around him.

It wasn't, however, tight enough, as the next thing Julian felt was a sharp pain in his forehead and a hot rush of liquid on his lip as he collided with the windscreen.

Just minutes before he'd been in the pub with Big Brian and Adam, having a few drinks and a few laughs as he tried to forget about his run-in with the cockney gangster the night before. It had been a pretty normal evening, a good time, and now this.

This pain. This confusion. This ache in his back and the throbbing in his head.

He remembered Adam's driver going home, leaving them on their own, and Big Brian's suggestion that the least drunk of them should drive Adam back to his place. The least drunk of them, Big Brian had decided, was Julian.

He'd agreed even though he could hardly walk in a straight line, and now he was staring out of the smashed windscreen at the lamppost he'd just crashed the car into.

A groaning sound came from beside him, and although it hurt him to do it, he turned his neck just enough to see Big Brian in the seat next to him. He was staring ahead, dazed, the cone of chips that had moments ago been in his hands now spread out over the dashboard of the car.

Julian could see that his hands were bleeding from where he'd cut them on something, and that reminded him of his own pains. Reaching up a shaking hand, he felt blood on his head from where he'd slammed into the windscreen, then dotting his mouth with his finger, he came away with more blood from where he'd bitten down on his lip upon impact.

Adam - who'd been sitting in the back - was seemingly OK, though everyone was more than a little shaken.

Julian, who until now hadn't really ever been fazed by much, was starting to reconsider his change of direction in life. Two near misses in two days was a little too much of a close call for his liking.

All three of them lurched out of the car - each of them holding their bodies in various places, as though that would somehow stop them from hurting - and Julian staggered to the side of the road. The car was on the pavement, its hood smashed inwards, the engine smoking slightly.

All three of them tried desperately to flag a car down, but no one would stop. Julian didn't really blame them - with his busted lip and bleeding head, and Big Brian's bleeding hands, they looked like they'd been fighting with each other.

They stayed there like that for another ten minutes or so, and then they gave up.

None of them said a word as they started on the two-mile walk home, but by the end of it, Julian's entire body was screaming.

When Julian got back to the flat, he spent a long, long time in the shower, trying to wash all the blood off his body, not to mention cleaning out all his little cuts and scrapes. He knew that he should have gone to a hospital to get himself checked out, but there was a reason he couldn't do that - the same reason they'd just left the car abandoned at the side of the road instead of organising for it to be picked up.

The reason was that the car was hot. It wasn't stolen, exactly, but it *had* been supplied by Terry, and from what he could work out, Julian was pretty sure it had been used in a robbery. He hadn't wanted to ask any questions about it - plausible deniability and all that - and the last thing he needed was for the police to find out he'd drunkenly crashed it into a lamppost. So, they'd simply left it there, with Julian thinking they'd figure it all out when everyone had sobered up.

As he stepped out of the shower, the hot water only alleviating his pain a little, Julian tried not to think about it. London was great, sure, but he knew that he shouldn't have been getting involved in these kinds of things. He could feel himself slowly getting pulled into a world he wasn't sure he wanted to be a part of.

After drying himself off Julian crawled into bed, the pain in his head very much now matching the pain in his body. He just needed a good night's sleep, that was all. Things would look better in the morning. They always did. Didn't they?

Of course, that was only if he *could* get a good night's sleep. And, as it turned out, that was something Julian certainly wasn't going to get that night.

At around 3 a.m. he was woken by the sound of people moving around - talking loudly and banging into things - and Julian made himself sit up in bed, his head still thumping. If only he had some painkillers to hand, although right now he didn't think any normal painkillers would be able to help him much.

Just then the door to Julian's room slammed open, making him jump. It was Paul and Mick, each of them carrying a suitcase, stuffed full.

"What's going on?" Julian asked sleepily. "What's with all the noise? What time is it?"

Mick placed his suitcase on the floor before casually replying, "Well, mate, looks like the settee's on fire. Soon the whole lounge will be going up."

Julian leaped out of bed, frantically scrabbling for his crumpled jeans and t-shirt. As he put them on, he glanced over at Paul and Mick.

"Well, what are you just standing there for? Shouldn't we be . . . you know . . . *doing something?*" Julian could hear the panic in his voice but he didn't care - if ever there was a time to panic, it was now.

Paul shrugged. "Look, I'm not a firefighter. We thought we might climb out your window."

Julian glanced at the tiny window in question before violently shaking his head. "That's not going to work, not unless we can all lose five stone immediately." He glanced at their suitcases - which presumably held their most prized possessions - and shook his head; they were at least twice the size of the window. "Have you phoned for the fire brigade?"

"Yes, but there's no other way out," said Mick, who still didn't sound *that* bothered by the whole life-threatening situation. "We can't get through the lounge; it's too risky."

Shaking his head - and realising that, as usual, *he* was going to have to take control of everything - Julian grabbed the sheets off his bed before stuffing them in the sink in the corner of the room. He turned the taps on while he looked back over at the others. "We need to throw these over the settee. Are you going to help me or not?"

The two men nodded, and grabbing the now soaking wet sheets, Julian sprinted out into the lounge, where Big Brian was running around in a daze, picking up burning items with his gloved hands and throwing them through the nearby window - again, one too small for them to attempt climbing out of. He must have still been completely drunk.

The room was unrecognisable. Flames blazed around the fabric settee - making it look like some kind of seating area from hell - and a thick cloud of smoke hung in the air, immediately tickling the back of Julian's throat and making him cough.

Rushing over to the settee, Julian took one end of one of the sheets while Paul took the other, and together they threw it over the sofa. Mick helped him with the second and then Julian yelled at them both to go and get more from some of the other beds.

The wet sheets had put out most of the flames on the settee, but the fire had now spread to the curtains, and Julian was worried where it might go next. Before they knew it, the whole flat could be going up in flames.

By now the smoke in the lounge had become so intense that Julian could barely see the others - they all just looked like strange grey blurs in the distance. Man-shaped blurs, but blurs nonetheless. His eyes were watering and his mouth was getting more dry and parched by the second - he could taste the smoke on his tongue, could feel it burning at the back of his throat.

The pain in his head and body was being completely eclipsed by the effort of trying to breathe while at the same time avoiding inhaling any smoke, and keeping his hand clasped over his nose and mouth, Julian got down on the floor like he'd seen people do in films.

He was trying to find his way to the door - to the outside world, to freedom - but the settee somehow seemed to constantly be in his way, and with all the smoke surrounding him he was more than a little confused and disoriented.

Julian could feel himself getting light-headed - the dizziness almost threatening to take over his entire body - and just as he felt his eyelids starting to close of their own accord, the atmosphere in the room suddenly changed, as if someone had just flipped a switch.

A door had been opened somewhere, and now there seemed to be more people in the small lounge than there had been before.

By now Julian was lying down next to the settee - almost using it as some kind of shelter against the rest of the smoke-filled room - and although he couldn't see anything in the thick fog of smoke that surrounded him, he could hear people moving around.

At one point he felt a sharp pain in his side, the sensation waking him up a little as he realised that someone had stumbled over his body. Talk about kicking a man when he was down.

The next thing he knew, strong arms were being wrapped around his torso, pulling him upwards and dragging him across the floor, away from the settee. As he was being pulled through the smoke he started coughing again, and when he opened his eyes, they immediately started stinging.

A few seconds later a strong breeze brushed against Julian's face - the sweetest thing he'd felt, well, *ever*. He was acutely aware of being outside, although it took him a while to realise what that actually meant: he was out of the burning flat. He was away from the fire and the smoke. He'd been saved.

He just had time to wonder if the others were as safe as he was when they appeared next to him - Big Brian, Mick, and Paul had also been brought out by the firefighters. They were in various states of disarray, their faces covered in dirt, their hair sticking up at random points, their eyes glazed over. Going by how he felt, Julian assumed he must have looked just as bad, if not worse.

He was now sitting on the cold ground, trying to get his breath back while one of the firemen kneeled down in front of him.

"Don't worry," he was saying, though his voice sounded like it was coming from miles away, "we'll get you off to the hospital in no time. But first, can you tell me - is there anyone else left in the flat?"

Julian tried to think through the haze in his mind as he glanced at the people beside him. "I . . . I don't know," he answered honestly. His head was killing him, but even through the pain and discomfort, something was niggling at him, something he couldn't quite grasp in his confusion . . .

Mick, Paul, Big Brian . . . who else was meant to be here?

"Arthur!" he shouted out suddenly, bolting upright. "Old Arthur's still in there! He must still be in bed!"

With that the firefighter was gone, and Julian leaned back against the wall, sighing. He was glad he'd remembered Arthur; he just hoped it wasn't going to be too late.

The other three sat closer to him then - Mick patting him on the leg while they waited - and after what seemed like an eternity, two firefighters emerged from the flat, an extremely disgruntled-looking Arthur being supported on either side by the two large men.

Julian breathed a huge sigh of relief. While he'd been waiting he'd been having visions of Arthur lying in his bed, unaware of what was happening while he slipped into unconsciousness, never again to wake . . . but the reality was somewhat different.

For one thing, he was still incredibly drunk, and with that drunkenness had apparently come a level of strength that Old Arthur didn't normally possess; as the firemen led him out of the flat he shrugged them off before running around in circles, screaming, "Fire! Fire! Fire!"

Well, Julian thought to himself, he wasn't wrong.

Even though his head was still thumping and he felt like he'd been run over - repeatedly - by a truck, Julian managed to get to his feet and walk over to Arthur, who was still shouting out that same word over and over again, as if he were stuck in some kind of loop in a dream.

"Arthur," Julian said, trying to keep his voice low and soothing. "It's OK, Arthur. Everyone got out. We're going to be OK."

Arthur stared at Julian, his eyes glazed with drunkenness, and eventually he started nodding. "OK," he repeated back to him. "We're going to be OK."

The next day Julian woke up in a strange room, his head still thumping, wondering where the hell he was.

Then, rather slowly, it all started coming back to him: the car crash, the fire, the hospital . . .

He tried to think back through his hazy memory of the night before. It had taken a while for them all to be checked over, and while everyone had been given the all-clear, they were still more than a little shaken up by the whole experience.

So now they were all staying in a shabby hotel near the flat, and Julian was trying to ignore the pounding sound that had just started on the door to his room.

"Julian!" hissed Big Brian from outside. "Open up, will you?"

Dragging himself out of bed - and groaning the whole time - Julian ambled slowly over to the door. As soon as he'd undone the chain and the lock and had pulled it open, Brian barged in, motioning for him to close the door behind them.

"What's going on?" asked Julian, who - for just a split second - thought there might be another fire. Now that *would* be bad luck after the last couple of days he'd had - although didn't they always say bad things came in threes?

"We need to talk," said Brian, looking serious - something that didn't really come very naturally to him at all, the expression sitting strangely on his face.

"OK . . ." replied Julian as he walked over to the bed, perching on the end of it before looking over at Brian.

He sat down in the armchair next to the mirror. "It's about the car. We have to go to the police."

Julian shook his head as he tried to think through the pain of his headache. "Why on earth would we do that? I don't want to get into trouble."

"But we'll get in trouble anyway," Brian pointed out, "and especially you - you were the one driving, remember?"

Julian groaned. "Of course I remember. What of it?"

"Fingerprints, man," Brian explained. "Your fingerprints are all over that steering wheel and god knows where else. Not to mention all those people in the pub who saw us getting drunk, who probably saw the car in the car park, and who may have seen us drive off in it . . . there'll be witnesses, just you watch. If we don't tell the police something, we'll look even more suspicious."

Julian's head was pounding more heavily now. "So what are you saying? Go and admit I was driving drunk? That I was driving a car that was involved in a robbery not so long ago?" He stared at Brian. "Not gonna happen."

Brian sighed. "You don't need to mention the alcohol. Just say you were driving along normally and then you swerved . . . say you were avoiding a cat or something, and that you ended up hitting the lamppost. People do that all the time; it's totally believable."

Julian frowned. "But won't they ask why I didn't report it right away? Why I didn't try and get medical help until after the fire?" They still had no idea how the fire had started - whether it was an accident or some kind of foul play - and right now, Julian didn't have the mental capacity to even try and get to the bottom of that particular mystery.

"Concussion," Brian replied. "You had a concussion and couldn't remember what happened. Say you think someone gave you a lift home in their car but you don't remember who, and that generally you can't remember much else at all. Keep it vague. You'll be fine."

"It's not much of a cover story," Julian pointed out, after thinking it over for a while.

"Trust me; it'll work," was all Brian had to say. "They'll never link it to the robbery, or anything else for that matter."

"OK, fine," said Julian, who just wanted to get rid of Brian so he could get more sleep. "I'll go in a couple of hours; I just need to clear my head a bit first."

Reluctantly, Brian agreed, but not until he'd made Julian promise that as soon as he woke up he'd go straight to the police station.

Julian promised, and finally, Brian left him in peace.

After crawling back into bed, Julian waited for his head to stop swimming, and a few minutes later he was sleeping soundly, though he had horrible dreams that he only just remembered when he woke a few hours later - nightmares of being trapped in a police cell, of being interrogated, of having his fingerprints done and his mugshot taken.

When he finally woke up - sweating and shaking a little - for a split second he thought he was back home at his mum's pub. In a boring yet safe place. Then reality hit, and a sinking feeling wound through his entire body.

He had to go to the police. He had to tell them about the car. He had to lie.

So, even though it felt like an absolutely monumental effort, Julian dragged himself out of bed, had a shower, got dressed, and then left the hotel, stopping only briefly to ask a passer-by where the nearest police station was.

Once at the station, he told the man at the reception desk why he was there, and after a brief wait on an old, hard chair in the waiting area, Julian was taken through to a small, simple room that featured a table and two chairs. It was one of their regular interview rooms, but it immediately put Julian on edge - it reminded him of the interrogation room from his dream.

"So you're here about the Fiat car we found on the side of the road?" the officer asked as they both sat down.

"Yes," muttered Julian, whose headache was threatening to return with a vengeance. Suddenly, he was very, very nervous.

"Can you tell me exactly what happened?"

Julian shrugged, trying to appear casual while inside his heart was thumping madly against his ribcage. "A cat ran out into the middle of the road - *right* in front of the car - and I just panicked." He shrugged again. "The next thing I remember, I'm turning the steering wheel madly, just trying to avoid it, and then there was . . . just blackness. I must have got a ride home from someone because I don't remember anything else until I came around at my flat."

Just then another officer opened the door and came into the room. He was a Scotland Yard officer, tall and muscly and incredibly intimidating.

"So you don't remember what happened at the point of impact?" he asked. Clearly, he'd been listening to Julian's story from the next room.

Julian frowned, as though trying to sort through his memories, when in reality he was trying to remember the explanation he'd come up with on the walk to the station. "Since I woke up, I've had a few flashbacks - bits of memory coming back at random times - and I think I remember a lamppost. That's it." He shrugged again, raising his eyebrows and smiling slightly as if to apologise for his lack of memory.

The Scotland Yard officer looked down at some papers in his hands - papers Julian couldn't read from where he was sitting - and cleared his throat. "And how long have you been the owner of the Fiat?"

Julian's stomach churned. They *knew* - they knew it was dodgy!

He paused for a moment before replying, hoping they'd put the hesitation down to his foggy memory after the crash and not the fact that he was stalling for time while he tried to decide what to say. "Not long, actually," he finally replied, hoping he sounded confident rather than terrified, "I bought it from a man in Fulham a few days ago."

The officer stared at Julian, waiting for him to say more, and when he didn't he prompted, "You get a receipt for it? Any paperwork? Anything?"

Julian shook his head, giving the officer his little half smile again. "Afraid not. It was a quick deal - I just needed something to get around in. You know how it is."

The officer didn't agree with him or even nod. Instead he asked Julian, "And when you bought it, did you look at the car tax?"

Julian shook his head again, a little slower this time. "Afraid not. Why, is there a problem?"

The officer stared at him for a few more moments before replying, "The Fiat had the car tax from another car."

"Oh," said Julian, frowning. "I didn't notice. I'll get it sorted as soon as I can."

"And," the officer added, glancing down at the papers again, "the vehicle has been found in connection with an armed robbery. Do you happen to know anything about that?" The officer was the one smiling now, as if he was thinking, 'Got you!' He just looked so smug. So did the other one.

Julian gulped. He had a feeling it was going to be a long interview.

CHAPTER 23

Several hours later, Julian emerged from the interview room feeling far more exhausted than he had since he'd first come to London.

In all honesty, he'd been beginning to think he would never make it out of there.

Fortunately, Julian had Reggie on his side, and when he'd heard from Big Brian where Julian was and what he was doing, he'd sent a solicitor over to the police station, who'd proceeded to sit in on the interview.

Unable to detain Julian for questioning any longer, the police had to let him go, and when Julian got outside and saw Reggie waiting for him in his big flashy car, he couldn't help but smile.

Reggie always came through when you needed him.

And now he'd come through again, giving Julian the chance to be his driver on a more full-time basis, now that Jimmy was more involved in other stuff - although what kind of stuff, Julian didn't know and didn't really *want* to know.

Being his driver, Julian started to learn a whole lot more about the enigma that was Reggie, especially as he conducted a lot of his business calls using the Cadillac's car phone; Julian would only ever hear one side of these conversations, but that was usually enough to give him the gist of what was going on. Occasionally he would ask Reggie questions about his dealings, which he either would or wouldn't answer, depending on what kind of mood he was in.

So, slowly but surely, Julian was able to build up in his mind the sort of 'business' Reggie ran, going by the little snippets of information his boss occasionally gave him.

Soon, however, it became increasingly clear to Julian just how corrupt Reggie really was, especially when he found out about one of the contracts he had with a car manufacturing company - basically, Reggie was bribing officials from the union to supply membership documents to his workers. And it didn't just stop there; Julian also found out that one of the officials collected lead crystal, and that Reggie had given him thousands of pounds' worth of expensive crystal as part of some kind of 'deal'. It all sounded very illegal, which worried Julian, but it also sounded pretty damn thrilling too. Especially the crystal part.

One side of Reggie that Julian didn't know about, however, soon came to light during a terrible night that Julian would remember for years to come. He knew that Reggie could be intimidating and ruthless when it came to business, but what he didn't realise was just how *scary* the man could be when it came to his personal life. If he'd known that, Julian would have been more careful - much more careful.

To start with, Julian didn't realise he'd been doing anything wrong. He was used to seeing Reggie out and about with a multitude of women; they seemed to be attracted to his charisma, not to mention being fascinated by all the crazy stories he'd tell anyone who'd listen. He was the king of the one-night stand, and never once had Julian heard Reggie talk about a woman as though he truly cared for her. He liked having fun with women, and he clearly enjoyed their company, but it never seemed to go any deeper than that.

Which was why he was so surprised at Reggie's reaction when he caught Julian talking to Samantha, a woman he'd hooked up with just the once several weeks before. Samantha was a firecracker - tall, thin, and with long brown hair, she looked like a catwalk model - and while Julian usually preferred a figure that was a little curvier, he couldn't deny there was just something about her.

"Julian," he said in a gruff voice, "talk to me outside for a moment."

They were in one of their local pubs, and thinking it was something to do with a job, Julian followed Reggie outside without any concerns.

Once they were alone, however, Reggie's demeanour changed. His eyes wide, he got right up in Julian's face, glaring at him as he said, "I don't have many rules, mate, but hooking up with one of my birds is a big no-no, alright?"

Julian held his hands up as he backed against the wall. "Hey, Reg, I was just talking to her. We weren't doing anything, I swear."

Julian stared at him for a few more seconds - the tension between them growing bigger and bigger with every passing moment - and then he eventually stepped back, giving Julian room to breathe again. His eyes were still wide, though, and crazy; he looked like someone on drugs who was having a rather nasty trip.

"Keep it that way," he spat, before turning and walking off into the night. Apparently he'd had enough of the pub for one evening.

Julian watched him go, his fear soon turning to relief, and then anger - who was Reggie to tell him who he could or couldn't get with? What right did he have, when he slept around with so many people? It wasn't like Julian had been talking to his girlfriend or his wife, and that *was* all they'd been doing - talking!

Julian didn't get angry very often, but he was angry now, and purely to spite Reggie and his ridiculous behaviour, he marched back into the pub, took Samantha's hand in his, and led her over to the bathroom. He didn't care who saw them go - on some level, he wanted this to get back to Reggie.

They had a quick fumble in one of the cubicles, the sex rushed and awkward (both of them had already had far too much to drink), and once they were finished, Julian kissed Samantha on the cheek and went home.

He barely remembered doing it the next morning, so he was blissfully unaware that in Reggie's eyes, his days were now numbered.

Julian had already learnt from his 'colleagues' that Reggie was not a forgiving person, and even if he really liked the person who'd done him wrong, he felt it was his duty to punish that person in whatever way he saw fit. Sometimes that would be enough and they'd go back to being friends afterwards. Sometimes, friendship was simply no longer on the cards. Really, it depended on Reggie's current mood.

He'd heard this before and hadn't really taken it in, but by the end of that night, he would believe every word of it.

Yes, that evening Julian learned a very valuable lesson: never get on the wrong side of his boss. Ever.

It was nearly 10 in the evening and the night was cold, dark, and windy - not a night to be out and about, but one to be spent inside in a nice warm room with some nice warming alcohol and maybe a nice warm woman too. But sadly, that wasn't to be.

Reggie had told Julian he wanted to "go for a drive," and as Julian was his driver he didn't really feel he could refuse, especially after their little 'spat' outside the pub.

So, Julian picked him up, surprised to see Mick there with him too. Where on earth did the two of them want to go at this time of night? If they wanted to go drinking, they usually went to one of their locals within walking distance.

When Julian asked Reggie where he wanted to go and Reggie replied, "Just drive - I'll tell you where to turn," something didn't quite feel right. Why hadn't Reggie just given him the address of the place he wanted to visit, like he usually did?

He glanced at Mick in the rear view mirror, who just nodded at him in acknowledgement, without saying a word. Considering how chatty Mick usually was, this seemed a bit strange. In fact, it all seemed more than a bit weird - the atmosphere in the car had suddenly turned thick with tension.

All of a sudden, Julian wanted to be anywhere - anywhere else in the whole entire world - other than driving that Cadillac into the dark night.

After a few left turns and a few right turns, on and on until Julian wondered where the hell Reggie wanted to go, Julian found himself driving along a narrow dirt road, seemingly in the middle of nowhere. They were surrounded by trees - looking increasingly strange and spooky in the darkness - and Julian could have sworn it was getting colder and colder the further they got into the woods.

Eventually, Reggie told him to stop. "Keep the headlights on," he told him before getting out the car, and Julian watched as Mick got out too.

A second later Julian also got out of the car, and he was just slamming the door shut when he felt something being shoved against the back of his coat. It felt like a gun.

For a brief moment Julian honestly had no idea what the hell was going on, and then it dawned on him: Samantha. Reggie knew he'd hooked up with Samantha and now he was dishing out his 'punishment'. That was why Mick had looked so sombre, and that was why there'd been a weird atmosphere in the car during the whole ride. Now it all made sense.

But pulling a gun on him in the middle of a forest? What the hell was Reggie thinking? If he was trying to scare him, it was working. Should he try and run? Call Reggie's bluff?

No, he would just have to go along with whatever this was and trust that Reggie wasn't about to do something monumentally stupid - even if the gun suggested otherwise. What else could he do?

"Move," grunted Reggie from behind him, and with shaking legs, Julian started walking.

As he went, Julian shivered; it was incredibly cold out here, especially with the wind blowing through the trees, and he was only wearing a thin coat. Sighing, he looked around at his surroundings - nothing but tree trunks and darkness - wishing they were at least somewhere near civilisation. Of course, there was a reason why they weren't.

"So, I hear you got with Sam," Reggie said, breaking the eerie silence that had descended on their little part of the woods and making Julian jump. "Even after our little chat, you went and got with her. What's the deal?"

"No deal," said Julian, trying to keep his voice level. "No big deal at all. It's not like you two are exclusive, right?" He laughed, hoping to lighten the mood.

It didn't work.

"That, mate, isn't the point," Reggie replied, his words only just audible. "I asked you not to go near her, and you did."

"No, you *told* me not to go near her. There's a difference," Julian replied. He really didn't want to rile Reggie up any more than he already was, but deep down, he never thought Reggie would actually hurt him. Actually shoot him. That would be insane!

"No one tries to ruin my reputation!" Reggie shouted, raising his voice in an instant. "*No one*, you hear me?"

Julian nodded enthusiastically - now, he had to admit, he was getting a little worried. "Agreed. I'm sorry, Reg. If I could take it back, I would."

Reggie shook his head, slowly, though the gun in his hand remained totally still. "That, I'm afraid, just isn't good enough." He sighed, as though he really didn't want to be here, doing this, saying these words. "The damage has already been done."

Reggie pushed the gun deeper into Julian's back, and all of a sudden, a wave of fear rushed over him. What if he'd been really naïve? What if Reggie absolutely was capable of shooting someone for hooking up with an ex of his? "C-come on," Julian stammered. "We're friends, aren't we? How long have we known each other?"

Reggie appeared to think about this for a moment, before replying, "Long enough for you to realise what would happen if you pissed me off, I reckon."

Julian didn't reply, and the next few seconds - with none of them saying a single word - were some of the longest of Julian's life. Was he about to die? Was this it? After everything he'd gone through, was *this* how it was all going to end?

Just when Julian thought he couldn't take the silence any longer, Reggie turned him around to face him, then gestured at the ground with the gun. "Kneel."

Lowering his head, Julian kneeled down on the muddy ground. He was physically shaking, and he felt a tear trickle down his cheek.

"What are you doing?" asked Reggie, and Julian could have sworn he heard laughter in his tone, "If I kill you now, *I'm* going to be the one stuck doing all the work, aren't I? And if there's anything I've learned in business, it's when to delegate." Reggie turned to face Mick. "Open the boot and bring me the spade that's in there," he ordered, before turning back to Julian.

As Mick disappeared from and then reappeared into his line of sight, Julian wondered how he could possibly have got himself into this situation. How had he gone from cheeky schoolboy, to a college student having an affair with a teacher, to this? To kneeling on the ground in the middle of nowhere, with a guy pointing a gun at his head?

"Alright, what's taking you so long?" Reggie asked Mick, bringing Julian out of his morbid thoughts. "Pass it over."

When Mick held out the handle of the spade to him, it suddenly hit him: he was going to die tonight. Yes, he was going to die, but not before being made to dig his own grave. The thought made him throw up in his mouth a little bit.

Despite the cold, Julian was sweating, a line of perspiration forming on his upper lip and another one settling into the frown lines on his brow. He stared into Mick's eyes as he handed him the spade, as if pleading with him to say something, to *do* something. Anything.

But there was nothing Mick could do, and Julian knew it; once Reggie got something into his head, he couldn't be persuaded otherwise.

When Julian had the spade in his hand, Reggie gestured at the ground next to him for a second time. "Get digging," he said, his voice clear and strong - at no point did he betray any feelings, not of doubt or sadness or guilt or anything. Either he really didn't care about Julian, or he was doing an excellent job of pretending he didn't.

"Come on, Reg," Julian whispered, resting the bottom of the spade on the ground while he held onto the handle for dear life. "Please."

"I already told you," said Reggie, "I'm not going to do all the work here. And neither is Mick; he's done nothing wrong." He pointed again at the ground, grinning widely. It made Julian shudder. "So what I want you to do," he continued, "is get down on your knees and start digging."

"Please," Julian pleaded again, and Reggie shoved the gun right against his chest.

"Do it now," Reggie growled, "dig."

And so - with shaking hands and tears in his eyes - Julian did exactly that, almost collapsing onto his knees and shoving the spade into the soil. The earth was damp and came out in a muddy clod, which Julian flung off into the darkness beyond the nearest tree. It made a wet splat as it landed on the ground.

"Quicker," said Reggie, who was still pointing the gun at him.

Julian hurried, but even so, digging a grave was not quick work, and Reggie and Mick just stood there and watched in the beam of the Cadillac's headlights, staring at him as he got dirtier and dirtier, witnessing a man digging his own grave.

After a while, Julian had made a hole in the ground that, while certainly not six feet deep, was definitely deep enough and long enough to put a body into. It would probably be found as soon as a large rainfall occurred and washed away the topsoil, but he supposed it was fit for purpose.

Julian shuddered when he realised what he'd just thought.

He wondered if Reggie would tell him to make it deeper, but apparently Reggie thought it was fit for purpose too, as after bending over and inspecting the hole, he nodded at Julian - as though to tell him it was a job well done. Which was ridiculous. Julian could feel a hysterical bubble of laughter working its way to his lips, but he managed to keep it down.

"Now, I don't feel like dragging a body of dead weight around either," said Reggie after a brief pause, "my back's not what it was. Do me a favour and lie down in it, will you, Julian?"

By now Julian was shaking uncontrollably, but he made no show of resistance as he lay down on the damp ground. He did briefly think about just standing up and running - better to die trying to escape than just lying down and dying, surely? But honestly, that just sounded exhausting, and he wasn't sure he could physically bring himself to do it.

When Reggie moved over to the shallow grave and towered over the now trembling Julian, Mick looked away; apparently, he just couldn't watch.

By now Julian was audibly crying, sobbing in his grave, but after a moment or so, he realised the sound of his own crying wasn't the only noise he could hear - no, he could also hear . . . what was that? Laughing?

He looked up to see Reggie chuckling at him, as though they'd just been sharing the world's best joke.

"Jesus, Julian! You didn't think I was actually going to shoot you, did you?"

Julian's heart leaped in hope as he stared at Reggie. "What . . . what . . ." was all he could say.

Reggie laughed for a few seconds longer, and then started strolling back towards the car, tucking the gun into his trousers as he went.

After opening the passenger door, he turned back towards where Julian was lying on the ground, still trembling. "You *ever* do *anything* like that again, and I won't be quite so forgiving. You understand me, Julian?"

Silence greeted this question, and Reggie asked again, louder this time, "*Do you understand?*"

From his horizontal position, Julian nodded. "Yes, yes, I understand."

"Good." Reggie turned to face Mick, nodding towards the car. "We'll let Julian find his own way home."

Mick nodded in return, taking one last look at Julian before heading back to the Cadillac.

Julian was still crying, and now he'd wet himself too. The spade lay forgotten beside him.

He waited until the car had backed away, and then he hunched over on the ground, throwing up the entire contents of his stomach. Through blurry eyes, he watched the Cadillac's tail lights as his boss drove off into the gloom.

Soon, the darkness swallowed the car completely.

CHAPTER 24

After his terrifying night in the woods, Julian didn't think he'd ever feel the same way around Reggie again, but as time passed, things started getting - weirdly - back to normal.

Julian could have run, sure; he could have gone back home and tried to forget Reggie even existed, but Reggie knew where his mum's pub was, and he knew he'd be able to track him down.

No, his best bet was to keep working for him, and to keep a close eye on him. The whole keep your friends close and your enemies closer thing. Plus, Reggie had told Julian that the gun he'd used on him hadn't even been loaded. It didn't make things right, but it helped a little - if Reggie could be believed, anyway.

Even so, Julian never forgot, and he never even dared speak to one of Reggie's female acquaintances without permission ever again. He'd learnt his lesson there.

In the weeks following that night, Julian thought of it often - the trees and the car headlights and his hands gripping the handle of the spade - but soon other things pushed the memory out of his mind. Mainly, Reggie's business in Libya.

Ever since he'd come back from Libya his boss had been telling wild and crazy stories about his time there, which - as usual - Julian didn't know whether to believe or not. Especially when Reggie started saying that he'd met Gaddafi of all people. Julian hadn't questioned that particular story; he was still very much aware of wanting to stay on Reggie's good side.

Bribing the officials with the 'escorts' had apparently worked, as Reggie won the Libyan contract, and soon he was sending out a team of people to set up the site. The contract was for 180 days, with the work involving the fitting out of all the interiors of tank hangers and stores for the Libyan Army. When Julian heard Reggie had got the job, he was more than impressed with his boss.

And he was even more impressed - and proud of himself - when Reggie told him he wanted Julian out there too, to help him and to be his 'man on the ground'.

Reggie trusted Julian to get things done, and had been impressed himself that the story of him digging his own grave in the woods hadn't been leaked to any of their friends or business associates - Julian sure knew how to keep his mouth shut, and that was a quality Reggie very much admired in people. Especially people he did business with.

So, it was decided. Six other people were to join Julian during his flight from Heathrow to Libya, and as a bit of a leaving present, Reggie had booked them hotel rooms near the airport for the evening before their flight, giving them £250 each with direct instructions to spend the money on alcohol - Libya was a dry country, so if they wanted to get wasted, they needed to do it before boarding the plane, getting it out of their systems all at once.

After quite a bit of discussion in Julian's room at the hotel, they decided to head to Soho to catch a 'show', and several strip clubs and bars later, the seven of them found themselves in Stringfellows, most of their money now gone but each of them without a care in the world.

Julian had been to these types of clubs before, but there was something else about Stringfellows, with its grand balcony looking down over the dance floor, its sparkling chandeliers, and, of course - the women. Every waitress who worked there wore a black body suit, similar to a swimsuit with a low basque, showing off just enough cleavage to get a man excited. These were paired with fishnet tights and heels. It certainly made getting each drink a lot more interesting.

Yes, Julian was having a great time, thinking only about how much fun he could have that night and not about the awful hangover he was inevitably going to suffer through the next morning.

But for now he was downing shots and dancing to the music, the loud, thumping bass vibrating through his body as he eyed up the women in the club - both the ones who worked there and the ones visiting, of which there were surprisingly quite a few.

One woman in particular immediately caught his eye, and not just because she was drop dead gorgeous - although she was, with her long, chestnut-coloured hair and deep brown eyes, not to mention her slim body and legs that went on for miles - but because she was by far the classiest thing that establishment had probably ever seen.

She would have looked a little out of place on her own, with her long silver ball gown and her diamond necklace, but she wasn't alone; she was sitting with a group of suits who were clearly having some kind of business meeting. There were five of them, all deep in discussion while they each took turns looking at a folder full of documents.

It was a bit of a strange place to do business, Julian thought, but then again, why not? There were good drinks, good music, good entertainment . . . in fact, perhaps it was the *perfect* place to do business.

The woman looked to be at least half the age of most of the men there, and she also looked incredibly bored. So bored, in fact, that she was sitting slightly away from the group of businessmen, watching a couple of waitresses move around the floor. She didn't look like she was enjoying herself too much, though, so Julian ruled out the possibility that she batted for the other team.

He had to admit, however, that watching her watching two scantily clad women was turning him on, his brain immediately picturing all three of them back in his hotel room. Not that that would *ever* happen.

After a while, the woman turned to look at Julian, making him jump. He realised he'd been staring at her from his position near the bar, and he could feel himself going red.

She didn't seem to mind - she winked at him, an action that seemed completely at odds to how sophisticated she appeared, sitting there in that ball gown of hers.

Just then, another man in a suit moved over to their seating area, leaning down and whispering something in her ear. Julian's heart sank. So she had a boyfriend then - or, more likely, a husband. Of course she did. She was stunning.

But then, as he watched, the woman said something back to the man, clearly annoyed, before standing up and storming off. Trouble in paradise perhaps? Julian could make that work for him. Possibly.

Downing the rest of his drink, Julian strolled off in the same direction as the woman, hoping to run into her so he could work his charm before she went back to her partner, but when he actually found her - just around the corner from the women's toilets - he saw she was crying.

"Oh," he said awkwardly, not prepared for finding her like this, and not prepared for how he'd feel once he spoke to her; his heart was fluttering madly in his chest and for a moment, he felt thirteen again, all nervous and uneasy. "Sorry . . . I . . . er . . . are you OK?"

The woman wiped her eyes. "I'm fine, thank you. Just . . . annoyed."

"Oh?" Julian asked again, thinking he might still be able to turn this around. "Anything I can help with?"

She looked him up and down, clearly liking what she saw. "That's sweet of you. What's your name?"

"Julian," he said as he held out his hand. "And who may you be?"

"I'm Veronica," she replied, shaking his hand, and before Julian even realised he was going to do it, he lifted it to his lips, kissing her gently on the knuckles. At this, a thrill ran through his entire body.

"Nice to meet you."

"Likewise," Julian replied, in his semi-drunken mind picturing himself as some kind of suave James Bond-type. Well, he *was* wearing a suit; he was half way there already. "So, who's annoying you and what can I do about it?"

Veronica rolled her eyes as she took her hand back from Julian. "It's my chaperone." She noticed the shocked look on his face and added, "I'm here with my father and his business associates - which is just as fascinating as it sounds - and he always makes me have a chaperone whenever we go out." She glanced around, a mild look of distaste on her face. "Usually, it's to seedy places like this."

"Wow," said Julian, who wasn't quite sure how to react to this news. "So your father is . . . important . . . then?"

Veronica nodded. "He's an ambassador. He likes to take me with him when he entertains clients and associates - you know, just in case there's someone influential who's looking for a wife." She rolled her eyes.

"Oh, so you're not married?" Julian blurted the question out before he knew he was going to ask it, adding what he hoped was a smooth-looking smile at the last minute.

Veronica smiled too, a wide one that showed all of her perfectly white, perfectly straight teeth. If she wanted, she could be a movie star. "No, I'm currently single. How about you?"

Julian could feel his heart fluttering in his chest again - he could be onto something here. "Very much single," he replied, "and unfortunately flying out to Libya tomorrow. So tonight is my last night in London for quite a while." He grinned. "I was hoping to make it a night to remember."

Veronica's eyes flashed then, as though she'd found an opportunity to be naughty and very much wanted to take it. "I see," she said slowly, drawing out the words.

"It's a shame you have a chaperone," Julian added, wondering if they'd be able to sneak out of the club without him noticing - that's if Veronica wanted to. God, he hoped she wanted to.

"It *is* a shame," she whispered, and she was just about to open her mouth to say something else when her expression changed to one of annoyance.

"Miss Morrison," a voice came from behind Julian, "your father is asking for you."

Julian turned to see the guy from before - Veronica's 'chaperone', apparently - and his heart sank; he'd been hoping for some more one-on-one time with this woman. Everything about her just intrigued the hell out of him.

"Is this man bothering you?" he asked her, not even looking at Julian.

"No, I'm fine, Michael. I'll be there shortly," Veronica said, all emotion now gone from her voice. Her smile had disappeared too, and while she still looked beautiful, Julian wished it would come back.

Michael, however, wasn't budging, and the next thing Julian knew, he was pushing past him and grabbing her by the arm.

Veronica shouted out, but she allowed herself to be dragged past Julian, much to his surprise. Was she just going to end their conversation before it had even begun? How unfair was that?

As she passed him, however, she just managed to whisper in his ear, "The Dorchester. Room 103. Come after 2 a.m."

Julian nodded as the man pulled her away. "Come on, Miss Morrison. Your father is wondering where you are."

It didn't appear that her chaperone heard what she'd said, and for that Julian was thankful. He'd just been given an incredible invitation, and he didn't want anything to get in the way of it. Even now he could picture how that silver ball gown would look falling to the floor, revealing the voluptuous body beneath. He couldn't wait.

Once Veronica had gone out of sight he looked at his watch - almost midnight.

Now suddenly excited - and with no thought whatsoever for the flight he had to catch in the morning - Julian made his way back to the bar, where Veronica and the guys in suits were just leaving, having apparently wrapped up their business meeting.

As she left, Veronica glanced over at Julian, sending him a secret smile that made him go weak at the knees. He smiled back, though he was quick to turn away right after in case her chaperone or her father saw. He felt like he was back at school, sneaking around behind the teachers' backs. All he needed was a forbidden hayloft.

There was just something about this woman - an intense connection that he'd felt almost immediately, unlike anything he'd ever experienced before. He just hoped she'd felt it as well. He supposed he'd find out soon.

The next hour or so went by pretty quickly and before he knew it, Julian was pulling up outside The Dorchester, a far fancier hotel than the one he was staying in.

Soon he found himself outside room 103, and desperately hoping that she'd given him the right room number, he tapped lightly on the door.

A few seconds later the door swung inwards, revealing Veronica, still wearing that amazing ball gown. Upon seeing her again, a shiver ran up Julian's spine - but a good shiver, not a bad shiver. A thrilling shiver.

She smiled as she let him in, then made sure to lock the door behind him.

"I'm so glad you came," she said as she led him over to the desk in the corner and poured him a glass of clear liquid. "I thought maybe Michael had scared you off."

"Your chaperone?" Julian asked. "No chance. Where is he, by the way?" he added, pretending to look scared.

"They're on another floor, don't worry. Here," she handed him a glass as she took another one, "let's make a toast. To your last night in London."

Julian clinked his glass lightly against hers. "To my last night in London."

As he drank, he looked around the room, really taking everything in for the first time. This place was plush, with thick cream carpets and silky white covers on the bed, not to mention the huge bathroom he could see through the open door and the little kitchen area in the corner. This girl - or perhaps, her dad - sure had money. And lots of it.

Not that any of that mattered; he was mesmerised by the girl herself, not how rich she may be. And 'mesmerised' truly was the word - for the first time in a long time, Julian was feeling incredibly nervous about what was going to happen. There was just something special about this woman, and he didn't want to mess it up.

"So," she said, watching him taking in their surroundings, "are you here to check out the room or do you want to check me out instead?" Her voice was flirty and light-hearted, like she was already having a good time.

Julian immediately turned back to face her, watching in awe as she untied her halter neck and let her incredibly expensive-looking ball gown fall to the floor, pretty much exactly as he'd imagined it in his mind. He felt his heart skip a beat as he looked at her.

Wearing just her black underwear and her silver high heels, Veronica then stepped out of the dress, leaving it pooled on the floor as she moved closer to Julian.

After finishing his drink and placing it carefully on the desk - his hand shaking a little in anticipation - he wrapped his arms around her, taking pleasure in her soft, smooth skin. "You're cold," he observed as he trailed his hands around her back, slipping them under her bra and then under her knickers.

"Well," she replied, placing her hands on his chest and feeling his torso through his shirt, "you'd better warm me up then."

Julian was more than fine with that arrangement, and soon both of them were tumbling onto the bed, Veronica giggling while Julian wondered how on earth he'd got so lucky as to be falling into bed with such a beautiful woman.

The next morning Julian woke up feeling happy but without knowing why. At first he had no idea where he was, and then, looking around the fancy hotel room, things slowly started coming back to him.

He had a headache, but it wasn't bothering him as much as it usually did. After all, how could you focus on the bad when you'd had such a wonderful night?

Turning his head - slowly; he still didn't want it pounding any more than it already was - Julian saw Veronica lying next to him, her long brown hair spread out across her bare back. She was sleeping on her front, the sight of her slender figure sending a thrill through his entire body all over again, but it wasn't the usual thrill he got after sleeping with someone - there was more to it this time. It wasn't just physical . . . it was emotional. Spiritual, even.

He stared at her for another moment or two, and then he looked beyond the beautiful woman he was sleeping next to, over to the bedside table and the clock sitting on top of it.

Julian sat up with a start, causing Veronica to jump.

"What?" she asked, staring at him through bleary, sleep-filled eyes. Beautiful eyes. "What's wrong?"

"Is that time right?" Julian asked, really hoping that the clock was wrong.

She glanced at the clock, nodding. "Yeah, why?"

"My flight!" Julian exclaimed as he jumped out of bed, madly searching around the room for his clothes. "I'm going to miss my flight!"

"Oh," said Veronica, who clearly just wanted to go back to bed. "Grab a taxi, you'll be fine." She was still very much in sleep mode, and even through his panic, Julian just had time to note how sexy she sounded when she was half asleep.

Within two minutes Julian had got dressed, and with one last glance at the clock, he made his way to Veronica's side of the bed, kneeling down and kissing her on the lips. "Last night was great, really incredible." He sighed. "I'm sorry I've got to rush off."

"That's OK," she replied sleepily, but just as Julian stood up, ready to leave, she pulled on his sleeve to stop him, shouting out, "Wait!" Suddenly seeming much more alert, she retrieved the hotel's pen and little pad of paper from the bedside table drawer, scrawled something down, and gave it to Julian. "My address. Keep in touch."

Julian put the piece of paper into his pocket without looking at it, leaned down to kiss her again, and then he was gone, running out of the hotel room and desperately hoping he wouldn't run into Veronica's father or chaperone on the way out.

He hated having to leave her so soon but he simply couldn't miss this flight. If he did, Reg would kill him (although hopefully - he thought to himself, only half joking - not literally).

His luck was in, however, and after emerging onto the cold, wet London street, he hailed a taxi, quickly giving the driver the address of the hotel he was staying in.

On the journey there, he took the paper out of his pocket, squinting at the badly-written words; Veronica either had terrible handwriting or she'd still been half asleep. To make matters worse, the ink had smudged on the paper - probably from him shoving it into his pocket too quickly - and some of it was a blur. He could just about make out some of the words, but really, it could have said anything.

For a moment he thought about asking the driver to turn around and head back to the Dorchester so he could get her address again, but deep down, he knew he wouldn't have time. So, that was it. He crumpled up the bit of paper, wondering if he'd somehow be able to track her down after he returned from Libya.

Sighing, he looked out the window, taking in the sights of London as he passed. He couldn't quite believe he was about to get on a plane to Libya - that was, if he even made it in time - and that this was the last he'd be seeing of England's capital city for quite some time. Even though he was excited, the thought did make him a little sad.

Soon the driver was pulling up outside the hotel, having made good time, and Julian ran in. He grabbed his stuff in record time, made a quick pit stop in the bathroom, handed his key in to the person on the reception desk, and was back in the taxi before he knew it.

When he finally got to the airport, the board told him that his flight hadn't started boarding yet, and he breathed a huge sigh of relief, though he looked so jittery and nervous going through security that he got taken aside so the security officer could pat him down.

Julian kept glancing at the clock, at the seconds ticking away as he stood there getting searched.

Eventually he was allowed through, and he more or less flew through the airport to find his gate. Of course, the gate he needed was the very last one on the concourse, and by the time he got there he looked like a crazy person - red face, sweating, hair sticking out at odd angles, and completely out of breath.

His fellow business associates were already there, calmly waiting to board, and as Julian collapsed into a seat next to them, groaning, they all burst out laughing.

"Have a good night then, Julian?" one of them asked, grinning.

Julian just about had the energy left in him to nod. "The best."

Moments later it was announced that the plane was boarding, and Julian dragged himself to his feet, feeling more hung over than he had in a while - and that was saying something.

When he finally found his seat, right at the back of the plane, he sat down next to a man and a boy, who he soon found out were from Libya and were father and son. He chatted politely to them for a while in (broken, on their part) English, then settled back in his seat and closed his eyes, hoping he'd be able to get at least some sleep on the way there.

Much to his surprise he fell asleep straight away, waking a couple of hours later feeling a lot more refreshed than when he'd got on the plane. As his mind came back to the present and he realised what people were talking about, he even discovered he'd slept for most of the flight, and that they were now hovering over Libya.

Leaning slightly over the father and son next to him, he peered out of the tiny plane window. He could just about see the ground below them, the bright sunlight reflecting off something on the runway and almost succeeding in blinding him as he gazed out.

After a moment or two he realised that the people next to him looked worried, and after glancing around the rest of the plane, he noticed everyone else wearing similar expressions of concern and fright. The cabin staff were all seated at the other end of the plane, and while there were constant messages coming over the speaker system, they were all in Arabic. Julian couldn't even begin to guess what the pilot was saying in his native language, and as usual on planes, the tone of voice being used was calm and collected, as though nothing bad was happening. No clues there.

"What's wrong?" he asked the passengers next to him, hoping they'd understand.

The father looked at him, frowning. "Cattle on runway," he said, "circling around airport."

Just then a large clunking noise came from beneath the plane's undercarriage, quickly followed by several more, slightly quieter - but just as alarming - sounds further up the cabin.

"What was that?" Julian asked, looking back at the man and his son.

The father just shrugged. "Cattle," he repeated.

Julian considered leaning over and peering out the window again - trying to see the supposed cattle on the runway - but part of him didn't want to; part of him didn't believe the cattle story at all. Not one bit.

The other passengers were starting to look a little panicked now too, but Julian tried to calm himself, taking deep breaths and attempting to look on the positive side: they were clearly at the airport in Libya, so it wasn't like they were flying over the middle of an ocean or anything, and there *could* be cattle on the runway somewhere, he supposed . . . though that didn't explain those ominous clunking sounds, did it?

They kept circling around the runway for what seemed like far too long, but eventually the plane landed, giving the passengers hardly any warning before it started to descend, then thumping rather clumsily onto the ground and causing everyone to grab their seats - or the hand of the person next to them - in fear.

As the wheels touched the ground and the bumpy ride finally became smoother, everyone on the plane cheered, a round of applause echoing throughout the cabin.

Julian glanced at the father beside him - who looked more than a little relieved - and beyond to the window, where he could now see some flashing blue lights as several vehicles approached.

After finally getting off the plane, Julian followed the crowd to a small building next to the airport, where their luggage soon arrived on a tractor and trailer.

As he waited to find his bag, Julian turned to a staff member and - hoping they spoke English - asked about the cattle on the runway.

The man stared back at him for a moment before replying, "What cattle? There are no cattle."

"Then what was the problem with the plane?" Julian asked, unsure whether he actually wanted to know the answer or not.

"Landing gear would not come down," he said simply, "nearly had a crash landing."

Julian nodded, trying to appear casual as he spotted his group from London in the crowd. After grabbing his bag, he made his way over to them.

"Rough ride, huh?"

"Just a bit," replied Julian, thinking he'd better not repeat the staff member's words to the rest of the group. "Can we get out of here now?"

CHAPTER 25

Soon, Julian and the rest of the group were settled at the hotel in the centre of Benghazi, which was housing everyone on Reggie's crew. It was a pretty huge place, and nice to look at too - with its exterior archways and pillars, not to mention all the palm trees. It was also just a short ride into the desert; every day (or night, if they were on a night shift) the workers would take a mini bus to the site, each of them taking it in turns to drive.

Their actual place of work was also a little different compared to anything Julian had ever seen before. It was an army base, for one thing, and for another it was still under construction; the outer walls were still being built, and when Julian and the group first got there, the entrance was more than a little ramshackle. Basically, there were two oil barrels with a pole across the top - acting as a rather primitive barrier - and even though there was nothing but desert on either side, there would still be an armed army guard waiting at the 'barrier', making sure no undesirables got through into the army base.

While they were working there the tank hangers got built, and it was Julian's and the rest of the group's jobs to install the mezzanine floors and racking. As they worked, routine checks had to be made inside and underneath everything. At first Julian didn't know what they were looking for, and when he asked, the only reply he got was, "Scorpions."

Compared to London, this was a whole different world.

As time went on, Julian began to befriend one of the guards - one of the few who spoke good English, incidentally - eventually finding out that the tanks moved from Tripoli to Benghazi all the time. These tanks (Russian-made) were pretty useless - in Julian's humble opinion -

with no air conditioning and machine guns that didn't work. But still, it was pretty cool to be anywhere with tanks, he supposed.

The hotel they were staying at had mostly male guests, and while there were some foreign female cabin crew staying there, they were all kept hidden away on a separate floor - a separate, *guarded* floor.

It took Julian a while to get his head around all the differences between Libya and London, but he didn't let little things like that stop him for long; he'd soon found out that the only time he could meet these women was when they were in the coffee lounge near the reception, so Julian started spending most of his free time there.

He would often think of Veronica whenever he was hanging out with the women at the hotel, wishing she was there with them, and that he could take her back to his room - just to spend time with her, even if nothing else happened. He just wanted to see her face, feel her hand in his. Not for the first time, he kicked himself for failing to get more contact details for her.

But life went on, and before Julian knew it, it was Christmas day - the one day where all the crew had been given the whole day off work - something everyone had very much been looking forward to for a long time.

A meal had been organised at a local restaurant for all of the workers, which again was a completely different experience to any staff meal Julian had attended back in England. This was mainly due to the lack of booze, although looking at the bar, Julian thought he could see the spots where the optics had been prior to the abolition of alcohol.

So, instead, the group drank mixed soft drinks - with Julian pretending there was a shot of vodka in his - and after the meal, they went to the pictures to see *Robinson Crusoe*.

The small theatre was filled with cheers and whoops as Crusoe and his man Friday rolled around on the floor in a fight, and upon seeing the men holding hands, Julian exchanged a look of bewilderment with the guys sitting next to him.

That was . . . new.

All in all, it was a rather different Christmas, though Julian and the others made sure they had fun; just because they weren't at home, it didn't mean they couldn't enjoy themselves.

That night in his room, Julian thought of his mum, all alone at the pub - apart from some of the regulars who would no doubt go there even on Christmas day, not wanting to be alone either - and sighed. He hoped she was OK, hoped she was managing to have at least some kind of fun festive time.

He also thought of Veronica, as he often did, hoping she was having a nice Christmas too, wherever she was and whatever she was doing.

After Christmas, life went on as normal (or as normal as it ever was in Benghazi for Reggie's workers) and Julian's coffee lounge visits started to pay off. He'd been hanging out with some local Libyans, and after a few days they started to mention a place they often visited - a building that was known rather mysteriously as 'Hotel Christmas'.

"What's Hotel Christmas?" asked Julian, immediately intrigued - after all, he was always looking for ways of 'spicing things up'.

"How about we go up to your room and tell you?" one of the guys replied, gesturing to something in a bag he was holding.

At this, Julian's interest was piqued even more. "What's that?"

"Just a little 'flash'," he whispered back. "You got anything in your room? Any juice or anything?"

Julian grinned. "I've got some orange juice."

"Great," said one of the others, "let's go."

Julian led three of the local Libyans up to his room, and soon he was drinking orange juice with 'flash' in - the first alcohol he'd had in what felt like years. Despite the rather harsh taste, and the pulpy texture of the juice, the fact it was alcoholic made it taste delightful as it slid down his throat, and he immediately wanted more.

"So what's Hotel Christmas?" he asked again, reaching out for the bottle of flash.

"Hotel Christmas," one of them replied, "is the place to be."

As they drank, they told him all about it - how it was a place where they could go and dance and have fun - and Julian thought it sounded great, especially with the lack of fun around the hotel.

So, wanting more of the flash, Julian asked the locals if they'd take him there, to which they agreed.

Julian wanted his co-workers from England to go with him, but after locating them in the coffee lounge and explaining his plans, he realised that none of them had even the slightest inclination to go to a random building with some random locals.

This didn't stop Julian, and soon he and the locals were on their way to a village several miles away, all of them piled into an old car that sounded like its engine was about to give up at any moment. They passed around the bottle of flash - which was rapidly diminishing - as they drove through the village, Julian looking out of the open window at the houses dotted here and there; short, white, rectangular buildings that appeared to be plain and functional, at least compared to the relatively fancy-looking hotel they'd just come from.

Their first stop was at the flash brewer's house, and once they were sitting in his living room, he joined them with another decanter of homemade alcohol.

He proposed a toast - which Julian didn't understand a word of - and they all raised their glasses, throwing the strong liquid enthusiastically down their necks. Julian was a little more enthusiastic than most, however - most of it went down his shirt, much to his annoyance and everyone else's amusement.

Soon they were leaving the house, their next stop being the mysterious-sounding Hotel Christmas, though the building itself didn't look too mysterious - it seemed like any other normal Benghazi building to Julian, though he could just about hear some faint music coming from inside.

As they approached the doorway - with Julian in the lead - a guard appeared out of the shadows, standing in front of him and looking him up and down.

"You drink?" he asked Julian, his voice low and quiet, which somehow was far more intimidating than if he'd been shouting.

"No," replied Julian, somehow managing to slur even that one tiny word. It was always the way, wasn't it? Just at that moment when you need to appear completely sober - even if you're only very slightly tipsy - you come across looking as though you've had at least ten pints.

Julian stood up straight and tried again. "No, sir."

The guard was staring at him, his expression blank. He was beginning to make Julian incredibly uncomfortable. "Papers," he said after a long pause.

"Papers?" repeated Julian, looking at the others around him, all of whom were staring at the ground - so much for their help. "My papers are back in the hotel," he carried on. "I work for your army."

The guard continued to stare at him, and Julian had half convinced himself that he was going to be let into the hotel without any further problems whatsoever when the guard reached out and grabbed him by the throat. Then, pushing him against the wall, he shouted out loudly for assistance.

Other guards appeared at once, each one grabbing one of the locals, and before Julian realised what was happening, every single one of them was being bungled into a Land Cruiser.

"Wait!" shouted Julian, his heart thumping wildly, "We just came to have some fun, we're not here to . . ." He trailed off when the cold, hard shape of a gun was pushed against his temple, and he immediately thought of Reggie, making him dig his own grave in the woods. He shuddered.

The vehicle started, and after a relatively short journey it came to an abrupt halt. Julian and the others were pushed out and then led across the gravel ground towards a squat grey building.

One by one they were shoved through a metal door and into a room where another guard was sitting behind a desk, staring at them as they entered. Speaking in Arabic, he told everyone to empty their pockets; Julian soon got the gist of the command when he saw the local Libyans giving up their money, keys, and other things, and reluctantly, he did the same.

It slowly dawned on Julian what was happening, and his heart sank as he was led inside a cell - one that already had two occupants. The locals were taken into the next cell along, and then - with a loud slam that made Julian jump - the metal doors were closed behind them, sealing them inside.

In the next cell, Julian could still see and talk to the locals he'd come in with, and when he sat down on the cold concrete floor, they warned him not to admit to any drinking.

"If we stick with the same story," one of them whispered, "we'll be OK."

Julian wasn't so sure, but as the guards were now too far away to hear them, they started coming up with a plan. Julian was to say that he'd drunk some bottles of Underberg as medicine for his bad stomach, which had made him appear drunk - the slurred speech and so on.

Under no circumstances was he to admit to drinking alcohol, or say where he got it from; as the locals told him, Julian could be charged for corrupting Libyans to drink, the punishment for which was to receive several lashes - something Julian definitely didn't want to be on the end of.

After leaving them to 'stew' in the cells for a while, the guards came back and all of the new arrivals were led out, one by one, to see a doctor. As planned, they all denied drinking alcohol and were all returned to their cells. Julian told his story about the Underberg, and the doctor smelled his breath, but luckily he couldn't distinguish between the medicine and any alcohol. Or at least, that's what Julian hoped. On the surface, it seemed that their plan had worked.

Of course, they weren't going to let them off that easily, and Julian soon learned they were to spend the night in the cells, a loaf of bread and some tins of tuna the only food that was supplied to them. Still, it was something to soak up the flash, he supposed.

That evening, Julian was sitting in his cell, contemplating how he'd ended up here, when a cigar appeared in front of his face. It was one of his cellmates.

"Oh, no thanks," Julian replied, unsure where this cigar had even come from as they'd been asked to give in all their personal possessions.

The man just kept holding it out, staring at him intently until Julian felt he had to take it.

"Thank you," he said, glancing at the others in the next cell. "I don't have any money, though . . ."

The man shook his head. "No, no. Nor did I. That's why I stole it."

It was the first thing he'd said in English, having been talking with their other cellmate in Arabic the whole time, and the words surprised Julian. "Right . . ." He looked over at the locals he'd come in with, shrugging.

"I heard him talking with his friend," one of them said. "He sold ammunition in exchange for those cigars. He got caught."

Julian nodded slowly. "Does that mean he . . ." He trailed off, and suddenly remembering that the cigar man had spoken to him in English, he turned back to him as he continued, "Are you going to receive lashes, then?"

"No," said the man, which made Julian feel a little better until he added, "in the morning they are to cut off my hand in public."

"Oh," was all Julian could say, though he made a mental note to try and stick on the straight and narrow from now on - he liked his hands and he planned on keeping them both.

Rather sheepishly, he handed the cigar back.

Julian and the others remained in their cells not only just overnight, but for the next day *and* the next night. Then, finally - when Julian had more or less given into the fact that he had no idea when he'd see the light of day again - he was taken to an official building in Benghazi where the prosecutor's office was; a tall, rather ramshackle-looking place with peeling paint and flaking plaster.

Despite the little story they'd come up with in the cell, Julian was told that he was going to be charged with Corrupting Libyans to Drink, and that a date for the court case would be issued in due time. He was then told to go back to his hotel to retrieve his passport, and also to ask the hotel to find an interpreter for him - this whole thing would be a hell of a lot harder otherwise.

Julian felt incredibly nervous as he stood there in that office, the prosecutor staring at him as if he'd committed a horrific crime, and that feeling didn't abate as he was taken back to his hotel; he felt like he could throw up at any minute.

When he arrived, he was annoyed to find the others from London sitting in the coffee lounge. They all looked up as he walked in, their conversation halting immediately, and it took just two seconds for them to start bombarding him with questions.

"Where the hell have you been?"

"Was it a girl, Julian?"

"You shacked up with her, mate?"

Julian walked over, sitting down on a comfy chair - the first actual seat he'd had in days - and then, making sure no one else could hear him, he gave them the whole story of what had happened, finishing his tale by telling them that he needed to make plans for his escape. He needed to get away from Benghazi, and out of Libya altogether.

He'd definitely had enough of this country, and he was worried what might happen if he stayed; a court case was not anything he wanted to get into right now, and he had no desire whatsoever to spend any more time in a Benghazi jail cell.

After a rather brief discussion, the others helped him come up with a plan, and after retrieving his passport from his room, he went back to the prosecutor's office. Julian was beyond nervous now, but he knew he had to do this. In his mind, he didn't have much choice.

The prosecutor placed his hand out, palm up. "Passport," he said, his voice harsh and abrupt.

Julian placed the passport in the prosecutor's palm, though he made sure he still had a firm grip on the document as he replied, "Receipt."

A crooked grin appeared on the prosecutor's face then, who immediately came back with, "Jail." He raised his eyebrows at Julian, taunting him.

So, Julian took back his passport, shrugging, and the next thing he knew, he was being taken back to jail, his heart sinking the whole way.

As he sat in his little cell - which was starting to feel more like home to him that the hotel room he hadn't stayed in for days - he sighed to himself. Well, that hadn't really gone according to plan.

Still, he wasn't about to give up, and the next time he was taken to the prosecutor's office, he did exactly the same thing.

"Passport."

"Receipt."

"Jail."

And so he went back to his cell. This was repeated another two times - with Julian's confidence in his plan waning a little more each time he went - but finally, he was given the receipt he'd been asking for; the prosecutor grudgingly writing it out for him on an official pad of paper.

Julian thought this was too good to be true, so when instead of taking him back to his cell, they took him to the hotel, he couldn't quite believe his luck. He was told that his passport would be sent to him the next day, and while he wasn't sure if that was the truth either, there wasn't much he could do about it.

So, he waited, and he waited, and he thought of Veronica and his mum and his flat and home. And he waited some more.

Much to Julian's relief his passport was indeed sent to the hotel the next day, and fortunately for him, the clerk on duty when it came in was a man he'd been speaking to on and off, and who he'd managed to befriend. Not only did he speak very good English, but he also used to be in the police, so he was a wealth of information just waiting to be cracked open.

When Julian went to the front desk to retrieve his passport, he glanced up at the clerk. "Do you mind . . . er . . . please could you check my passport for me?"

The clerk smiled; he liked Julian, and despite his past job, he had a soft spot for genuinely nice people who always seemed to find themselves in difficult situations. And Julian definitely came into that category. "Check it for what, sir?" he asked politely.

"Er," replied Julian, not really sure how to put this, "I need to know that there aren't any . . . you know . . . marks . . . on it . . . things that could be picked up when going through . . ."

"Security?" the clerk finished for him. "Of course. No problem."

Julian sighed in relief as he watched the clerk look through each and every page of his passport, that relief getting bigger and bigger as the clerk smiled back at him.

"There are no pin marks here. Nothing to be identified by security."

Julian smiled; things finally seemed to be going his way for once. "Thank you."

Now Julian's plan could really get under way, and as soon as was possible - without anyone looking upon him with suspicion - and with the help of the other boys in his group, he got together as many Libyan dinar notes as possible; he'd need as much money as he could get if he was going to pull this off.

The group also helped him purchase his ticket and organise the times of his transport, and soon - with all his dinar notes stuffed into his shoes for safekeeping - Julian was on his way to the local airport.

The airport terminal was hot and smelly, and as he made his way to the departure desk, he felt sick with anxiety. He just needed to get through these next few minutes, he told himself.

At check-in, he handed over his passport, holding his breath as the official studied it closely. The process seemed to take forever, but eventually the man at the desk nodded and handed it back. Julian tried to hide the relief from his face.

That relief was pretty short-lived, however, as the next moment the man told him, "As you are not Libyan, you will be last to board the plane. If there is no seat left, you will have to wait for the next plane. OK?"

Julian nodded, unable to say anything.

"Also," the official carried on, "if you are on the plane and a Libyan person wants your seat, you will have to give it up for them. No exceptions. OK?"

Julian nodded again, though inside he was screaming. All he wanted to do was to get out of this country - was that too much to ask? And it wasn't like he could just get a plane straight out either; first he had to get to Tripoli, and from there he'd be able to get another plane across the Mediterranean to Malta. Right now, Malta seemed like light years away.

Why did everything have to be so damn complicated?

After an agonising journey through security, and an equally agonising wait at departures - with Julian expecting at any moment for someone to come and tell him the plane was full and that he'd have to wait for the next one, or maybe the one after that - he was finally allowed on the plane, although he didn't let himself celebrate just yet.

Until the plane actually took off, his seat wasn't guaranteed, and as he watched the plane fill up, he got more and more agitated. The way things were going, he was expecting to be ejected from the plane just before take off - just when he thought he was safe - but to his huge relief, that didn't happen, and soon they were in the air, Julian clutching his passport in his pocket.

He'd never felt so stressed in his entire life, and he just wished he wasn't alone. Once more his thoughts turned to Veronica, wondering if he'd ever get to see her again.

Finally he landed in Tripoli, and while the security man searched through his pockets and hand luggage, they didn't bother with the shoes, and Julian managed to get on his next plane with his bank notes still undetected.

There was another agonising wait, another take-off, and another brief period of relief before - finally - the plane started descending.

Julian rubbed at his eyes, the stress and anxiety having completely exhausted him, and as the plane hovered above the tarmac in Malta, he took a deep breath.

He felt like he'd been stuck on this plane for days, and he couldn't wait to breathe in some actual fresh air - it was all he'd been thinking about for the past half an hour or so. Well, apart from Veronica.

A moment later his wish came true, and as the wheels touched down on the ground, Julian let out a half-nervous, half-triumphant laugh. He wasn't the only one, either; several of the passengers around him seemed to have been thinking the same thing, and were clearly just as relieved as he was.

CHAPTER 26

As soon as the plane came to a stop, Julian jumped out of his seat; he still felt an overwhelming urge to be off that plane.

He was a little nervous approaching the desk, but the only thing the tired-looking customs officer said to him as he passed was, "Welcome to Malta, Sir."

Nodding at him briefly, Julian continued walking towards the main area of the airport, looking around the large space for only a brief second before proceeding outside to the taxi rank. He wanted to get out of the airport as much as he'd wanted to get off the plane.

He was hit by a gust of warm air as soon as he emerged outside, the sun beating down on him as he ran over to the nearest taxi. Opening the door, he glanced at the driver as he scooted along the back seat. "I need to find a hotel, please," he said, pronouncing the words as carefully as he could in the hope of being understood. "I don't mind where. Somewhere small."

The driver nodded. "I have a cousin who owns a hotel nearby - very small. But good food. I could take you there and you could have a look?"

Julian agreed, leaning back into the seat as the driver sped away from the airport.

They carried on driving for some time, and Julian was just wondering where they were going when they pulled up outside the hotel. It was located in a narrow back street, nestled in between several terraced town houses. It wasn't exactly somewhere he would have expected a hotel to be, small or not.

"They'll have a room for you, Sir," the taxi driver said.

Julian nodded. "I need to exchange some money too - can I do that here?"

"Of course," he replied. "Anything you need."

Julian thanked him, paid the fare, and then headed into the hotel.

He entered into a small hallway, where there was the tiniest of reception areas: it was pretty much just a window into a little reception cubby, with a single chair propped up against the wall. The taxi driver wasn't kidding when he said this place was small.

As he looked into the cubby, Julian was greeted by a smartly-dressed older man. He had thick black hair and an impressive thick black moustache. Julian liked him immediately.

"Hello!" said the man at the small desk, smiling widely. "I'm Filippu, the owner. Welcome! Do you need a room?"

Julian introduced himself and asked about exchanging the money. Filippu did it right there and then, before letting himself out of the small cubby and leading him down a corridor. The paint job on the walls was peeling a bit here and there, and the whole place had a cheap and cheerful vibe to it.

"Are you here on business? If you don't mind me asking," the hotel owner said as they walked.

"No, not business," Julian replied vaguely. "Just travelling light. I hate getting bogged down with luggage, don't you?"

Filippu nodded knowingly as he opened the door into Julian's room. It was dark, and the hotel owner quickly went over to the curtains, drawing back the netting to reveal two large doors that opened onto a small balcony.

Julian looked around, nodding to himself at what he saw. The room was a little barren but obviously clean, with a stone floor and a few choice pieces of furniture: a double bed, a wardrobe, side tables, and a dressing table that was placed against the rear wall. Upon walking over to the balcony, Julian realised that it overlooked the cobbled street below, and through an alleyway between the houses opposite, he could see the ocean.

"This is great, thanks," he said to the hotel owner.

Filippu nodded. "The bathroom is just next door, in this outside passageway. Now, I'll just need your passport to register you and the money for however many nights you want to stay for. We can always extend your stay if you wish, just let me know."

He told Julian the rate for the room per night, and after thinking for a moment, Julian handed over enough cash for a week's stay, as well as his passport.

Filippu nodded, clearly pleased with the amount of notes he'd just been given, and then started retreating back along the corridor. "I'll get your passport back to you once I've made a note of your details," he said, and with that, he was gone.

Julian placed his holdall on the bed while he glanced again at his new surroundings. Luckily, there was one very important feature that he'd been hoping would be included in the room rate: a telephone.

Sitting down on the edge of the bed, Julian ran his fingers through his hair and picked up the receiver. First stop: his mum. He knew that Reggie and Johnny (on one of their many trips to the pub) had let slip about his stint in jail, and he also knew that his mum was, understandably, in a bit of a state about the whole thing. He knew he had to put that right, to stop her from worrying any more.

It took a while for the connection to go through, and just when Julian was about to put the phone down, thinking no one was going to pick up, his mum's voice came on the line.

"Hello?"

"Hi, Mum. It's Julian."

The relief in her voice was palpable as she exclaimed, "Julian! You're alright! You *are* alright, aren't you?"

"Yes, I'm fine," he said, wanting to calm her down as soon as possible. "I'm in Malta, and I'm going to have a little holiday here for a while. A bit of a break for a bit, that's all."

"Malta? On holiday? But Reggie said . . ."

"Don't listen to anything Reggie says," Julian joked. After a phone call from one of the London group still in Benghazi, his boss knew everything Julian had been up to. "Look, I'm safe, I'm well, I've just checked in to a nice hotel, and I'm going to relax on the beach for a few days. OK?"

"OK," she said eventually, although she still didn't sound very convinced by the whole thing.

"Bye Mum, we'll speak soon."

"Bye son. Be careful."

Julian placed the receiver back down, thought for a moment, then picked it up again. He dialled a different number, waited again, and then heard the 'click' as it went through.

"Reggie?"

"Julian, my man," came the reply. The words were a little slurred, and Julian assumed he'd been drinking. Possibly in his mum's pub. "How are things?"

"Things are fine," said Julian, "but I need to sort out my money. I'm still due my back pay."

"Yeah, of course," came the reply, "but first I want to hear everything! All the details."

Julian groaned. "I don't really have the time now, can you just arrange the payment for me, Reg?"

There was a pause at the other end of the line, and Julian was wondering if he was having another drink. Eventually he replied, "Sure, leave it with me."

Julian hung up and then stared out of the balcony doors, thinking of Veronica. After a while, he started pondering what to do next. He wanted to explore the area, but he was pretty thirsty too.

On the way out of the hotel he picked up his passport from Filippu, who was still in the little cubby, before heading outside. He ambled around for a bit before deciding on a little café/bar on the promenade - they had a few tables and chairs outside and he could see people drinking coffee and wine.

He ordered himself a tea and a beer before grabbing a seat outside, where he could look out at the view. The late afternoon sun was shining across the harbour water, creating dazzling patterns so bright they almost hurt to look at. It was really warm, and after removing his shirt, Julian relaxed back in his chair, doing some people watching as he drank first his tea and then his pint.

There was an English couple sitting at the table next to him, and as the guy raised his own glass at Julian, he said, "You've got a right good tan there, mate." The man himself was pasty white, and Julian smiled in response.

He supposed he had acclimatised pretty well, considering his own usually pale English skin. The past forty days had been mostly dry desert and blue sky, and as well as sporting the darkest tan he'd ever had, he was in pretty good shape too, all toned and lean. His stomach and torso in particular had changed dramatically - after all his exercising in Libya (and in jail, which he'd done to stop himself dying of boredom), he was completely ripped. He actually had visible abs for the first time in his life! Right then, he felt pretty damn good about himself, and he found he couldn't stop smiling.

The rest of the afternoon was pure bliss; he spent it drinking, relaxing, and making flirtatious eye contact with every attractive woman who passed - and there were a lot of them. They eyed his muscular body as they went, boosting Julian's ego even more.

Eventually he pulled himself away from the quaint little café and its amazing view and headed back to the hotel.

By now he was starving, he couldn't wait to go down to the hotel restaurant and have a big meal.

Like the hotel itself, the restaurant was pretty quaint, with an indoor area and then a small but pretty central courtyard full of little white tables and chairs. A sign told Julian that dinner was served between 6.30 p.m. and 10 p.m. and as it was almost 9.30, most of the guests had already dined and were onto their coffees or after dinner liqueurs.

As Julian hovered at the entrance to the courtyard, Filippu the hotel owner walked over, reaching out and shaking his hand. "Good evening, Mr Foster," he said, "would you like to sit inside or outside, Sir?"

"Outside," said Julian immediately, "and please, call me Julian." He smiled at the hotel owner, who nodded in return.

"This way, please." He gestured for Julian to follow him, before walking over to a table in the corner. It was set for two, and as Julian took one of the seats, Filippu removed the additional setting. "Here is the menu, Sir . . . I mean, Julian," the hotel owner said, smiling. "What can I get you to drink?"

Julian ordered a glass of wine from the menu at random and Filippu nodded. "That is a very good choice. It goes lovely with fish, if I may suggest."

Just then, a softly spoken voice behind him added, "If you like fish, we have bass as a special tonight."

Julian turned in his seat, his gaze settling on an incredibly beautiful Latino-looking girl. She was wearing a simple white dress, her long dark hair falling down almost to her waist. She was smiling, showing off her pristine white teeth and making her deep brown eyes twinkle. She was amazing.

"Ah, this is Angelina, my daughter," explained Filippu. "Excuse me, I'll just get your wine."

Julian stared at her for a few moments before realising what he was doing. "Sorry, I'm Julian," he said, holding his hand out. "It's nice to meet you."

Angelina moved closer to him so she could shake his hand, doing a little curtsy at the same time. "Are you enjoying your time in Malta?"

"I am now," replied Julian.

Just then her father came back, a bottle of wine in one hand and a corkscrew in the other. Smiling, he opened the bottle before pouring a small amount of wine into the glass on the table, which he handed over to Julian.

He took a small taste, nodded, and said, "That's fine, thank you."

Filippu waited until he put the glass down, then he poured the wine from the bottle again, giving him a rather generous amount. "Angelina will take your order. Enjoy your meal," he said before walking off to attend to another table.

"So what will it be?" she asked, taking out a notepad and pen.

"I think I'll go with the bass," Julian replied. "And the calamari for starters."

"Good choice. I'll get that for you right away."

Once she'd gone, Julian leaned back in his chair, taking a large sip of the cool, crisp wine. He could certainly get used to this type of lifestyle.

It wasn't long before Angelina brought him over the fish - they were right; it did go well with the wine - and for the rest of the night,

Julian watched as she moved around the courtyard, tending to the guests. In her bright white dress, she looked like an angel.

Angelina noticed him watching, and every so often she would turn to catch his eye, dazzling him with her smile.

Yes, Julian thought. He could *definitely* get used to this.

CHAPTER 27

Julian enjoyed his next few days in Malta - after everything that had happened to him recently, it was a nice change of pace, and that was putting it mildly.

He spent a lot of his time exploring the local area, eating and drinking and making a few friends here and there, Julian's casual charm working well for him as usual. He continued to go back to the café/bar/restaurant on the promenade where he'd spent his first afternoon in Malta, and soon he'd befriended the owner, Joseph, and his son, Geno.

Both of them knew Filippu and Angelina, and Joseph told Julian all about them - how Angelina's mother had died early on in her childhood, and how Angelina had subsequently spent most of her younger years caring for her father. When she grew up she met an English tourist and moved to England for several years. She'd only recently returned to Malta to help Filippu with the hotel.

Julian hung on Joseph's every word - he wanted to find out as much as he possibly could about Angelina. Despite seeing her in the hotel every day - and despite hanging out with her quite a bit - she still seemed very much an enigma to him.

The day after he'd learned all about Angelina's childhood, Julian spotted her outside the hotel, taking a break from working in the restaurant. She was sitting on the low brick wall, a glass of water in her hand.

"Can I join you?" he asked.

"Sure," said Angelina, smiling brightly. "How are things with my favourite guest?"

"I bet you say that to all the guests!"

Angelina raised her eyebrows. "Maybe I do, maybe I don't. I suppose you'll never know." She winked at him.

"Hey, Angelina," he said after a moment's silence, "what do you say about showing me around the island? Maybe we could get some food, some drinks, go dancing . . ." He trailed off, waiting to see how she'd react.

She didn't, not at first - she just carried on drinking her water. Then she looked over at Julian, smiling. "I can show you around the island, Julian, but it won't go any further than that."

Julian could feel himself turning red. "Any further?"

"I mean," she continued, "if you're looking for a relationship, I'm not your girl. I just got out of a long, complicated, horrible mess of a relationship, and I'm not looking to get into another one any time soon."

"Oh," said Julian, who wasn't entirely sure how to respond. "That's fine . . . I just, I like hanging out with you, that's all. I thought maybe we could hang out together more. As friends," he added quickly, after seeing her confused expression.

"OK," she said after what felt like an eternity. "As friends. I'd like that. And I can definitely show you around the place, tell you the best places to go to, the best food to eat. Are you free tonight?"

Julian nodded eagerly. He would have been free *any* night for her, and he had a feeling she knew it.

After their little chat outside the hotel, Julian and Angelina pretty much became inseparable - as friends. Every night she had off from the hotel restaurant, they would go out drinking and dancing until the early hours, and every day during her free time, they would go for lunch and sit by the water, looking out at the beautiful ocean. They talked about anything and everything, and Julian couldn't remember the last time he had such interesting conversations, with *anyone*.

Often they would go up to the hotel's rooftop garden, which was Filippu's pride and joy. He kept it as a private space for himself and Angelina, but he didn't mind Julian going up there - they too had become firm friends by now.

It was beautiful up on the roof, and not just because of the colourful plants and flowers covering most of the space - the view was incredible too. You could see for miles, and Angelina spent hours pointing out landmarks and other places to Julian, telling him all about her life and where she spent her time growing up.

When he wasn't spending time with Angelina, Julian would often talk with Filippu, learning all about his likes and dislikes. It soon became apparent that his biggest passion in life was his powerboat; he talked about it as if it were a person. He told Julian - extremely proudly - that he'd competed in and won a round-the-island race the very weekend before Julian had arrived at the hotel. Julian was extremely impressed.

"You must come this weekend," he told his new friend. "I'm marshalling a race for smaller craft off the island of Gozo. Angelina's coming; we're going to make a bit of a day of it. I'm taking a big hamper of food and drink - lobster, delicious fruits, wine, champagne . . . there's more than enough to go around. What do you think?"

Julian thought it sounded great, and not *just* because Angelina was going to be there. He was very much getting used to the Malta lifestyle, and because of this he kept extending his stay at the hotel. This pleased both Filippu and Angelina.

So, that Saturday, the three of them made the short journey across the bay to Filippu's powerboat.

Angelina had brought her large black camera case with her, but apart from his wallet and his sunglasses, Julian hadn't brought anything. The hamper Filippu had packed took up most of the back seat, anyway; when they first got in the boat, Julian had gone to sit in the back with Angelina, but Filippu had other ideas - he placed the hamper there, then indicated for him to sit in the passenger seat.

"I need you to navigate," he said.

The plan was to attend the event, and then go to the after party on the beach, which Angelina assured Julian was always a good time. Then they would leave in the early hours to get back to mainland Malta.

Julian was very much looking forward to it, especially the beach party, and as Filippu got himself seated and in position, he leaned his head back to soak up the sun. It was another glorious day in Malta.

Soon the engines had ignited, and a small cloud of smoke rose from the rear as the boat reversed out of the mooring. Julian watched Filippu as he kept to a slow speed, exiting the harbour enclosure and taking them out into the open sea. The breeze on Julian's face was incredibly refreshing, and he looked back at Angelina and smiled.

She smiled back, clearly relaxed.

"Hold onto your hats!" Filippu cried then, making the engines roar as he stepped up the power. The boat rose sharply at the front and Julian looked around at Angelina again, wanting to make sure she was OK.

She was gripping her camera case at the same time as securing the hamper on the seat, making sure they weren't going to fly out of the boat; she was obviously used to this.

Julian, however, wasn't quite so used to it, and he hung onto his seat for dear life as Filippu continued to surge forward.

"You want to drive, Julian?" he asked, laughing at the expression on his friend's face.

"I'm OK thanks," Julian just about managed to say in response. "Maybe later!"

Filippu stepped up the power even more. "I'll hold you to that!" he shouted over the sound of the engines.

Just then, the boat lurched downwards as Filippu reduced the throttle, making Julian's stomach churn. He took a deep breath, trying to calm himself down; the last thing he needed was to throw up in front of Angelina. That wasn't how he wanted her to remember this little trip of theirs.

By now they were approaching the small harbour on the island, which was full of powerboats as well as a seemingly endless throng of people, all getting ready for the race.

Filippu steered them in expertly, then helped Julian from the boat. "You look a little green, my friend," he said. "Perhaps you'd better stay away from the contents of the hamper for a while."

"Oh, I'll be fine. Soon, I'm sure . . ."

Angelina joined him on the jetty. "You'll get used to it, don't worry."

Julian nodded, looking out at the hustle and bustle of the race preparations. Filippu was talking to one of the organisers, who handed him a clipboard, a radio transmitter, and a first aid kid. He held the latter up to Julian. "You sure you don't need anything from here?"

Julian could feel himself getting red, but Angelina patted him on the shoulder. "Ignore him; he's just happy because he gets to be in charge and boss people around for a bit. Come on, let's get in our places."

Filippu was getting back into the boat, and upon hearing his daughter, he turned to face them. "You're not coming with me?" He looked at Julian. "It's very exciting at the marshal point. The boats go right past you."

Angelina groaned. "I was thinking we could watch from dry land."

"Nonsense!" shouted Filippu. "Get back in, Julian. Angelina, we can meet up with you afterwards."

"No, I'll come," she said. "I'll get some better shots from the boat anyway."

So it was agreed, and rather reluctantly, Julian got back in the boat, watching the jetty get smaller and smaller as they headed to the rear of the island, where they stopped next to one of the red sea buoys.

"So what do you actually have to do?" asked Julian, glad now that Filippu had stopped the engine.

"Well," he said, picking up his equipment and checking it over, "we have to make sure all the boats stay on course - you know, taking no shortcuts and cheating. Also, it is up to me to warn the others if there's an accident. Then I have to check off each boat as they come around, and keep track of how many laps they do. It's a very important job," Filippu finished proudly.

Julian nodded, impressed - he wasn't sure he'd be able to remember all that, or keep track of everything during the middle of a race - and then watched as Angelina took out her large, rather expensive-looking camera. Photography was one of her hobbies, she'd explained to Julian, and she took a couple of shots of him as a bit of a 'warm up'.

From their position right next to the course, Julian and his friends had a great view of the race, and watching the boats speed around the island, he felt a deep, burning desire to be a part of it. Every time a boat passed by - getting very close to their own boat at times - they would be rocked on the waves, and the noise of the racers was so loud he could barely hear anything else when they went zooming past. Everyone in the crowd was just so enthusiastic, cheering everyone on, and the click-click-click of Angelina's camera just added to the whole thrilling atmosphere.

All too soon the race was over, and Julian watched as a motor cruiser approached to collect everything back from Filippu, who had clearly had a great time. There had been no accidents and no shortcuts taken. A nice, clean race. On board the cruiser there were several bikini-clad girls, all of them talking animatedly about the beach party. Julian couldn't stop staring at them.

Angelina poked him in the side. "Bet you can't wait for the party now!" she said, glancing at the girls and making him blush.

"Yes, the party," said Filippu. "Angelina, I'll drop you off at the beach with the hamper. Julian, let's go for a quick drive in the boat, shall we?"

Julian wasn't at all sure about this after his little bout of seasickness, but thinking about the thrilling race he'd just witnessed, he agreed, and soon - after dropping off Angelina and the supplies - he was taking the driver's seat, with Filippu in the passenger seat next to him.

"Have you driven a boat before?" asked Filippu.

"I've been in one," replied Julian. "One of my relatives used to own a small speedboat. I had a go on it when I was a kid. They let me steer it a few times."

Filippu nodded. "Don't worry - it's like riding a bicycle. Just on water."

Julian started the engines, and after a few words of instruction from Filippu, he engaged the throttle. As the boat's bow began to rise he increased the power, then he stood up to try and get a clearer view of where he was going.

"Sit down, Julian!" Filippu shouted. "You're going to fall out!"

Julian - whose nerves were now totally gone and whose blood was pumping around his body faster and faster with every passing second - took his advice and sat down, probably just in time. He felt more excited now than he'd felt about anything for a long time.

"OK," said Filippu, seemingly calming down a little. "Go on, open it up if you want to."

Nodding, Julian pushed on the throttle, the boat surging forwards with a jolt and causing his entire body to get pressed back against the seat - he couldn't stand up now even if he wanted to, the pressure was that great.

His excitement quickly changing to fear, Julian decreased his speed immediately, taking a deep breath as the boat slowed down.

"That's it," said Filippu, "nice and slow." He was looking at the rear of the boat, where a wave of water was threatening to swamp the whole thing.

Julian - who himself was now a lot calmer - did as Filippu said, his heart rate slowly getting back to normal.

"You know," his friend said after a while, "you could be good with a little practice."

Julian had been thinking the same thing - despite the rocky start, the thrill he got steering that boat along the open water was unlike anything he'd ever experienced before. He just felt so . . . *free*.

After a few more minutes of Julian getting to grips with the boat, they headed back to the beach to find Angelina waiting for them. She'd used her time to arrange the blankets on the sand, and had also taken out the food and drink from the hamper. There were lots of other people on the beach, their own blankets and belongings arranged around several as of yet unlit fires that were dotted around the shore.

Julian sat down next to Angelina as she opened a bottle of champagne, the liquid fizzing over the sand as she leaned down and poured it into three plastic cups. Filippu took his and went over to talk to some of his friends, and as Julian sat there on the beach with Angelina - looking out at the ocean after his little adventure on the boat - he thought that no glass of alcohol had ever tasted sweeter.

"You having a good time?" she asked.

"The best," Julian replied truthfully.

And the rest of the night was just as much fun. Everyone mingled with everyone else, sharing food and drink as well as stories - Julian listened intently to the 'race chat', the participants telling tales of their time in races all over the island and even further afield. Julian couldn't help but be inspired, and although he was having a great time on the beach, he longed to be back out on the boat.

Once everyone had had a sufficient amount to drink, the party games began, and Julian took part in almost every one of them.

It soon got to the point where people were falling asleep on the shore, and while Filippu went off with some of his friends to sit around one of the fires (which had all been lit as soon as it had got dark), Julian and Angelina headed around the corner, where it was a little more private.

"You want to swim?" asked Angelina.

Julian frowned. "Believe it or not, I didn't bring my swimming trunks with me. I was planning on staying *in* the boat and *out* of the water."

Angelina shook her head. "You English boys and your swimming trunks! Who needs a swimming costume to swim?" With that, Julian watched - hardly believing his eyes - as Angelina pulled off her dress to reveal her bra and panties underneath. They were bright red, the perfect colour next to her rich, smooth skin.

"Right," said Julian, who kicked off his flip-flops before taking his t-shirt off. Standing there in his shorts, he started heading towards the water.

"Ah, Julian," came Angelina's soft voice from behind him. "What are you doing?"

He turned around. "Swimming?"

She shook her head again. "And what are you going to wear when you come out? Your shorts will be all wet."

He hesitated, unsure of what she was saying, then watched in awe as she took her bra off before slipping out of her panties. "Here, we swim naked!"

She walked towards him, leaning into him and pulling off his shorts in one quick motion. She threw them on the sand behind them, grabbed his hand, and pulled him into the water.

She splashed at him playfully, the water that surrounded them glistening under the moonlight, the waves sparkling like crystals. It was a magical sight, and Julian stared at the ocean for a moment or two before swimming over to Angelina and splashing her back. She smiled, and for just one moment, Julian thought something was going to happen between them. It certainly looked like she would be up for it, but at the same time, he didn't want to cross over the line. He'd told her he was happy being friends, and he was going to honour that.

If only she didn't look so amazing right now, splashing about in the water, her toned, curvy body sending shivers up his spine. How did he always manage to meet such amazing women?

After swimming for a few more minutes - with every single one of those minutes being absolute torture for Julian, who was trying not to get too close to Angelina should he get carried away - they headed back onto the shore.

They picked up their clothes, but they didn't want to put them on straight away. So, settling down in the dunes together, they looked out at the ocean, the moon still reflecting off the black-looking water below.

"I'm cold," said Angelina, pouting, and after only a brief hesitation, Julian moved closer to her, wrapping his arms around her shivering body.

It felt nice, lying there on the sand together, and for the first time since she'd taken her clothes off, Julian was content to just be there with her, without anything happening or potentially happening. It felt a little strange, but good.

Once they became tired of staring out at the ocean, they both leaned back and looked up at the sky. There wasn't a cloud in sight, and as far as the eye could see, the sky was lit up with a thousand twinkling stars. It was a magical night, with magical company. Julian was so glad he'd decided to stay in Malta a bit longer.

They lay there like that for another hour or so - eventually putting their clothes back on - and just as the dawn sun was rising over the sea, Filippu appeared beside them.

"Come on, it's time to go. I've packed the boat. You ready?"

Rather reluctantly, Julian nodded. He hadn't wanted this night to end, but there was one thing he was even more eager about, and as he followed Filippu back to the boat, he made a promise to himself: he was going to learn as much about boats from his friend as he could. He wanted to feel that exhilaration again, experience that thrill as he sped along the open water.

He couldn't wait.

CHAPTER 28

Julian stuck to the promise he'd made to himself, and at every available opportunity, he followed Filippu around, asking him as many questions as he could and pestering him until he took him out on the boat.

Julian loved learning from Filippu, and not just because of how he felt when he was out on the boat, which was amazing enough - what usually happened after the training sessions was a pretty good incentive to get out on the water as well.

Their lessons would always end in a small bay, where they would go to the same beach bar and club, which was pretty big and spread out over three levels. On the first level there was situated a kitchen area, a large patio, and a sun bed area, all of which led onto a jetty. The second level was for drinking and dining, with a bar and restaurant, and the third level led to the road and extra parking for guests not arriving via the water.

The bay itself was like something straight from a postcard, with all of its cute little villas and multi-coloured fishing boats. The water was always teeming with people - both locals and tourists - going out on boats or speeding by on water skis. It was the place to be, and Julian loved it more every time he went there.

Julian and Filippu often went out in the boat with Filippu's co-pilot Joe, and at the end of their sessions they would meet up with Angelina at the beach bar while Joe returned and moored the boat. It was a little routine they had quickly got into, and soon they were doing this almost every day.

As was quite usual on the island, Angelina knew the owners of the beach bar, as she'd gone to school with one of them, Toby. On top of this, Filippu was seeing a woman named Josephine, who lived in a villa very close to the beach bar. These things kept them coming back time and again, and Julian was more than happy with the arrangement.

One day at the beach bar, Josephine came along to meet up with Filippu, but she didn't come alone - she brought her neighbour, Penny, with her.

"Come and meet my friend," Josephine called to Julian, when she saw him across the bar, "she's gorgeous!"

Gorgeous was an understatement, and as Julian walked over, he didn't quite know what to think. Where had this woman come from? She was blonde, busty, and clearly rich, if the jewellery that adorned her body was any indication.

"It's nice to meet you," Julian just about managed to get out.

"I was thinking the same thing," Penny replied flirtatiously, looking him up and down in obvious approval.

"Darling," Josephine said to Filippu, "I think we should leave these two alone, don't you?"

Julian had no problems with that, and soon he and Penny were talking and laughing like they were old friends. He found out all about her - she was an ex-footballer's wife and a jeans model, and she had two children (who were currently away with their dad). She was indeed incredibly rich, but she didn't come across as being snooty or as though she were above anyone else.

They talked for hours, the attraction between them both instant and obvious.

By now time was getting on, and Julian suggested they go and grab dinner somewhere - his treat. Penny immediately agreed, and soon they were sitting down on the balcony of a nearby restaurant, dining under the stars as the waves crashed onto the shore beneath them. There was a slight sea breeze that sobered them up a little, but they soon put that right again by ordering two bottles of champagne with their food.

"So," said Penny, once Julian had paid the bill, "do you want to come back to my place?" She leaned over, placing her heavily adorned hand on his thigh.

Julian didn't have to be asked twice, and after only a brief stroll back to her villa, he found himself in Penny's bedroom, amazed - and not for the first time - at his luck.

Unfortunately, his luck didn't last too long that night.

It started off fine, with them slowly undressing each other in the semi-darkness, their only light source the glow of the moon beaming in through the large open windows. It gave Penny's skin an almost ethereal appearance, and Julian couldn't stop staring at her breasts in the glimmering moonlight, not to mention her lean, almost muscly abs. It made him hungry for her, *desperate* for her.

Gently, he caressed her skin, leaning down and kissing her first on and then all around both of her breasts, lingering at the nipples and making her groan softly. In response she pulled off his shirt before tugging on his trousers, pulling them roughly down to the floor. He stepped out of them and then leaned into her warm, welcoming body.

Penny was still wearing her jeans, but Julian simply couldn't wait any longer, and in a fit of passion he threw her down on the bed, making her laugh - a low, seductive kind of laugh that sent a tingle up his spine.

Julian pulled down his underwear before tugging on Penny's jeans and panties, lowering them just about enough so he could push himself into her, making her cry out in desire.

The alcohol they'd had at the bar and the restaurant was now very much doing its thing, and throwing all caution to the wind, Julian pushed into her as hard as he could, causing her to scream in response, even louder this time as she reached her arms up and grabbed him around the shoulders.

But Julian still wasn't done, and with a massive surge of adrenaline he pushed in even harder and further than before, pinning her down to the bed so much he thought he heard one of the wooden bed slats break beneath them.

Penny's grip on his shoulders increased, her nails digging roughly into his skin - not that Julian could really feel it; all he was aware of now was that intense throbbing down below, that almost agonising rush of lust that overtook everything else. Now harder than ever, he leaned down, kissing Penny between her breasts before sucking down hard on one of her nipples, making her cry out again.

With Penny's legs still half in her jeans, they rocked back and forth, Penny screaming at the top of her lungs when she climaxed, before going limp in his arms as she relaxed her entire body.

Julian shouted out too - all that pent-up desire and lust exploding out of him - and when he was done he kissed her briefly on the lips before quickly pulling out.

Unfortunately, that was his big mistake.

A second later Penny shouted out in surprise, and looking down, Julian saw a spurt of blood land on the sheets and the top of Penny's leg.

"Penny! Are you OK?" he asked, horrified at the sight of the dark red liquid now spreading out on the bed sheets.

"It's not me," she whispered, pointing at him, "it's you."

Julian looked down again, this time focusing on himself, and when he realised what had happened, he immediately wished he hadn't looked at all. Penny was right - it *was* him. More accurately, it was his foreskin, having clearly got caught on the zip on Penny's jeans.

Feeling incredibly light-headed all of a sudden, Julian reached down to grab his throbbing manhood, causing yet more blood to spurt out onto Penny's white sheets. By now Penny had wriggled out of her jeans and was standing next to the bed, her face as pale as the bedding. She looked like she was about to be sick, and Julian didn't blame her; if he was honest, he was amazed he hadn't thrown up yet.

She watched in horror as Julian agonisingly pulled the zipper out of his skin before jumping off the bed and running over to the toilet, leaving behind him a trail of blood - all over the brand new cream-coloured carpet.

In the bathroom, Julian tried not to focus too much on the carnage down below as he grabbed as much toilet roll as possible and wrapped it around his bloody penis. His hands soon got sticky with the blood, and after a wave of nausea washed over him, he reached out and grabbed hold of the sink to steady himself.

As he stood there, trying to stop his manhood from bleeding all over the tiles, he caught a glimpse of himself in the mirror - naked, apart from his mummy-esque bandaged penis - and he had to laugh; it was either that or start crying hysterically. Luckily the alcohol in his system was masking a lot of the pain, and he tried not to think too much about how it would feel in the morning. That was another problem for a few hours' time.

Needless to say, the mood at Penny's place changed considerably after that, and whereas normally Julian would be ready for at least another round before they went to sleep, that definitely wasn't happening this time.

No, instead Julian spent the next thirty minutes scrubbing the carpet while Penny stripped the bed and cleaned up the bathroom; not the most sexy of activities in the world. And all the while his penis throbbed, reminding him of the monumentally stupid thing he'd done to himself. If he hadn't still been pretty drunk, he supposed he'd be embarrassed.

After he'd finished with the carpet, Julian thought that Penny might ask him to leave, but although she didn't say much for the rest of the night, she let him stay; they spent the whole night lying together out on the balcony, the air still warm after the heat of the day.

It would have been quite romantic if Julian's penis hadn't been throbbing for the whole night, and when he woke up the next morning, his fears of the night before came true - he found himself in excruciating pain from the moment he opened his eyes.

Penny gave him some painkillers and some coffee, and then, after Julian had had a shower she offered to take him back to the hotel, where they could have some more drinks. She thought it might help dull the throbbing even more than the painkillers had, and Julian agreed.

The drive was spent mostly in silence, while Julian re-played the night before over and over in his mind. He just couldn't believe what had happened to him; in the cold light of day, he was mortified.

Soon they were there, and as he got out of the car, he turned to Penny. "Before we go in, I just want to say that I hope we can do this again some time." He laughed, trying to lighten the mood. "Well, perhaps not this *exact* same thing . . ."

While Penny didn't laugh, she did allow a half-amused smile to grace her lips for a few moments before focusing on parking her car.

Not that you could really call it 'parking' when it came to Penny; in an attempt to parallel park between two vehicles, she gently reversed into the front bumper of the car parked behind her, simply shrugging when she realised she'd collided with it. It was then that Julian noticed several different colours scratched on the bumper and boot of her car, as if she'd managed to crash into a car of every colour of the rainbow. Amused, he shook his head.

As Penny was getting out of the car - having finally decided that her parking was good enough - Filippu and Josephine strolled over to them, clearly having just arrived from Josephine's place. Julian hoped his friend had had a better night than him, though he didn't say anything, and he also gave Penny a quick, meaningful look for good measure, pleading with his eyes for her not to say anything. That half-smile appeared again, and she nodded slightly in acknowledgement.

After saying hello, all four of them walked into the hotel together, immediately deciding they should all sit at the same table and get some drinks in.

First, however, Julian had a bit of business to attend to, and after excusing himself, he headed out of the bar and through to the reception area toilets. Then, heading over to the furthest urinal from the door, he reached down and unzipped his jeans, carefully taking out his penis and starting to unwrap the paper he'd put on fresh that morning - not that it looked too fresh now. At least it had stopped bleeding profusely. That was something, he supposed.

Julian got straight to work, but he was so absorbed in what he was doing he didn't hear when the door to the toilets opened behind him, nor did he hear the footsteps as someone walked across the floor, coming to a stop just behind him and leaning over his shoulder.

"What the hell are you doing?" asked Filippu, making Julian jump.

He desperately tried to hide his manhood, but it was pretty clear that Filippu had already seen the mess down below; he started laughing heartily and slapping Julian on the back.

"I've never seen a man wrap it up before!" he shouted, making Julian flinch. "What on earth happened?"

"Please keep it down," whispered Julian, worried who might hear them; the last thing he needed was for this to get out and then to get spread around the whole club. "I just had a little accident at Penny's, that's all . . . the zipper on her jeans . . ."

He wasn't able to get any more words out before Filippu started laughing again, and annoyed, he walked over to the single cubicle, shutting the door behind him so he could re-do his wrap in private. He could still hear his friend laughing.

By the time he came out of the cubicle Filippu was nowhere to be seen, and after washing his hands, he headed back into the main bar area of the hotel, where his three friends were sitting at the table, several drinks in front of them. He immediately felt his mouth water.

He'd got about three paces across the floor, however, when he realised that everyone was staring at him, and when the laughter started, he glared at Filippu.

"Sorry," Filippu said as Julian sat down, "but that story was far too good not to share!"

Josephine stared down at her drink, while Penny just shrugged; she didn't seem bothered one way or the other, even though it was *her* zipper he'd got stuck on. He wished he could be as relaxed as she was.

Shaking his head, Julian reached out for his pint.

He was never going to live this down.

CHAPTER 29

The next Saturday (when news of Julian's little accident had both spread around seemingly the whole island and then been apparently forgotten once the people had found something new to gossip about), Julian, Penny, and Josephine were asked to watch Filippu at the international race of the year - an invitation-only event that many residents on the island looked forward to every year.

Julian was excited at the prospect of seeing another race, and that morning, Penny came to the hotel - along with Josephine - to pick him up and drive them all to the yacht club.

The drive didn't take too long, and when they got there, she did her usual infamous parking trick - this time bumping into both the car behind *and* the car in front in an attempt to get into the space.

Julian laughed as he shared a look of exasperation with Josephine, who also had a little chuckle.

"Come on, luvvies," Penny said as she got out the car and saw their faces, "that's what bumpers are for!"

Julian grinned; you had to love Penny's logic.

Heading into the yacht club, they were immediately met on the terrace by several waiters carrying trays of food and drink - an array of champagnes, wines, and cute little canapés.

"I could get used to this," said Julian, taking a glass of champagne and a few canapés off a couple of the waiters.

Penny smiled - of course, she *was* used to this. This was her life. Every single day.

Julian sighed; he had to admit, he did feel a little jealous of her lifestyle, not that he'd ever say anything to her - or anyone else for that matter.

After about half an hour of eating, drinking, and chatting, it was announced that the race was about to begin, and looking up at the sky, Julian smiled as he saw several helicopters zooming into the vicinity, hovering over the boats on the water. It was pretty spectacular, and yet again Julian wished he could be involved in something like this, instead of just sitting on the sidelines like usual.

He wanted to be out there in the thick of things, having fun and feeling the rush of the wind in his hair as he zoomed around the island. Perhaps one day, he told himself, before taking another sip of champagne.

Just then, a rather well-dressed man passed by the three of them, whispering to Julian, "You're lucky to have two women to yourself!" as he went.

"I'm afraid not! Josephine here is with Filippu; he's taking part in the race."

The man nodded. "Well, good luck to him then!" he shouted back, and then he was off, heading towards the toilets.

Julian focused back on the boats. The race was about to begin, and he was thrilled already. He wasn't the only one either; the place was buzzing, people from all over the island having turned up to cheer the racers on.

The three of them were soon joined by Angelina and her friend Toby, one of the owners of the beach bar they often went to. After chatting to them for a while, Toby caught the eye of a man standing in a group next to them - it was the man who'd congratulated Julian on being there with two women.

"Donny!" exclaimed Toby, reaching out and shaking his hand once the other man had joined them. "I didn't know you were coming."

Donny grinned. "Wouldn't miss it!" He nodded at the others in acknowledgment before winking at Julian.

"Donny's a photographer from the UK," Toby told the group.

"Oh?" said Angelina, her interest suddenly piqued. "I love photography! What kind are you involved in?"

Donny grinned again. "Glamour shoots mainly," he replied before adding, "but don't hold that against me!"

Angelina laughed - seemingly not at all put off by his job - and soon the two of them were engrossed in a conversation about lenses, filters, and other photography jargon that went completely over Julian's head.

It wasn't until Julian headed to the bar for another drink that he got a chance to talk to Donny himself; he followed Julian, needing a top-up.

"So," Julian said while they waited to be served, "what kind of work are you doing here on the island?"

Donny's eyes immediately lit up - it was clear he was passionate about his job. "I've been photographing people," he explained to Julian, "*important* people."

"And what happens with these photographs afterwards?" Julian asked, wondering what kind of 'important' people he meant.

"Well," said Donny, leaning forward and lowering his voice as though he were about to impart some big secret, "If I remove the backing paper from the photo I can heat seal it onto a canvas, making it look like a painting. They're in demand at the moment."

Julian nodded. "Clever."

Just then the bartender came over to take their orders, and while he was getting the drinks, Donny turned back to face Julian.

"So, what about you? What's your business on the island?"

Julian shrugged, trying to act casual. "Oh, I was just passing through . . . then I ended up staying for a bit."

Donny nodded as their drinks were served, and as they headed back to the group he said, "Plenty of opportunities here, if you know where to find them." He winked at Julian. "*Plenty* of opportunities."

The group continued to drink as they watched the race on the big screen out on the terrace, cheering and shouting as the boats made their way around the course. Just like last time, Julian felt a surge of adrenaline flow through his body as he watched, not to mention the almost overwhelming urge to get out there himself - to feel the wind in his hair and the sea spray on his face, to experience that sensation of freedom as he whizzed around the island and zoomed into first place . . . he wanted it all.

As the race leader came into view, all of the spectators approached the edge of the terrace to cheer the boats on as they neared the end of the course. By now everyone had had at least a few drinks and were all really getting into it; whoops and claps filled the air as the boats zoomed over the 'finish line'.

"Where's Filippu?" asked Julian.

Josephine, who had been counting each boat as they'd gone past, replied, "I think he came about tenth."

Julian nodded, a little disappointed for his friend. There had been 18 boats in the race, and he knew Filippu wouldn't be happy with that result.

The group carried on drinking and chatting while they waited for the racers to appear, and soon Filippu was walking onto the terrace.

"Well done, darling," said Josephine, greeting him warmly as she threw her arms around his neck and kissed him on the cheek.

Filippu shrugged. "There was a fuel issue. I tried my best," he explained as he shook hands with everyone else in the group. When he got to Julian he received several pats on the back, and when he got to Donny, he smiled warmly.

"Donny!" Filippu cried, before shaking his hand.

"You two know each other?" asked Julian.

Filippu nodded. "I know Donny's friend Anton - he's a ship's chandler. He actually introduced us to each other."

Donny grinned. "It's a small island, alright."

As Donny and the others started talking about the race again, Filippu turned to Julian, lowering his voice slightly as he said, "Have you met Anton? He's a bit of a shifty character. A . . . what's the word . . . wheeler dealer."

"I haven't had the pleasure," he replied.

The day continued in much the same vein - with more drinks and more talking - and after hanging out with his friends for a while longer, Julian settled down to talk to Donny; he found the man intriguing, and he wanted to know more about his photography business and how he made his money.

By the end of the evening Julian and Donny had agreed to meet up for lunch the next day to discuss a 'business opportunity' in the foyer of the Hilton hotel - a little more glamorous than the places Julian was used to. He was impressed.

As Julian walked in he spotted Donny sitting at a table, drinking a rather fancy-looking coffee, and after saying their hellos, Donny ordered Julian a cup of his own. Once it arrived, they got straight down to business.

"This is my plan," Donny said, taking another sip of his coffee and glancing briefly at their surroundings, as though making sure no one was listening. "The island was heavily bombed during the war," he explained, "and because of this, a lot of really valuable paintings were stored in vaults, deep underground."

Julian nodded, though he had no idea about any of this; it wasn't exactly the kind of thing his friends usually talked about.

Donny continued. "They've never been seen by the public, so I'm going to photograph them and reproduce them on canvas, like I told you. Then they can be publicly displayed, and people can enjoy the artwork without having to see the originals."

Julian nodded again, thinking this through. "So how do I come into this?" he asked eventually. It was what he'd been wondering ever since Donny had set up this meeting the night before. Why him? What could he do that other people couldn't? Or, perhaps, wouldn't?

"Well," said Donny, finishing his coffee, "I need someone to get involved both financially and physically. You see, in order to get this off the ground, I need money. And one way of getting money is by looking at supply and demand. Do you know what's in demand over here, in terms of vehicles?"

Julian thought briefly of the boats they were watching yesterday, wondering where this was going, then shook his head.

"Diesel transit vans."

That was the last thing Julian expected Donny to say, and seeing his confused expression, his new friend smiled.

"They're pretty much always in demand over here - you see, the Maltese government offers a significant discount on diesel fuel when it's used for work purposes."

Julian nodded, slowly beginning to understand. "So you want to supply a transit van? A diesel one?"

Donny grinned. "Bingo. We'd have to go back to the UK to buy it, then drive it back, along with some other goods to help us in our venture. Is that something you'd be up for?"

Julian agreed immediately. He loved Malta, but a trip back to the homeland would be nice; he missed England. "So that's it?"

"Not quite," replied Donny. "We'll need some other stuff too. Ice machines, things like that, we can always make money from. And I can organise the special paper I'll need for the canvas process. So, are you in?"

Julian nodded. "I'm in."

"Great! In that case, I think this calls for a celebration," exclaimed Donny. "Let's order something a bit stronger than this." He gestured at his now empty coffee cup.

"I couldn't agree more."

After a couple of celebratory drinks Julian headed back to the hotel, and on his way in, Filippu called to him from his little cubby hole in the reception area.

"Julian! Where have you been on this fine day?"

He went over to the little window, leaning down to talk to him. "I went to meet Donny, to discuss some business."

Filippu frowned. "What kind of business?"

Normally Julian probably wouldn't have told him - at least not all the details - but the alcohol had relaxed him and he found himself telling Filippu everything.

"So what do you think?" Julian asked, wanting his friend's opinion even though he'd already agreed to the work anyway.

Filippu was silent for a moment while he processed everything. Then he looked up at Julian, frowning. "Well, it's correct what Donny said . . . about the diesel and everything . . . but you do realise it could take a while for customs to clear the goods on your return?"

Julian shrugged. "I can deal with that."

Filippu nodded. "Just be careful . . . and if Donny ever tries to get you to do anything with or for Anton, say no, OK? Just don't get involved."

Julian agreed, though in truth, the more Filippu warned him against this mysterious 'Anton', the more Julian wanted to meet him. That was just his nature.

After promising Filippu that he'd be careful, Julian went back to his room. He was so excited he wanted to start packing immediately.

A couple of days later Julian found himself, yet again, on a plane, though this journey wasn't anywhere near as stressful as his last one. Donny sat in the seat next to him, and the whole way back they went over their plan, laughing and joking like old friends.

As they landed, Julian peered out of the plane window, smiling as more and more of London came into view. He really had missed England, and even though he would only be there for a short time, he was glad he'd come - it was like charging up a battery; he just needed to get a fix of his home country and then he'd quite happily make his way back to Malta.

After a few hours of wondering around London while Donny dealt with some business of his own - a few hours during which Julian visited some of his usual haunts - they both met up to go and collect the van and the rest of their goods. There were several boxes containing various items, and a huge pile of backing paper that Donny would be using for the pictures. It seemed like an awful lot to Julian, but he didn't question it - he was sure Donny knew what he was doing.

"You ready for a long drive?" asked Donny once they were both sitting in the van.

Julian nodded; he'd picked up some food for the road and was quite looking forward to their little road trip. "Let's do it."

Soon they were on their way, heading south to Dover where they got on a ferry to mainland Europe. The crossing was a bit rocky but soon they were in France, and then (after a quick overnight stay in a hotel) they made their way to Italy, travelling through the alps and down into Naples.

It was here that they had a few hours to kill while waiting for the ferry over to Malta, and Julian and Donny spent the time wandering around the narrow streets of Naples, taking in all the hustle and bustle of the busy day as they passed street beggars, market traders, cafes, and bars - there were just people everywhere, talking, smiling, laughing . . . it was a great atmosphere and Julian loved it immediately.

Donny, however, didn't have such a great time; while he was distracted by a man selling jewellery on a street corner, another man crept up behind him and picked his pocket - Julian just about managed to see Donny's wallet disappear into the thief's coat before he was gone, running away through the crowd and seemingly vanishing into thin air.

"That was everything I had on me!" Donny groaned. "I've got literally no money left now, the bastard!"

Julian sighed. "I've got money. I'll pay for whatever we need."

Donny grinned. "Thanks mate. I'll pay you back, I promise."

After heading back to the docks they got on the ferry, Julian spending the first few minutes standing next to the railing and looking out at the water. A thick smog was hanging over Naples, smothering the city, and Julian knew how it felt - he was so tired, so exhausted. After a while he went to the cabin he was sharing with Donny, lying down gratefully on one of the small beds.

He'd loved being back in London for his brief stint, but if he'd never left England, he wouldn't have had the opportunity to see sights like he'd seen on this trip. He felt sorry for anyone who never got the chance to travel.

When they arrived in Malta, Julian was expecting a delay in customs like Filippu had told him, but what he wasn't expecting them to do was seize the van - which was exactly what happened.

"What's the problem?" asked Donny politely.

The official - tall, large, and generally intimidating - was glancing down at their paperwork. "Is this the only document you have?"

Donny nodded. "Yes. It's the only document we need, isn't it?"

The official shook his head, slowly and agonisingly. "Where did you purchase this van? We need the document of sale."

"That's the document of sale," replied Donny, getting a bit exasperated now.

The official shook his head again. "We need more information. Is this the correct phone number?"

Donny leaned over the paper to look at the phone number. It was the company he'd got the van from. "Yes, that's it."

"OK, wait here," the official said, before marching off and leaving Julian and Donny alone in the little waiting room.

"I thought you said there wouldn't be a problem," Julian groaned.

"There won't be," insisted Donny. "He'll phone the guy, he'll confirm everything, and we'll be on our way. Five minutes tops."

Julian wasn't so sure, and over an hour later, he *definitely* wasn't sure.

Soon, however, the official came back, handing Donny the piece of paper and gesturing to the car park. "You're free to take the van and your goods."

"Finally," said Donny, walking out.

Julian thanked the guard and followed him.

CHAPTER 30

After getting back to Malta, Julian decided it was time for a change of scenery; while he loved staying at the hotel, it wasn't the most economical way of living, and now that he'd realised how much he liked the island, he decided to get something a little more permanent.

So, after asking around and talking things over with Donny, the two of them decided to move into a villa together - Anton, Donny had said, could supply one to them at a great rate. Filippu wasn't very happy with this, but Julian was happy. The villa was small but clean and tidy, and it wasn't too far away from the hotel so he could still easily keep in touch with Filippu and Angelina.

He'd wanted to meet up with Penny again, but Filippu informed him that she'd gone back to the UK to reunite with her husband. Julian was a little disappointed to hear this, but a tiny part of him was relieved too - at least there was no chance he would re-live his zipper nightmare with her again.

He and Donny were getting on like a house on fire, having fun when they were home together but making sure not to spend *too* much time together - that was a sure fire way to get annoyed with your housemate. So, in the day, Donny would go about his business, taking meetings and organising things, while Julian would spend time with Angelina and Filippu, mainly at the beach bar, drinking and chatting. It was a pretty good set up for Julian, and he was loving every minute of it.

As he soon found out, Donny had a lot of friends, though whether most of these people were actually friends or business associates, Julian was never quite sure.

At one point he went with Donny to the airport to pick up some of these friends. Donny said they were there on holiday and had booked into the Hilton, making Julian picture some rich, suave-looking business associates, so he got a bit of a shock when at the airport Donny greeted a tall, beefy man with a bald head, and an extremely thin man whose neck and arms were completely covered in tattoos. Donny sure did know some colourful people.

And then there was his photography business; before Donny could even get going on the work with the painting replicas, he got commissioned to do some other photography work on the island. As he explained to Julian, he'd previously been asked to photograph government ministers, and now the same person wanted him to photograph a beauty contestant who'd been a finalist in the Miss Malta competition. She needed new shots for her portfolio.

As soon as Julian heard those words - 'beauty contestant' - he sat up straight, asking Donny question after question about the woman and begging him if he could tag along to the shoot.

Finding Julian's reaction hilarious, Donny agreed. "But don't be all sleazy or anything; I'm a professional. I'm sure she's used to guys hitting on her all the time."

Julian pretended to be offended. "I think you'll find I'm the least sleazy person ever, Donny."

"Yeah, yeah," his friend joked.

A couple of days later, Julian and Donny headed off to meet Maria, the beauty contestant and most recent subject of Donny's photography business.

After Donny's words of warning, Julian didn't want to come across as being at all sleazy or like he wanted to hit on the woman, but as soon as he saw her, he couldn't stop looking at her. She was the epitome of a beauty queen, with long, slender legs, big brown eyes, and long, straight brown hair that went down to her lower back. She was tall as well, something she emphasised rather than tried to hide. She appeared to encompass a mixture of Maltese beauty and Italian charm.

As soon as they got there, Donny became instantly suave and charming - not his usual self at all, at least not when he was around

Julian and Julian alone. "Maria," he said, "so lovely to see you. May I introduce Julian; he's my manager and financier."

Julian could feel his face going red; they'd agreed beforehand that Donny would say Julian was his manager, but hearing it out loud sounded a little odd.

"Hello Julian," Maria said, smiling. It was a sweet, innocent smile - she wasn't trying to be charming or to impress anyone - and it made Julian pay even more attention; most of the women he came across were overly confident, some of them complete man-eaters. He could tell immediately that Maria was different.

"Hi," he replied, rather nervously. "You look wonderful." Julian cringed; he'd been deliberately trying not to come across as if he were hitting on her, and what did he go and say, as soon as he'd walked through the door? He could see Donny shaking his head at him out of the corner of his eye.

This time it was Maria's turn to blush, and she shook his hand quickly before turning back to Donny. "Shall we get going with the shoot?"

Donny agreed, and Julian helped his friend set up the equipment before relaxing on a seat in the corner of the room, where he could watch Donny work his photography magic.

Not that he *had* to work much magic with Maria - she was stunning. The woman was just so photogenic; she was made for the camera. With every shot Donny took, he smiled, clearly getting some good stuff.

Maria wasn't the first beauty queen Julian had met, but she was definitely a whole different breed compared to Marjorie. She just seemed so innocent, so completely unaware of the effect she had on men - not to mention the effect she was currently having on Julian.

He really hadn't wanted to come across as being seedy or anything like that, and he'd promised himself he wouldn't ask her out, but looking at her posing for the camera - her deep brown hair swinging in front of her face, her big eyes staring into the lens, her full lips forming into the perfect pout - Julian came to the conclusion that he'd be mad not to try it.

So, as Donny was packing up, Julian strolled over to Maria, smiling the best non-sleazy smile he could muster. "That was great," he said enthusiastically, "you're a natural with the camera."

"Oh, I don't know about that," she said quietly, "I always feel a bit silly doing all that posing."

"Nonsense," Julian replied encouragingly. "Look," he said, hoping he was going to sound professional and polite, "I don't usually do this with clients of Donny's - work boundaries and everything - but I was wondering if you'd like to spend some time together? Perhaps this weekend? We could have a nice, quiet day on the beach, relax a little. What do you think?" He mentally held his breath while she considered his proposal. He could almost feel Donny's eyes staring into his back, but he ignored him.

"Actually, that sounds really nice," Maria said after a couple of seconds. "I'd love to."

Julian walked out of the photo shoot feeling incredible, and not even Donny rolling his eyes at him could bring him down. "What?" he asked, feeling immediately defensive.

"Nothing, man. I'm just amazed she said yes; I get the feeling she doesn't date much."

This time it was Julian's turn to roll his eyes. "We're not dating; it's just a day at the beach."

"Yeah, yeah," said Donny.

That Sunday, Julian - who had hired a car for getting around the island -picked up Maria from the Main Square, smiling as he took her in: she was wearing a floral wrap dress, a large sunhat, and sunglasses, and she looked like a movie star.

"You look lovely today," Julian said as he got out of the car and moved around to the passenger side.

Maria smiled. "So do you."

Julian held open the door for her, and as she sat down on the passenger seat, her dress fell to one side, revealing the most perfect legs Julian had ever seen - long and suntanned.

On the way to the beach Julian saw a man on the side of the road, selling watermelons. "What do you think?" he asked Maria, gesturing at the road trader. "We could have a little picnic on the beach?"

Maria agreed, and Julian indicated before pulling over to the side of the road. They picked out two large, juicy-looking watermelons, and the trader cut them into segments before wrapping them up.

"Let me pay," said Maria, but the road trader shook his head.

"For Miss Maria, they are free," he explained.

Maria smiled sweetly at the man, and Julian wondered just how much free stuff this woman got given to her all the time.

They got back in the car with the watermelons - Maria holding them as Julian drove - and before too long they were pulling up into one of the car parks near the beach.

As they strolled along the sand, Julian started to hear people talking, saying Maria's name and pointing her out to friends and family members. She was obviously more well-known than he'd realised, and clearly modest too - she didn't appear to notice the attention she was getting at all. Unless she was just used to it.

When they found a good spot Julian laid out the towels he'd brought with him, and as he sat down, he looked up at Maria, letting out an involuntary gasp. She had removed her wraparound dress and was now standing there in her lemon yellow bathing costume, showing off every curve of her beautiful body.

And that was the start of a lovely afternoon for both Julian and Maria. They talked, they swam, they ate the watermelon, and then they talked some more, finding out as much as possible about each other. It was nice and comfortable.

As they spoke, however, Julian could feel a niggling feeling deep in his gut, telling him to come clean - he really liked this woman, and he didn't want to lie to her any longer.

So, after taking a deep breath, he announced, "Maria, I'm sorry but I have to tell you - I'm not Donny's manager. I do have a financial share in the business, but that's about it."

A small smile played on Maria's lips. "I sort of figured that out for myself." She shrugged. "You seemed more interested in staring at me and asking me out than in what Donny was doing at the shoot."

Julian could feel his face getting red. "Right, sorry about that."

"It's OK," she replied. "It was nice to get some attention from someone who wasn't a photographer."

"Oh come on!" Julian cried out, before he could stop himself. "Sorry, but . . . have you *seen* you? You must get asked out all the time!"

Maria shrugged. "I haven't always been a beauty queen, you know." She stared into the distance for a moment before carrying on. "I've spent the last ten years caring for my mother - she was sick, and my sisters are all younger than me, so I had to step up and do everything." She shrugged. "Well, my mother died recently, and as my sister is now eighteen, she's kind of taken over for me - to give me a break from looking after everyone. So I haven't exactly had time to date anyone at all."

"I'm so sorry," Julian replied, kicking himself for being all jokey earlier. "I had no idea."

"Thank you. Her death was . . . awful, but expected. I'm just happy she's not in any pain anymore." She took a deep breath, wiping her eyes quickly to stop the tears from falling down her face. "Anyway, that's when my life really started, I suppose. My sister wrote to the organisers of the Miss Malta Beauty Pageant, and the rest is history. I never would have even attempted something like that by myself."

Julian frowned. "Why not?"

Maria shrugged. "Lack of confidence, I guess. Anyway," she added, looking out at the horizon, where the sun would soon be setting. "I'd better be getting back. Thank you for a lovely day."

"Thank *you*."

They packed up their towels and headed back to the car, and after Julian had driven her back to the square, he switched off the engine and turned to face her.

"I had a great time today," he told Maria. "I'd like to get together again, if you want to?"

Maria smiled. "That sounds great."

"Well," Julian replied, more confident now, "It's my birthday on Wednesday and I've booked the Promenade Café for me and some friends; we're going to have a curry night. Will you come?"

Maria nodded. "I'd love to."

Wednesday came around soon enough, and Julian was more than excited at the prospect of all his friends getting together for a night of food and fun - he just hoped Maria would show up like she'd promised. Her presence would make the night extra special.

He'd reserved a long table on the upper deck of the café, and Joseph and Geno had really gone to town with the decorations, putting up streamers, balloons, and banners to wish him a happy birthday.

When Julian got there, he saw that several of his friends had beaten him to it - as well as Joseph and Geno, Filippu, Angelina, Tony, Josephine, and Donny were there, as well as Donny's friends that Julian had gone to the airport to meet. Not only that, but when he entered the lower bar area, he was greeted by a rousing reception of 'Happy Birthday' being sung to him.

"You're getting old mate," said Donny, handing Julian a pint.

Filippu laughed. "He is far younger than you, Donny!"

Julian smiled, his grin getting wider when he saw Maria hovering in the doorway of the bar. "You came," he said as he went over to her.

"Of course I did," she replied. She leaned over and kissed him on the cheek. "Happy birthday, Julian."

Julian felt a little shiver crawl up his spine as her lips touched his skin. "Thank you. I'm really glad you're here."

From then on the night just got better and better, and Julian simply couldn't have asked for anything more. He was surrounded by friends - many of whom he now thought of as his own special Maltese family - and with Maria being there, it was the icing on the cake.

After the food and (a lot of) drink, the dancing started, continuing into the early hours as the sun set and the twinkling fairy lights on the terrace came on. Everyone was having a blast, with Donny doing dodgy dancing and making people laugh, and Angelina moving in that special sexy way of hers.

Julian, however, couldn't keep his eyes off Maria as she swayed to the music; it was innocent enough, and yet somehow she appeared to be even sexier than Angelina in her short white dress that showed off her smooth, tanned skin.

Soon people started getting tired, and Julian's guests vanished one by one as their taxis arrived to take them home. Soon he and Maria were the only guests left, and after leaving Joseph and Geno to clear up, Julian escorted Mary into a taxi, ready to take her home.

"Did you have a nice night?" she asked as the taxi drove off.

"The best," he replied, thinking wistfully of past birthdays.

Maria smiled, her lips suddenly illuminated in the moonlit glow coming through the car's window, and as she glanced out at the view, she whispered, "Well it doesn't have to be over yet - how about we go for a walk on the beach before I go home?"

Julian told the taxi driver to pull over and let them out early. At this time of night the beach was completely deserted, and as they started strolling along the shore, Julian took Maria's hand in his.

"This is so romantic," she said as she skipped across the sand; she was now holding her shoes so she could go barefoot.

"It is," Julian agreed, bringing up her hand and kissing her on the knuckles. "It's a beautiful night. Almost as beautiful as you."

Maria stopped walking then, turning towards him.

Julian leaned forwards to kiss her, winding his arms around her body as he felt the soft material of her dress and the softer skin beneath.

She returned the kiss immediately, but when Julian leaned in even closer, pressing his body to hers, she took a tentative step back, breaking the kiss.

"I'm sorry," he said, almost stuttering, "I didn't mean . . ."

"No, it's not that," Maria replied, biting her lip as she looked down at her bare feet, "I just . . . I told you that I've never had a boyfriend before."

Julian nodded. "I know."

"Well, I've never done . . . *that* with anyone before, either." She took a deep breath, as though trying to calm herself down. "You see, I believe in saving myself . . . for marriage."

Julian sighed; he was more than a little disappointed. On the other hand, however, he was pretty impressed. In this day and age, saving yourself was easier said than done, and he liked that Maria was staying true to herself; there was something very . . . inspiring about it. "I understand," he said, taking a step back himself. "Duly noted. You don't have anything to worry about with me."

That made Maria smile - a real, contented smile. "That means a lot." She took his hand in hers again, moving slightly closer to him. "And if you're OK with not taking things all the way, then I'd very much like to kiss you again."

"So kissing's OK?"

Maria nodded. "We can have fun. But if you could respect my wishes and stop when I ask you . . ." she sighed. "I know it's not ideal . . ."

Julian lifted her hand up again, kissing the soft skin on her fingers. "I would be quite happy to just kiss you all night," he said gently.

Maria leaned forwards to kiss him, more slowly and deeply than before.

Even though Julian could feel himself getting hard, he tried to repress it - he could always deal with that later; right now he was just going to enjoy being in Maria's company, enjoying her warmth, her lips, her body . . .

As the kiss intensified they sank down to the sand, lying on the beach as Maria placed her long, lithe body over his. The feel of her on top of him got Julian even more aroused, and yet again he had to reel it back so he wouldn't lose control.

Maria moaned as they carried on kissing, and Julian placed his hand on one of her long, smooth legs. He thought she'd tell him to stop, but she just moaned even louder, and getting more confident now, Julian brought his hand up even further, carrying on underneath her dress until he got to her small, lacy underwear.

Yet again Maria didn't say anything, and although Julian had no desire to go against her wishes, he knew she'd tell him if he was crossing the line. So, slowly, he placed his hand underneath her panties, pushing his fingers deep into her warmth.

Maria gasped, but instead of pulling away like Julian thought she might, she pushed her body in closer to his, making his fingers go in deeper. "Julian," she moaned.

"I'm sorry," he whispered, "is this OK?" He pushed his fingers in even deeper, trying to find her sweet spot.

She moaned again. "Don't stop!"

Julian did as he was told, and as he moved his fingers around inside her, he reached out his other hand until he found her breasts, her nipples raised through the thin fabric of her dress. He caressed them while his other hand caressed inside her, and soon she was writhing around on top of him and moaning even louder.

By now Julian was harder than ever, but at no point did he think about going against her wishes - he would just have to deal with it. What he *did* want to do, however, was show Maria just how much fun she could have without having full sex, and the way she was responding, he thought he was doing a pretty good job of it.

"Julian," she moaned again, before leaning down and kissing him deeply.

He increased the rhythm of his fingers, also increasing the pressure on her breasts, and after another minute or so, Maria pulled away from him, arching her back as she screamed into the night. In the moonlight, she looked like the most beautiful thing he'd ever seen.

A moment later she was leaning down on him, nuzzling her face into his neck while she tried to catch her breath. Julian took his fingers out and wrapped his arms around her, holding her close.

"That was . . . incredible," she breathed. "But . . ." she faltered for a moment, looking up at him, "I didn't mean . . . it doesn't count, does it?"

Julian shook his head. "It doesn't count. Like you said, you can still have fun, can't you? Wasn't that fun?" He was grinning now, even though his entire body was stiff with anticipation, something that wasn't going to get sorted out for a while.

"It was. Thank you."

Julian kissed her gently, holding her for another minute or so before whispering, "Let me take you home."

CHAPTER 31

As Julian got out of the taxi and approached the villa, he noticed that the light was on. This wasn't unusual, with Donny being up all times of the night, but for some reason this time it made him stop in his tracks.

As he let himself in, he saw Donny in the kitchen. "You still up?" he asked, actually glad for the distraction from thinking about Maria.

"Check through your things," Donny replied, all serious, "someone's been in here."

Julian immediately went on the alert. "What? What do you mean?" He glanced around the villa, seeing the drawers open in the lounge and several objects scattered on the floor.

Upon entering his bedroom, he noticed that the wardrobe doors were open, the contents dispersed all over the floor. His suitcase was open on the bed as well, but upon further inspection, he realised nothing was missing.

What a birthday present to come home to, he thought, laughing bitterly to himself.

"Made you a coffee," Donny said from the doorway, making Julian jump. "Anything missing from your case?"

Julian moved over to his housemate, taking the drink from him with a shake of his head before asking, "What the hell's going on, Donny?"

He shrugged. "Beats me. Thought we'd been robbed, but all my camera stuff's still here." He shrugged again. "Unless the thieves were stupid, I think they were looking for something specific."

Julian stared at his friend, trying to read his face, but Donny looked as bewildered as he felt. He was just about to open his mouth to ask if anything else had been taken when their villa was suddenly filled with a bright light - headlights from a vehicle that was approaching outside. Two vehicles, as Julian soon saw, walking into the kitchen.

Before he even had a chance to adjust to the light and figure out who it was, the villa door banged open as several Maltese policemen entered the kitchen.

Within minutes he and Donny had been arrested and taken into separate police cars, Julian's heart thumping the whole time. What was going on?

Julian tried to speak to the police officers in the front of the car as the vehicle started moving, but they wouldn't answer him at all, and the longer the journey went on, the worse his bad feeling got. Whatever this was, it wasn't something he'd be able to get out of easily - that much he could tell.

When the car finally stopped, one of the policemen opened the door and pulled Julian out, not trying to be gentle. He stumbled on the ground, and when he looked back up, he realised he was looking at a prison - Valletta jail.

As he was led inside Julian got flashbacks to Benghazi, flashbacks that only intensified as he was taken to and pushed inside a cell. The only difference here was that he had the cell to himself; there weren't any other prisoners, waiting for the morning when they'd get their hands cut off.

No one explained anything to him; no one even spoke to him as he was locked in the cell and left on his own. He couldn't see Donny anywhere, or anyone else for that matter, and after an hour or so of waiting for something to happen, he realised it wasn't going to - at least not until morning, perhaps.

As he leaned his head against the wall, he whispered, "Happy birthday," to himself, and then he thought of Maria.

It wasn't until the next afternoon that something actually happened, by which point Julian really was on the verge of going crazy. He'd hardly slept, apart from a brief doze now and then, and his neck was cricked from the strange position he'd been sitting in for most of the night. He was also dying to know just what the hell was going on - it was driving him mad not understanding why he was there, or what he was supposed to have done.

So, when a policeman came to get him from the cell and took him to an interview room, part of him was relieved - hopefully now he'd get some answers at least.

That relief completely left his body, however, when he got into the interview room and saw who was waiting for him, sitting at the table and smiling at him like he was an old friend.

Julian stopped in his tracks, hardly able to believe his eyes. It was the Scotland Yard officer who'd interviewed him in London - the very same one. He had a smirk on his face that seemed to say, 'fancy seeing you here!'

Next to him sat a man who was clearly a Maltese police officer, though not one of the ones who had brought him in.

Whatever this was - and he still had no idea what it could be - it was serious. Very serious indeed.

"Julian," the Scotland Yard officer said then, sounding far more cheery than the situation warranted, "have a seat. It's good to see you."

Julian had no time for fake pleasantries; as soon as he sat down in the empty chair, he asked the officer, "What's this about? I haven't done anything wrong."

The officer raised his eyebrows. "And what about your friends?"

"You mean Donny?" Julian asked. "I'm not his keeper; I don't know what he gets up to."

The officer tilted his head. "And Anton? I believe you rent your villa from him?"

Julian nodded. "Yeah, so? He's not exactly my friend."

"And how about Mr Bowman and Mr Seaton?" he asked.

"Who?"

"Now now," the officer said, tutting, "we know you went to the airport to pick them up with your good friend Donny."

A wave of fear washed over Julian then. Just what the hell had Donny got him into? "I didn't know their surnames," he said eventually.

The officer frowned. "Interesting. And I suppose you don't know what they've been up to either?"

Julian shook his head, a sick feeling blossoming in the pit of his stomach. "I really don't know them. I was just tagging along with Donny."

"OK," said the officer after a few moments, "here's what we're going to do. I'm going to tell you what you're involved with, and you're going to tell me everything you know. Is that a deal?"

Still completely bewildered, Julian nodded.

And then the officer started to talk.

Finally, Julian thought to himself, he was going to get some answers, but as he listened to what the Scotland Yard officer had to say - with the Maltese policeman watching him like a hawk for any signs of recognition or recollection - he just got more and more confused.

The charge, the officer told him, was for forgery. Apparently, Donny had been illegally printing foreign money and the police had already arrested a gang of his associates as they travelled on the M6 in the UK. Not only did they have two million dollars on them, in cash, but they also had a rather impressive array of firearms as well.

The connection had been made between the UK and Malta - with Donny at the forefront - and as Julian had been both living with and working with Donny, he was just as much a suspect as his new friend was. It was the biggest scandal Malta had ever seen, and Julian was stuck right at the centre of it.

Once the officer had finished, he sat back in his seat, eyeballing Julian.

"That's . . ." Julian sighed. "I want to say that's ridiculous, but I don't suppose it is, really."

"And what's that supposed to mean?" asked the Maltese officer - the first thing he'd said since Julian had entered the room.

Julian signed again. "Filippu - my friend - he warned me against Anton, told me not to get involved with him. And I didn't; renting his place was the only 'business' I've had with him." He swept his hand through his hair as he took a deep breath. "I can't believe this."

"So you're telling me," the Scotland Yard officer said, "that you were unaware of this entire enterprise?"

Julian nodded. "Of course! I came to Malta because I wanted a break. I just wanted to live somewhere sunny and warm, have some fun, make some new friends. Relax. The last thing I wanted was to be caught up in something like this!"

The Scotland Yard officer stared at him for a long, long time, clearly trying to make Julian sweat so much he'd start confessing, but Julian just stared back at him, looking helpless.

Eventually, the officer said, "You know what, Julian? I believe you."

"What? Really?" Julian asked before he could stop himself, before quickly adding, "I mean, thanks."

The officer shook his head. "In my line of work you quickly get the knack for being able to read people. To see when they're telling the truth and when they're . . . *bending* the truth. I believe you had no idea about Donny's forgery business. And anyway, apart from your association with the man, we have nothing to connect you to it." He sounded exhausted, like this case had been running rings around him for months. For all Julian knew, it probably had.

"So what happens now?" Julian asked after a while, the silence beginning to make him antsy all over again.

The officer glanced at the Maltese man next to him, then back to Julian. "You'll have to stay here for a while longer, while we get this mess sorted out. If all goes well, then you'll be free to leave."

Julian couldn't believe it. "Seriously?"

The officer nodded. "As long as no evidence suddenly comes to light that involves you . . ."

Julian shook his head. "It won't."

"Well then, that concludes this interview," the officer said, standing up. "We'll come and get you soon."

With that, Julian got taken back to the cell, which he wasn't exactly thrilled about, but at least he felt better now that he'd had some answers. He wasn't happy with what Donny had done, but deep down he knew that Donny had done him a favour by never mentioning it to him - if Julian had known about the scheme, even a little bit, that interview could have gone a hell of a lot differently.

Within a few hours he found himself leaving the prison and being driven back to the villa he shared with Donny.

At least, he *had* shared it with Donny - as he found out from the policeman on the drive back, Donny was being deported and had already been taken to the villa to retrieve his belongings. Anton was being charged as well, and Julian made a mental note to thank Filippu for all his warnings about him.

By the time Julian had got out of the police car and had entered the villa, Donny and most of his belongings were gone, and he felt relieved.

After inspecting the kitchen and the living room, Julian headed into his room, where his suitcase was still on the bed, open and half full. Without trying to think too much about why he was doing it, Julian finished packing his suitcase with the remainder of his clothes, took one last look around the villa, and left, before going to stay at Filippu's hotel.

Filippu was happy to see him, though not surprised - gossip moved fast on the island, and he knew everything. He welcomed him back with open arms and gave him the room he'd had before; seemingly he'd kept it free while filling up the other rooms of the hotel, should Julian decide (or be forced) to come back.

Julian thanked his friend and made his way to his room, where Angelina soon joined him.

"Hey you," she said, "have I gone back in time or something?" She was grinning.

"I know, I know," Julian replied, "I should never have left."

Angelina went over to him, giving him a big hug. "I'm just glad you're OK. I thought you might have been charged or deported like the others."

Julian shook his head. "For a moment there, I thought the same." He put his suitcase on the bed, opening it and starting to take his clothes out.

"Here," said Angelina, "let me help you." She began to lift his washing out, and between them, they soon emptied the case.

"Thanks," Julian said, and as he lifted his case up to place it on top of the wardrobe, he stopped in his tracks.

"What is it?" Angelina asked, noticing the expression of confusion on his face.

Frowning, Julian shook the suitcase before placing it back on the bed. "This is heavy," he said, "even though it's empty . . ."

Intrigued, Angelina took a step closer as they bent over the case, staring at it as though it would somehow come to life and start telling them its secret.

After a moment or so, Julian started inspecting the case in detail, soon realising there was more to its interior than met the eye. "This has got a false bottom!" he exclaimed, feeling the surface of the material.

Angelina watched, wide-eyed, as Julian pried open the newly added partition of the case to reveal a secret compartment underneath. And that wasn't the only surprise - hidden away in the concealed space was a whole load of notes. English bank notes, in both £20 and £50 denominations.

Angelina stared at the notes, her mouth hanging open, before eventually whispering, "There must be thousands of pounds there!"

Julian nodded. He was feeling oddly numb all of a sudden. "Thousands of *fake* pounds."

"What's that?" Angelina asked, the tone of her voice startling him out of his reverie. "There's a note."

Feeling like he was in a dream, Julian reached out to pick up a scrap of paper that had been shoved into one corner of the compartment. It was a handwritten note, and Julian recognised the handwriting immediately - it was Donny's.

'Julian,' the note read, 'please accept this as payment for our road trip. I said I'd pay you back after my wallet got stolen, didn't I? D.'

Angelina raised her eyebrows. "What are you going to do?"

Julian let out the breath he'd been holding in. "I have absolutely no idea."

CHAPTER 32

What Julian did next was pretty simple, once he'd really thought about it: he went home. He thought that being back in London would at least allow him to think more clearly, and he'd have far more options in his home country than he would in Malta.

It was hard saying goodbye to his friends on the island - Filippu and Angelina in particular - but he knew it had to be done. He just hoped he'd be able to see them again some day.

There was a huge risk with getting back to England, so he thought he'd take the slightly less dangerous route and drive back instead of getting a plane. His days of horrible, stressful flights were over - at least for now - and he thought his case was less likely to get searched if he was driving instead of flying.

Luckily, his hunch was correct, and he managed to get back to London - with his suitcase of 'cash' intact - without any problems.

If only that was the only thing he had to figure out.

Then there was the money: all that lovely money Donny had left him, but money that Julian had no idea what to do with. After all, it was fake, and if he got caught with it Scotland Yard would come down on him like a ton of bricks.

He thought about hiding it somewhere, and he even thought about burning it all, but he couldn't quite bring himself to do that. With that much money, he could set himself up for life, and that was far too tempting to just throw away.

He'd spent years struggling to get by, doing jobs and other things he didn't particularly want to do just so he could have enough cash to live on, and he wanted that life to stop.

The first thing he did was get in touch with Terry. He knew Terry had contacts - not to mention experience with laundering money, especially forged money - and he needed help.

"So how do you want to do this?" asked Terry. They were sitting in a local pub, in the corner where no one could hear them. "What kind of business do you want to launder the money through?"

Julian shrugged. "What are the options?"

Terry leaned back in his chair, taking a swig of his pint. "We could do it through the casinos - several different ones. I know a guy who's an ace at counting cards. Then there's horse racing, things like that. Pay in the fake money, get back real money."

Julian thought for a moment. "If I went down the casino route, how would that work?"

"I'll sort everything out, I get a cut. Twenty percent."

Julian nearly choked on his beer. "No way! Five percent."

"Fifteen."

"Ten, and that's my last offer."

Terry stared at him for a moment. "Alright, ten."

Julian nodded. "And when can you start . . . sorting it out for me?"

Terry grinned. "Straight away. Just give me the money, mate. I'll get it done in no time."

Terry was true to his word, and not only did Julian find himself with freshly laundered money, but he also found himself with a profit. He started paying Terry a bigger cut, and he started getting even more money back.

This meant he could relax a bit, and really start thinking about what he wanted to do with his life. So, when he sat down and *really* thought about it - after a brief trip home to visit his mum - it came to him.

It was as he was thinking about Filippu and Angelina, and all the great times he'd had when they'd watched the boats racing around the island, that he realised that's what he should be doing: racing powerboats. He knew it would give him that adrenaline, that feeling of power and freedom, and once the thought had occurred to him, he wanted to get out on the sea as soon as possible. He wanted it more than anything else.

Before now that dream had been exactly that: a dream. But now he had the funds, and now that dream was within reach. He could afford to get a boat, could afford to have that lifestyle - the lifestyle he'd wished he could have back in Malta.

When he'd got back to London, he'd rung Penny, just wanting to check in and see if she was OK - he knew she was married and back with her husband, but he felt like he needed to speak to someone who was at least some kind of link to Malta; despite being born in England, he was feeling a little homesick for the beautiful island.

Penny was happy to hear from him, and after chatting to him for a while about his plans, she suggested he meet one of her friends, Katherine.

Not only was Katherine a fan of racing of all kinds, but she was also an actress, one who had the kind of lifestyle that Julian had suddenly found himself experiencing. In fact, she was about to leave for Jersey to film a TV show - some police drama he'd only vaguely heard of.

Penny set up a meeting, and one Saturday Julian found himself sitting in a café opposite a cute woman, getting on like they'd been friends for years; she was just so easy to talk to, and they hit it off immediately.

Katherine had a rather striking look. She was small and petite, with short black hair that had been cut into a rather choppy bob. She wore thick black eyeliner all around her eyes, and deep red lipstick that made her stand out from the crowd. She was edgy - not the kind of girl Julian usually went for, but attractive in her own way.

It seemed Penny had already filled her in on Julian's ambitions with powerboat racing - which immediately got Katherine interested - and soon they were discussing how Julian should go about getting into the racing circuit. As it turned out, Katherine had an old friend who was involved in the World Powerboat series, held annually in no other location than the Channel Islands.

Julian couldn't believe his luck - for once, everything seemed to be going right for him. Everything was falling into place, slotting together, and actually going well . . . *finally.*

"So when do you leave for Jersey?" Julian asked, after they'd had their third round of coffee.

"In a few days," said Katherine. "Why, you trying to get another date in before then?"

Julian grinned. "Actually, I was thinking of heading to Jersey myself. Thought maybe I could go with you."

That made Katherine laugh. "Well, you're certainly forward, aren't you?"

Julian just smiled back, saying nothing, allowing Katherine to fill in the gap.

"OK," she said after a moment, "why not?"

"Really?" Julian asked, for just a moment losing his confident persona.

She shrugged. "Sure."

And that was how Julian ended up in Jersey - even blagging himself onto the set of the police drama as an extra. It helped that he knew one of the actresses, but he liked to think it was partly down to his talent and charm as well.

It was while he was in Jersey that the next phase of his life really began, and yet again, it was heading in the right direction - the *best* direction, in Julian's eyes.

One of the other extras on the set, Jerry, knew a man on Guernsey with a powerboat, and not only that, but the man was a retired racer. Julian asked for an introduction with the man - Robert - and a few days later, he got a boat over to Guernsey, with a view to pick the man's brain.

"Julian," Robert said as he spotted him at the ferry port. "Good to meet you!"

Robert was tall, but a little chubby. His skin was tanned, like he spent a lot of time in the sun, and his face was more than a little wrinkled.

"Hi," Julian said, shaking the man's hand. "How did you know it was me?"

"Jerry described you to me. Plus, you're the only single man who's come off that ferry!"

"You got me. Thanks for agreeing to meet up."

"Of course, of course," Robert said. "Let's get a drink, shall we? Then I can tell you all about my illustrious racing career."

Five hours later, Julian was sitting on Robert's balcony, looking out over the island with an ice-cold beer in his hand - the latest pint of many.

He and Robert were getting on wonderfully, and had been speaking of nothing but powerboat racing since Julian had first set foot on Guernsey. Julian was learning a lot, and that was on top of everything he'd already learned from talking to Filippu.

"So," said Robert, as he came back onto the balcony with some sandwiches for them both, "when are you going to ask me?"

Julian stared at him, confused. "Ask you what?"

"About my boat," Robert said, handing him one of the plates. "I know you don't have one, and *you* know *I* have one. So when are you going to ask me if you can use it?"

Julian put his plate down on the little table next to him, unsure what to say.

"I'll tell you what. Why don't you rent it off me? I'm not ready to part with it - not yet - but I'd sure love to see it in another race. Maybe even see it *win* a race?"

Julian shook his head. "I swear, I didn't come over here with an ulterior motive. I really did just want your advice."

"Well, you got it." He smiled. "You also got a boat, if you want it?"

Julian thought about it for exactly two seconds before answering, "I want it."

And so started the next few months of Julian's training, under the careful eye of Robert. It was the perfect set-up: Julian wanted to learn how to be a powerboat racer, and Robert wanted someone to pass his wisdom on to. Just as Julian couldn't wait to feel that adrenaline rush when he finally took part in a race, Robert didn't want to let that feeling go - even if it wasn't him actually doing the racing anymore. In his eyes, he was racing by proxy, living vicariously through his new, young friend - his new, young friend who could have a promising racing career ahead of him, if he listened to Robert's instructions.

And Julian, for his part, hung on every word Robert said, soaking in as much of his knowledge and experience as possible. He was hungry to learn more, hungry to get going, even though it was a good few months before he entered his first race.

It was a small local race, one that was meant for beginners, and Julian smashed it: he got first place easily. He felt that adrenaline he'd been lusting for, that sense of freedom and that satisfaction when he finished way ahead of the rest. It was addictive - far more addictive than alcohol or drugs. As soon as he completed the race, he wanted to go again. And again and again.

Robert coached him every day, even let Julian stay with him on Guernsey while 'training', and during every race, Robert would be there cheering him on. Sometimes Katherine would be there too, and once even Penny and her husband came to see him. He thought that would be a bit awkward, but much to his relief it seemed that Penny had never mentioned the zipper incident to him; in fact, he didn't appear to know that Julian and Penny had ever been together at all.

Life was good, but there was one thing that would make it even better, one thing that would be the cherry on top - he wanted to enter the World Powerboat Championships, and he wanted to win.

Robert thought he was aiming a little high, and he told him this time and time again, but Julian wouldn't listen. Ever since that first race, watching with Filippu and Angelina, Julian had known that was what he wanted to do, and he couldn't think of anything better than coming first in the World Championships.

So, as soon as he could, he signed up and then he stepped up his training with Robert, going out on the boat more and more, for longer and longer sessions. In his dreams Julian pictured himself coming out on top for the whole championships, whereas in reality, as a relative beginner he wasn't allowed to compete with the big boys in Class 1 -

first he had to prove his worth in the lower class. Then, if he was good enough, he might get sponsored or asked to drive in the top class.

Even so, the upcoming race was all Julian could think about, all he dreamed about - whereas before he often had fantasies about bedding beautiful women, now his fantasies consisted solely of winning the big race, of holding up that trophy, of everyone shouting his name and cheering for their champion . . .

He was going to do it. He just knew it.

And then, one day, he woke up in the morning with a nervous yet thrilling energy buzzing all around his body, and he felt more ready than ever.

It was the day of the World Championships.

He didn't feel like eating, but Robert made him have a bit of breakfast, to keep his strength up for the race. He ate in a daze, yet again thinking of that moment when he'd be announced as the winner.

He wanted to prove to himself that he could do it, that through training and determination, he could achieve whatever he wanted to achieve.

He couldn't wait.

After breakfast, Julian and Robert headed down to the ferry port, where there was already a large crowd gathering - people with picnic baskets and cameras, reminding him again of the first race he attended with his friends back in Malta. He could feel the same excitement as he'd felt then, but now it was magnified by a thousand. A million.

As well as the crowd of spectators, the race sponsors had set up their hospitality tents on the promenade, a whole sea of different coloured marquees stretching almost as far as the eye could see. Each one was manned by several people, with most of them also featuring a scantily-clad hostess, handing out canapés and drinks and chatting enthusiastically to the people in the VIP area.

Julian watched, enraptured, as huge, low-loading transporter lorries with stainless steel sides delivered a whole fleet of boats, not to mention the helicopters that were currently flying in; he knew they would be following each of the top performing boats to report back on their positions. And then there was the parade - a long procession of lorries, cars, and spectators, everyone enjoying the atmosphere as they made their way to the main area. It was quite the sight to see, and his heart skipped a beat as he took everything in.

It was a scorching hot day, and Julian kept sipping at a bottle of water he was carrying around with him, trying to keep his body hydrated and his head clear. The swarming crowds were starting to make him nervous, but when Katherine appeared, giving him a hug and a kiss before heading off again, Julian started to feel a little calmer. He had people out there rooting for him, wishing him to do well, and that meant the world to him.

He'd told his mum about the race, but she didn't have the time to come over to the island, and even if she did, she'd told him she was worried about watching him get hurt. He'd told her there was no way he was going to get hurt. In fact, getting harmed in whatever way hadn't even occurred to him as something to worry about: the only fear he had was that he might not come first and that his hopes would be dashed.

He'd told Filippu and Angelina as well (not to mention Phil back in England), and even though they hadn't been able to make it, he knew they'd be rooting for him too. He wished they could be there with him.

Just as he was thinking this, he turned around in time to catch a glimpse of a familiar face, though for a few seconds he couldn't quite place it.

He tried to find her face in the crowd again, and when he did, it hit him: it was Veronica. The ambassador's daughter. The one he'd met in Stringfellows, and the one he had to leave behind when he got on a plane to Libya. The one he'd spent so long thinking about when he was in Benghazi, the one whose address he hadn't been able to read on the smudged note. The one who had got away.

Was she there for him? he wondered. Had she somehow heard that he was taking part in the race and had come over to support him?

His heart racing in his chest, he made his way through the crowd until he was right beside her. "Veronica!" he said, almost shouting, even though she was mere inches away from him.

At first she didn't recognise him - which wasn't surprising considering he'd probably changed quite a lot since they'd first met; he was tanned and toned now, muscly even, and his new, rich lifestyle meant he could afford the very best clothes - and then her lips turned up in a little smile, although it wasn't the full-on grin he'd been expecting. It was subdued, somehow . . . polite. Nothing more.

"Julian," she said, her voice barely above a whisper. "What are you doing here?"

"I'm racing today," he said, the pride evident in his voice. "Are you here to watch?"

She nodded, although she looked a bit awkward about the whole thing, and it wasn't until Julian looked at the man standing next to her that he realised why: they were holding hands, and upon closer inspection, they were both wearing wedding rings.

"Oh," Veronica said, looking down at her hand and then at the man next to her. "This is my husband, Malcolm. Malcolm, this is Julian . . . an old friend."

Malcolm - who was tall, broad-shouldered, and good-looking in a generic sort of way - nodded. "Nice to meet you."

Julian's heart sank. He honestly thought that if he was ever able to meet up with Veronica again, that would be it: she'd be the one, and he'd never have to even look at another woman for his entire life. She was marriage material . . . it just seemed someone else had got in before him.

Julian just about managed to mumble, "Nice to meet you too," and then he was gone, weaving his way around the people in the crowd as he ran away; he just couldn't look at Veronica any longer. It was messing with his head, and today, he needed to focus on the race.

He would allow himself to process everything later. After he'd won . . . after he'd shown Veronica exactly what she was missing.

So, he made his way to Robert's boat, a boat that had been promised to him as his own after the race.

Robert was waiting on the jetty for him, but when Julian walked over, he frowned. "What's wrong with you? You look like you've just seen a ghost."

"You could say that. A ghost of my past."

"Are you OK?" Robert asked, clearly concerned. "You can't afford to be distracted during the race, not even a little bit."

Julian nodded. "I'm fine. My focus is completely on the race. I promise."

"OK then," he announced, rubbing his hands together, "let's do this, shall we?"

"Let's do this."

It was time. They'd already had the safety checks and practice sessions the day before, and now it was time to prove to everyone that he had what it took. That he could go out there and win this thing.

Julian's heart was hammering in his chest as he got his boat into position, his navigator and co-pilot - a middle-aged man who had a lot of experience in racing - by his side. Whereas most of the Class 1 boys had to have a driver, navigator, and throttle man, Julian just had a navigator and his trusty crash helmet, should anything bad happen.

He allowed himself to look back at the crowd for just a second before focusing back on the water. He could see Robert, but who knew where Veronica and her handsome husband were? He just hoped they stuck around long enough to watch him win.

And then, just like that, they were off, all of the boats zooming along next to each other, some of them pulling ahead of the others straight away.

Julian tried to block out all of the negative thoughts that were trying to bombard his mind as he made the boat go faster and faster, but inevitably they soon started breaking through the barriers he'd put up, stabbing at him like tiny little knives.

He thought of Veronica in the club, looking bored next to her father and his friends, Veronica in her hotel room, the gown slipping down to the floor to reveal her incredible body, Veronica in the bed, groaning and writhing around on top of him, and finally, Veronica, handing him the piece of paper with the address on.

If only he'd read it before putting it in his pocket, if only he'd asked her to say it out loud too, if only he'd taken the time to go back once he realised the note was illegible, if only he'd never got on that plane to Libya in the first place . . .

If only. If only.

Julian could feel the sun on his face, the spray from the sea on his skin, could even feel that rush of adrenaline he got during every race, but none of it was having the same effect as it usually did. He knew he was supposed to be listening to the navigator, to his directions and lap times, but his mind couldn't quite focus on the man's voice, shouting over the sound of the engine.

She was married. Veronica was married.

Had she been married all along? Or did she have a whirlwind romance while Julian was in Libya and Malta, marrying the guy after only a few months of dating him? Did it even matter anymore?

She was married, and it was clear she hadn't given Julian even a second thought after he'd left her hotel room that morning.

Julian sighed. He could see the people cheering on the race from the edge of the island, and even though they were hardly more than tiny blurs of colour as he whizzed past, he imagined he could see Veronica and her husband, holding hands and having a lovely romantic day out.

Grabbing hold of the lever, Julian forced the boat to go faster, pushing it as hard as he could and not caring about the other boats and obstacles around him. There was no way he was going to let Veronica see him lose this race; despite everything, he still wanted to impress her.

So he pushed the boat faster and faster, the roar of the engine filling his ears as he tried to shake the memories of that night with Veronica out of his head. By now Julian had forgotten that he even had a navigator on board; the man simply didn't seem to be important anymore.

Opening up the throttle, Julian took his place behind the leading boat, heading down towards Herm Island. The sound of the exhausts was exhilarating as he jumped washes at full throttle, landing perfectly each time. His co-pilot managed the settings of the trim tabs and the engine trim while Julian steered with one hand, adjusting the throttles to achieve the best possible speed for the boat. At 70-80 mph, managing the throttles, trimming the tabs and the engine, and reading the waves was no easy task.

By now the engine was almost screaming, deafening Julian as he surged ahead, and as he willed the boat to go as fast as it possibly could, he turned to take one more look at the island, convinced he'd see Veronica there again, staring at him and perhaps even cheering him on.

It was as he turned his head, to try and seek out one face in a crowd of thousands, that it happened.

He'd got too close to another boat's wake - a boat he hadn't even realised was there, as he hadn't been listening to his navigator - causing the bow to pull too high out of the water.

He lost control of the steering, and before he could even think about getting the boat back on course, the huge jagged rocks and the sheer grey cliff face loomed up in front of him. He didn't even have time to gasp.

Upon the point of impact, everything went black.

Julian's last thought was of Veronica.

And then even that faded away.

EPILOGUE

The memorial was held a few months later; with Julian's body never having been found, they couldn't have a funeral, but certain people in Julian's life wanted to commemorate him in a less official way.

The crash had made headlines all around the world, publicising the Championships in ways that had never happened before, and making Julian incredibly famous, but not for the reason he'd been hoping for.

Because of this posthumous fame, the memorial was a large affair, with people from every corner of his life turning up to pay their respects. There were teachers from his boarding school days, staff members from the college, business associates of Reggie's, and even random people he'd met in pubs in London - they all wanted to come and say goodbye, even if there was no actual body to say goodbye to.

The memorial was a bit of a strange one, which was no surprise considering the circumstances, but even with all that, there was a definite imbalance to the attendees - at least 80% of the people at Julian's memorial were female. It was like they were still attracted to him, still drawn to him, even in death.

You could say a lot about Julian, about the mistakes he'd made in his life and all the things he perhaps shouldn't have done, but one thing was for sure: he certainly made an impression on people, and on the ladies most of all.

The memorial was held on a beach in Guernsey, not far from the crash site, and the locals were treated to a whole parade of young, beautiful women as they lined up to say goodbye to the man who'd had at least some impact on their lives. Many people didn't even realise it was a memorial they were attending - in truth, it looked like it could be a photo shoot for some glossy fashion magazine, with all of the models milling around and chatting about some guy they used to know.

From a table outside the nearby café, a thirty-year-old man watched the strange gathering with interest, sipping his coffee as he took in the scene before him. His hair was a little long and unkempt, and he sported a full beard. He looked like any normal tourist on holiday.

There certainly were a lot of people at the memorial, but there were some missing too.

Take the victim's family, for instance. There wasn't anyone there who could have been his mother, or his father, or even anyone who looked upset enough to be a close friend. The man's coach, who had trained him ready for the World Championships, wasn't even there, which if anyone had been paying proper attention, would have struck them as being more than a little strange.

The man outside the café smiled, feeling a little sad as he watched the memorial. Of course, they were always sombre occasions, meant to celebrate a person's life but more often than not managing to focus on the sadness of their passing.

But still, he smiled, watching as the women talked to each other in front of a large photograph of the man who, at one time in his life, had been destined to become a world racing champion. In another life, in another world . . .

The man thought back to that day. To waking up on a Herm Island beach, his lungs filled with water and his head throbbing like he had the hangover from hell. To the woman who'd found him and who'd helped him back to her house, all the time trying to convince him to go and see a doctor. He'd refused.

He'd been disorientated for a while, but when he finally came to his senses, he quickly made a decision. He already knew that everyone had presumed him dead, and he thought he could use this to his advantage.

All the mistakes he'd made in his past, all the women he'd loved and lost, all the illegal activities he'd been caught up in, everything . . . he could just wash it all away, like his limp body had been washed onto the shore of this island.

He could start over again.

He could be anyone he wanted to be.

And that's exactly what he did.

He'd let some people know the truth - Robert, his mum, Phil from school, Filippu, Angelina . . . but the rest, he simply let them believe what they wanted to believe. Including Veronica.

After all, anyone who really knew him wouldn't just accept the fact that he was gone, not when there wasn't a body to prove it. Anyone who *really* knew him would know he had the strength to survive.

The navigator who'd been with him had just about recovered by now, he knew - a broken leg and a few broken ribs were the worst of his injuries, and Julian was glad that had been all.

Julian finished his coffee just as a woman came out of the café, holding a little parcel with a couple of cakes inside. She kissed him on the lips and then wove her arm around his.

"Are you ready to go home?" she asked, glancing only briefly at the gathering on the beach.

Julian stared intently into the woman's eyes, the woman who'd rescued him a month ago on that lonely, deserted beach. The woman he was pretty sure he was going to marry one day.

"I'm ready," he said, smiling at her. "I'm more than ready."

Made in the USA
Columbia, SC
23 December 2017